"I think I'm in love,"

Callie told Marcus with a sigh.

The expression on his face was almost comical.

Callie saw a mixture of surprise, fear and something else, an almost blush hinting at pleasure, but she wasn't sure. And she didn't have time to puzzle it out. She needed to correct any misunderstanding her words might have created.

"Oh," she said. "Not with *you!*"

That might not be exactly true. She wasn't sure. She wasn't sure of anything after the kiss they'd shared....

Dear Reader,

Once again, we're back to offer you six fabulous romantic novels, the kind of book you'll just long to curl up with on a warm spring day. Leading off the month is award-winner Marie Ferrarella, whose *This Heart for Hire* is a reunion romance filled with the sharply drawn characters and witty banter you've come to expect from this talented writer.

Then check out Margaret Watson's *The Fugitive Bride,* the latest installment in her CAMERON, UTAH, miniseries. This FBI agent hero is about to learn all about love at the hands of his prime suspect. *Midnight Cinderella* is Eileen Wilks' second book for the line, and it's our WAY OUT WEST title. After all, there's just nothing like a cowboy! Our FAMILIES ARE FOREVER flash graces Kayla Daniels' *The Daddy Trap,* about a resolutely single hero faced with fatherhood—and love. *The Cop and Calamity Jane* is a suspenseful romp from the pen of talented Elane Osborn; you'll be laughing out loud as you read this one. Finally, welcome Linda Winstead Jones to the line. Already known for her historical romances, this author is about to make a name for herself in contemporary circles with *Bridger's Last Stand.*

Don't miss a single one—and then rejoin us next month, when we bring you six more examples of the best romantic writing around.

Yours,

Leslie J. Wainger
Executive Senior Editor

Please address questions and book requests to:
Silhouette Reader Service
U.S.: 3010 Walden Ave., P.O. Box 1325, Buffalo, NY 14269
Canadian: P.O. Box 609, Fort Erie, Ont. L2A 5X3

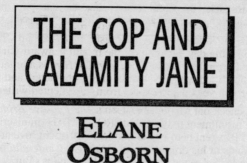

THE COP AND CALAMITY JANE

ELANE OSBORN

Silhouette®
INTIMATE™MOMENTS®
Published by Silhouette Books
America's Publisher of Contemporary Romance

SILHOUETTE BOOKS

ISBN 0-373-07923-0

THE COP AND CALAMITY JANE

Copyright © 1999 by Elane Osborn

This edition published by arrangement with Harlequin Books S.A.

® and TM are trademarks of Harlequin Books S.A., used under license.
Trademarks indicated with ® are registered in the United States Patent
and Trademark Office, the Canadian Trade Marks Office and in other
countries.

Printed in U.S.A.

Books by Elane Osborn

Silhouette Intimate Moments

Shelter in His Arms #642
Honeymoon with a Handsome Stranger #748
The Cop and Calamity Jane #923

ELANE OSBORN

is a daydream believer whose active imagination tends to intrude on her life at the most inopportune moments. Her penchant for slipping into "alternative reality" severely hampered her work life, leading to a gamut of jobs that includes, but is not limited to: airline reservation agent, waitress, salesgirl and seamstress in the wardrobe department of a casino showroom. In writing, she has discovered a career that not only does not punish flights of fancy, it demands them. Drawing on her daydreams, she has published three historical romance novels and is now using the experiences she has collected in her many varied jobs in the "real world" to fuel contemporary stories that blend romance and suspense.

To Lynn,
for years of sharing chocolate fever,
support and encouragement, and,
most of all, for all the laughs.

Chapter 1

It was happening again.

Callie Chance sat at the end of the bed, dazed and stunned, her bare feet growing colder by the second. Moving her head slowly, she took in the disheveled and very damp jumble that had been, a mere hour earlier, a tidy if somewhat cramped and dreary motel room.

The sound of a mop swishing over tiles drew her attention to the bathroom on her left. In front of that door, a yellow-brown stain formed a ragged half-circle in the faded mustard carpet. Atop this lay a glop of what looked like cottage cheese, remains of the ''popcorn'' ceiling that had given way beneath the water that had poured into her room from the one above.

Callie released a slow, shuddering sigh.

This really shouldn't come as such a surprise, she told herself. At a very young age she'd learned to expect such disasters to hit from time to time. She could clearly remember her mother warning that she'd have to be very careful if she didn't want the occasional mishaps to escalate into a continuous flow of calamities.

Shivering, Callie crossed her arms around the flannel night-gown she'd thrown on while she was still wet from her recent, rather ill-fated bath. Blast it! She *had* been careful, watching nearly every word she spoke, each step she took, almost her every thought, not to mention carrying good-luck charms, praying and lighting candles. And still people around her tripped and fell, failed at math tests, lost jobs, lost loves.

Until two years ago, when she had found a sanctuary on Cape Cod. By some miracle her life and, more important, the lives of those around her had settled into a safe, secure routine, unmarred by misadventure of any sort. And so, she thought that she'd finally managed to escape her "curse," as her mother had called it. Thought it was safe to love again.

Callie's fingers tightened into a fist. She should have known better, should have remembered how quickly good luck could turn to bad. Fortune had alternately smiled and frowned on her repeatedly in the last few days. And since arriving in San Francisco her luck had been in a constant flux, first up, then down, then up again, until that last final crash. Now, not only were all the hopes and dreams she'd arrived with completely shattered, but a new catastrophe lay around her in a wet, untidy mess.

"Hey, that's a good one, Scanlon. *Cat*astrophe is just what this is."

These joking words, so aptly echoing Callie's thoughts, brought her attention to the two men entering her motel room. The speaker wore a crisp navy blue suit and trendy turquoise tie. With his wiry body, bright red hair and heavily freckled face, he didn't look much older than eighteen. Since he'd introduced himself to Callie ten minutes earlier as police detective Rick Malone, she figured he must be somewhere in his mid-twenties.

"But, hey," the man went on, "this thing *could* change around. With a little bit of luck, forensics will find a fingerprint or two up there and let us clear this cockamamie case."

Luck?

Callie shivered again. She considered warning these two that the only sort of luck they were likely to find in *her* vicinity was the bad sort, but the decision was taken out of her hands by the second detective.

Dressed in a brown suit, he was taller than the first man and broader of shoulder, with black hair and an angular face that tightened as he gave his partner a narrowed, sideways glance. His name, he'd told her before he'd been called out to the balcony, was Detective Marcus Scanlon.

"Malone." Scanlon's voice was deep and slightly gravelly. "One thing you're going to have to learn about me, and quick, is that I don't believe in luck. Good *or* bad."

Oh, really?

The absurdity of his statement almost surprised a laugh from Callie. Her lips twitched slightly as she wondered just what kind of innocent soul would totally discount the forces of luck. Not that she expected people to keep a running tally of good and bad influences, like she did. But to claim it didn't exist? Foolish.

Detective Scanlon didn't look foolish. When he pulled a chair from the table in the corner to the end of the bed and took a seat across from Callie, she got a much closer look at him, almost uncomfortably close.

His face was unquestionably attractive. His high forehead was defined by the slight widow's peak dip of his thick black hair. His nose was long and straight, his jaw a bit wider than his face and sharply angled.

"Miss Chance, I'm sorry for the interruption." He spoke softly, as he drew a notebook from his breast pocket, with no hint of a smile. "We just have one or two more questions for you. First off, the motel manager has you registered as C. J. Chance. Would you tell me what the *C* and the *J* stand for?"

Detective Marcus Scanlon's eyes locked onto Callie's as he spoke. They were such a dark shade of blue that they appeared almost black, revealing little about the man's thoughts, except perhaps his determination to suck the complete truth out of Callie's every reply.

That, Callie told herself, Detective Scanlon could not have. Not the *whole* truth, anyway. She wasn't in the mood to have someone poke fun at her true name, not after the day she had just struggled through.

Easing her stiff lips into a half smile, she answered softly, "The initials stand for Callie Jane."

After a quick scribble in his notebook, Scanlon raised his eyes to hers once again. His gaze seemed to demand more. Callie shifted on the edge of the bed. She didn't know what else the man could possibly want from her. Before he and his partner had left the room, she'd told them that she was twenty-seven years old, had recently lost her job in Cape Cod and had arrived in San Francisco earlier in the evening.

"And *Callie* would be short for?"

Scanlon's question brought Callie's musings to a sudden halt. She fought off another shiver as she studied the hard lines of the detective's face, sizing up the odds that he'd believe her if she responded with a well-practiced shrug and the breezy insistence that "Callie" was the name she'd been given at birth.

She might have tried that approach earlier, when Detective Scanlon had first entered her room. A wide smile had lent an almost boyish expression to his sharp features as he began questioning her while his partner wandered the room, apparently inspecting the water damage. A moment later, the two detectives had been called onto the balcony that ran the length of the second floor. A second smile from Scanlon along with his reassuring words, "We only have a few more questions," had set her at ease.

Well, that was then, this was now. Now that his face was separated from hers by a scant two feet, the only hint of a smile she could see was a tiny skeptical tilt at the left corner of his wide mouth. The vertical creases on either side of his lips and the web of lines etching the corners of his narrowed eyes suggested that he'd passed his thirtieth birthday by several years, putting him well past "boyish."

And aside from the fact that Callie was being questioned about some sort of crime involving the room above hers, the no-nonsense glint in Scanlon's eyes warned that *this* was not the time to fudge on any details.

Meeting his hard gaze, Callie pushed a lock of still-damp hair off her face. One day, she promised herself, one day *soon* she would have her first name legally changed. But at this particular moment, with a representative of the law staring so pointedly into her eyes, she decided it was best to just bite the bullet, answer honestly and face the ridicule she knew would follow.

"My name is Calliope," she said quietly, then with a quickness born of long experience went on, "That's right. Like the pipe organ in a circus parade."

Detective Scanlon surprised her. Most people responded with a quick laugh and a joke or two when they ferreted out the name she'd been saddled with at birth. But this man's only response was the lift of one eyebrow as he gazed deeply into her eyes.

She'd just begun to release a sigh of relief, when Detective Malone spoke up. "*Calliope?* Geez. Did your parents have some sort of Big Top fetish or something?"

Holding the unreleased air in her chest, Callie turned to where Malone stood in front of the bare aluminum rod that served as the room's closet. His smile held the hint of a smirk. Familiar territory for Callie, including the little jolt of pain that had accompanied similar mocking jests she'd faced as a child. And, just as she had then, she curved her lips into a well-practiced smile and lifted her shoulders in an off-handed shrug as she answered him.

"Well, sort of. It seems that my mother was deeply into Native American culture at the time of my birth. She was particularly taken with the idea of naming her child for the first thing she saw after it was born."

Rusty eyebrows lifted over Malone's pale blue eyes. "Don't tell me."

"You guessed it," Callie said with just the right hint of wryness. "I had the misfortune to be born on the day the circus came to town." She paused for one beat, holding back the fact that during her childhood the circus was in town *every* day. "But, hey, I figure it could have been worse. I *could* have been named Clown-on-Stilts."

Malone chuckled, and the fireman who'd been mopping the bathroom stepped to the door to shake his head and smile at Callie.

Pah-rump-bump, she thought as she grinned back, amazed at how automatically the self-protective reflexes had kicked in, despite her weariness and the dull ache in the region of her heart.

That's it, Callie, she told herself. *Keep 'em laughing. Make the jokes first, before they can come up with the teasing names, before they can hurt you.*

Not that she thought any of these people would purposely try to hurt her. They had jobs to do, after all. Already the fireman had moved back to the bathroom to continue swishing his mop over the drenched tiles. And, after shaking his head at her, Detective Malone lifted his sharp eyes to study the ceiling again.

"Miss Chance?"

Detective Scanlon's raspy voice held no hint of ridicule. Still, Callie tensed as she turned to him, her mind echoing, *mischance.* For what must be the thousandth time, she wondered what her mother had been thinking when the woman had decided her new name should be "Mrs. Chance." Did she for one moment realize that her daughter would be called Miss Chance—a word that meant accident, mishap, misfortune? The very curse Callie had been fighting all her life?

Of course not. Her mother had been young, and too self-involved for that. And it was all water under the bridge anyway. Maybe she should just apply to have both her first *and* last names changed.

"It *is* Miss, isn't it?"

Detective Scanlon's quiet question brought Callie's attention to the man's hard gaze. She froze, fighting to keep from glancing at her left hand. The diamond ring that she'd worn publicly for the first time today was no longer on her third finger, she reminded herself. It was safely crammed into one of her purse's many compartments.

"Yes," she replied. "Miss, it is."

Callie had clenched her jaw as she said these words, making them sound a trifle defensive. Understandable, she decided, considering that she'd arrived in San Francisco with the belief that her marital status, along with her less-than-lucky last name, would soon be changing. But in the hour it had taken to get from the airport to the motel, she'd learned in the most painful way imaginable that this was not to be.

And less than two hours after *that,* she'd discovered that the woman in the room above hers had been involved in some nefarious crime which, so far, no one had seen fit to explain.

These detectives had every right to ask her about the second situation, of course. It was their job to interrogate possible witnesses. But they had no right to delve into the first. Her love life, or the debacle it had turned into, was none of their business.

The events that had conspired to bring her to the sorry state in which she currently found herself would become story material some day, of course. New friends and acquaintances would howl at the tale she would spin out of this evening's experiences. But she wasn't ready to tell that tale yet. It wouldn't come out funny right now, only pathetic. And the one thing Callie couldn't stand was to appear pathetic.

Or, to be precise, *more* so.

At this very moment Callie knew she probably resembled some overgrown lost orphan—with not a hint of makeup to cover her hated freckles, and with her neither-red-nor-brown hair tangling about the shoulders of the pink nightgown that wasn't quite long enough to cover her bare feet.

The only good luck she could see in the current situation was that Detective Scanlon didn't seem interested in any of that. He had shifted back in his chair somewhat. His midnight eyes revealed nothing of his thoughts, but Callie imagined she could see a whisper of a smile tugging at the edges of his mouth.

It disappeared as he spoke. "Well, Miss Chance, now that we have the basics covered, I need you to tell me everything that happened after your arrival at the motel. I'm particularly interested in knowing whether you came in contact with any person or persons in the room above this one."

The brief sight of that ever-so-tiny twitch at the corner of Scanlon's full lips made the man seem a bit less intimidating. Relaxing ever so slightly, Callie kept her eyes on the man's mouth as she replied, "Well, sort of."

Marcus Scanlon felt his frown tighten as he stared at the woman seated across from him. It had been a long day, near the end of a seemingly interminable week, a week in which very little had gone right. First, he'd been saddled with a new partner, a transfer from Miami, who was at the best cocky, and at the worst an out-and-out jerk. Then, he'd barely managed to fill Malone in on their caseload, when they'd been assigned to the most ridiculous case imaginable.

So why, instead of being exasperated by this woman, who *might* be a witness to a crime, or *might* be a possible suspect, did he find himself constantly fighting back a smile? His reaction bordered on insanity, especially since the arrival of Miss Callie Chance had destroyed the perfect stakeout.

He could hardly blame his response on physical attraction, considering that she reminded him of a drowned kitten. Of course, he had noticed that the slightly damp flannel gown did a lousy job of hiding some nice, lean curves. She smelled good, too, kind of musky and flowery at the same time. Her face, framed by rust-colored hair that tumbled wildly to her shoulders, was a little on the long side, but the freckles highlighting her wide cheekbones drew attention to her eyes.

They were a pale, cool shade of green with just the slightest glimmer of blue that he found rather restful, when they weren't shadowed with suspicion. But the wary expression, along with that wide, too-bright smile of hers raised all sorts of questions, along with certain doubts that he found not at all amusing.

The reason behind his desire to smile was most likely, then, a simple combination of frustration and exhaustion, brought on by too many long hours on the job. The remedy was just as simple: a decent night's sleep—something he had little hope of getting until he finished procuring Miss Chance's statement.

"Sort of," he echoed. "Would you mind telling us just

what *sort of* contact you had with the occupants of that room, Miss Chance?''

Marcus thought he saw her flinch before she replied, ''Brief and embarrassed. You see, the motel manager has a rather heavy accent. I thought Mr. Rajustani said I was to have room thirty-nine, so I went to the third floor and put my key into the lock. But it wouldn't turn in either direction, so I took the key out and flipped it over, thinking I'd stuck it in upside down. However, before I could give it another try, the door flew open.''

Scanlon finished scribbling in his notebook, then lifted his eyes to hers and asked, ''Can you describe the person who opened the door?''

''Well, it was a woman, but by the time the door was completely opened, she was already walking away, so I only saw her back at first. I heard her say something like, 'I sure hope you found—' then she stopped speaking and sneezed several times. By then, I'd looked down at the red plastic tag on my key and noticed the number *twenty*-nine. Realizing the mistake I'd made, I said, 'Excuse me,' and moved toward the stairwell to the left of the room. It was at that point that the woman turned toward me. However, it was dusk, and the only light in the room came from the bathroom area behind her, so I didn't get a very good look at her face.''

She paused. Her frown of concentration told Marcus that she was trying to remember something. He was just about to prod her when her eyes met his.

''I do remember her hair, though. It was very dark, and big.''

Marcus frowned. ''Big?''

''Yes—like they wore it in the late fifties and early sixties. Teased high and wide.''

Scanlon nodded slowly, his eyes narrowing.

''Nothing else?''

''Her eyes were very large, heavily made-up.'' Callie paused and shook her head. ''That's about all I can remember about her. However, after I turned from the door and started down the stairs, I ran, literally, into a man coming up. I'm not sure, but I think he was going to that same room.''

Marcus raised his eyebrows. ''What did *he* look like?''

''I—'' She shook her head. ''I don't know what he looked like. But he was about five foot ten, maybe five eleven. He was wearing—''

''You can't describe his face, but you know how tall he was?''

Scanlon saw the young woman stiffen. That bright, artificial smile she'd been wearing faded as her eyes narrowed.

''I happen to be five foot ten,'' she replied evenly. ''I worked for a contractor once, where I learned that stair risers are about seven inches in height. The top of the man's head reached just to my chin. You do the math. As for his face, I was about to say that he wore a baseball cap, and since I stood above him, I was only able to catch a glimpse of one ear and his chin. And that glimpse was very brief. He'd dropped something when we collided, and as I moved by him, he was bending to pick it up.''

''I see.''

What Marcus saw was that Miss Chance had wrapped her arms even more tightly around her body. Her eyes were slightly narrowed and her lips were drawn in a tight line. All of this told him that she didn't like having her honesty questioned.

And for some absurd reason, this made him want to smile.

He frowned instead. He knew all too well the dangers of trusting before he had all the facts. And this woman still raised far too many questions, both in his mind and gut, for him to trust anything she said or did.

''Did you notice anything about the cap—team name, insignia?''

Callie shook her head.

''Okay. And what makes you think this man might have been going to room thirty-nine?''

''I heard a door open and close above me. Also, I had gotten the impression that the woman was expecting someone.''

Marcus lifted his eyebrows slightly, offering silent congratulations for her observation, then started a new line of questioning.

"It was your call to the manager about water leaking from the ceiling in your bathroom that brought the fire department to the motel. How soon after you entered your room did this water problem start?"

"I'm not sure."

Scanlon gave Callie a sharp look that revealed more clearly than words that he was growing impatient. Feeling a tad testy herself, she returned his frown.

"Detective Scanlon, I've had a very long day, starting with a bus from Cape Cod to Manhattan, another bus to JFK, followed by a very long flight across the country. By the time I got to the motel, I was exhausted."

I just flew in from New York and, boy, are my arms tired.

The old gag flashed through Callie's mind so fast that she had to clamp her jaws shut to prevent the words from leaping out of her thoughts and onto her tongue. Not only was this hardly the time or the situation for jokes, but Detective Scanlon seemed determined to fight any inclination he might have to truly smile.

A shame. Those earlier bright grins he'd flashed at her had held such promise.

Callie shut her eyes. What was wrong with her? First that silly line leaping to her mind at such an inappropriate moment, and now this fixation on Detective Scanlon's smile. Hardly the sign of a healthy mind, given the reason the man was here.

Given the reason *she* was here, and not with the man she'd come to San Francisco to marry.

This thought sent a blend of pain, anger and disbelief shooting through Callie's chest with such suddenness that she had to swallow back a gasp. Her only defense against the building ache was to pull her thoughts back to the matter at hand.

"Actually," she started as she opened her eyes. "When I first stepped into my room, I couldn't decide what I wanted

more, a long soak in hot water or something to eat. I finally
decided to get some take-out to enjoy after my bath. I'd seen
a diner a block away as the taxi drove by, so I walked down
to get a sandwich and a container of milk. I was probably
gone twenty minutes or so. When I reentered my room, I
dropped my purse and the bag of food on the table in the
corner.''

Callie paused, thinking back to those moments. ''That's
the first I recall hearing the sound of running water overhead,'' she went on. ''This place isn't exactly the Plaza Hotel,
so I was concerned that there might not be enough hot water
to fill my tub. I stepped in to turn the faucet on, then came
back in here to unpack my nightgown and shampoo.''

''I assume there was plenty of hot water.''

Detective Malone's wry quip pulled Callie's attention to
the man. Again, the slight hint of a smirk greeted her as he
gazed pointedly at her damp hair. Giving him a tight smile,
she replied, ''Yes. I had a nice, warm bath. But the whole
time I was bathing, I could hear water running in the room
above. I remember thinking that the woman must be taking
a very *long* shower. Then, after I'd rinsed my hair, I became
aware of a tinkling sound in my bathroom. At first I thought
maybe I'd left the sink faucet running when I filled a drinking
glass earlier. I looked over and saw that water was running
down the wall from the ceiling above my sink. Minutes later,
it was practically a waterfall.''

''That's when you called the manager?''

Callie turned to reply to Detective Scanlon's question.
''Yes.''

She hoped he didn't want to know much more. The next
half hour was a blur. A siren had wailed to a stop in front of
the motel, then a seemingly endless train of people had come
in and out of her room. First, the motel owner to inspect the
damage, then a fireman promising that someone would come
in to clean up the water in her bathroom, and finally a policeman to inform her that some detectives would be arriving
to ask her some questions.

Callie drew in a deep breath. Well, they had asked their

questions. Now she just wanted to be left alone, to deal with the mess her life had become, and figure out where she would go from here.

But first she had some questions of her own.

"Excuse me, Detective Scanlon," she began. "The uniformed officer told me that a crime of some sort had occurred in room thirty-nine. I'm assuming this was more serious than a hit-and-run involving an overflowing bathtub."

Detective Malone had stepped over to join them. The two detectives exchanged glances. Some sort of unspoken communication must have crossed between them, because Malone turned to Callie.

"We have reason to believe that room thirty-nine was occupied by a pair of felons. It appears they ran into a bit of bad luck. The sink faucet snapped off, creating something of a geyser, which flooded the room and spooked them into taking off."

At this second mention of luck, Scanlon's dark eyebrows moved together in a scowl. Callie, on the other hand, found herself fighting an almost irresistible desire to laugh out loud.

Should she tell them about her "curse," she wondered? Should she tell them what this might mean to anyone who had the ill fortune to be anywhere *near* her? Should she take this opportunity to reveal the nickname her mother had branded her with?

No, she decided. Telling Detective Malone that her mother had jokingly called her "Calamity Jane" whenever things started to go bad would only give him something more to smirk at. And since Scanlon claimed to believe in neither good luck nor bad, he would probably just scoff at the idea that someone could be a jinx, that their mere presence could call down all sorts of disasters, including, but not limited to, broken water faucets. He certainly wouldn't understand what it was like to have bad luck descend like a dark storm—a storm that had the nasty habit of raining disaster upon those around her, generally leaving her untouched except for an acute case of embarrassment and guilt.

Besides, Callie really wasn't up to sharing the litany of

accidents that had befallen the poor souls unfortunate enough to get swept up in one of the many bouts with misfortune that littered her past. The mere thought of revealing the "bird incident" with Maynard the Magician, for example, was enough to make her shudder.

So the urge to laugh about the geyser in the room above hers, along with the thieves rushing to escape the deluge, disappeared as quickly as it had come. This was replaced by a sense of sorrow, far older than the oh-so-fresh hurt of having been hit with the unavoidable truth that, in her case, falling in love inevitably led to disaster.

The switch from near-laughter to the beginnings of self-pity was almost too sudden. Callie's emotions had been in a state of suspended animation ever since the moment she learned the kind of liar and cheat she'd fallen in love with. Now, a deep sense of betrayal and disappointment mixed with anger at Dave for fooling her, and worse, fury at herself for having been fooled.

In an attempt to calm the volatile mix of emotions, Callie took a deep breath and forced herself to concentrate on what Malone had said about the people in the room above.

"So, they were frightened off," she said slowly. "Well, I suppose that means *something* good came out of this mess, then. The thieves were at least prevented from striking again."

Again, a look passed between the two detectives. This time it was Scanlon who replied.

"That's not exactly the case here." Scanlon paused, his eyes narrowing on Callie. "You see, earlier today a certain wealthy gentleman received a telephone message, ordering him to check into this hotel, room thirty-three, and bring a suitcase full of ransom money. After he informed us of this, we posted two officers, posing as man and wife, in one of the rooms across the courtyard to watch for the ransom attempt and apprehend these people. However, the attempt was never made."

He paused, and leaned toward Callie. "I believe the ransom call was made by one of the two people who checked into room thirty-nine. I also believe that your accidental arrival on their doorstep made them nervous. Fearing a possible sting operation, they caused that little flood themselves so they could escape unnoticed in the confusion stirred up by the arrival of the fire department. Luck had nothing to do with any of this.''

Callie's thoughts were too involved with his earlier words to react to the man's sarcastic reference to luck. Staring into his dark eyes, her heart sank to her stomach and all the breath left her chest.

''Ransom?'' she finally managed. ''Are you trying to say that because I showed up at the wrong place at the wrong time, that some poor child might—''

Scanlon's quick ''No!'' broke into Callie's words. The man's features appeared to soften ever so slightly as he shook his head.

''Not a child,'' he said. ''A cat. Our suspects stole an expensive, champion cat and were trying to extort an exorbitant payoff for the animal's return.''

Not a child, Callie repeated to herself. A cat.

A *cat?*

The shudder overcame Callie before she had a chance to suppress it.

She hadn't always felt this way about felines. One of her earliest circus memories was the excitement of watching Sheba deliver two tiger cubs, followed by the feel of one of the squirming, squalling bodies in her own chubby hands. Of course, that was before Ebony, the black panther, had escaped and—

''I have only one or two more questions, Miss Chance.''

Callie looked up at Scanlon. There was that word again, for the umpteenth time. Mischance. She was tempted to ask the man to stop calling her that, but she was too weary to do more than nod.

''What time did your plane arrive?''

''My—plane?''

Callie had expected to be asked if she could provide a more detailed description of the man and woman in room thirty-nine. She was *not* prepared to be questioned about the disastrous events that had brought her to this wretched motel.

"I don't understand," she said. "What does the time of my arrival at the airport have to do with what happened upstairs?"

She noticed that with this question she had finally managed to get Detective Scanlon to truly smile. However, this was just a slight flattening of his lips as he lifted one eyebrow, a gesture completely devoid of any amusement or warmth.

"We never know," he replied. "The time?"

Callie frowned. "Seven forty-five."

"And you arrived at the motel, when?"

"About an hour later."

After jotting in his notebook, Scanlon gazed deeply into her eyes, then raised his left eyebrow ever so slightly as he asked, "And the reason for your visit to San Francisco?"

It seemed like such a simple question.

Detective Scanlon's dark eyes said as much, holding Callie's with a look of guileless inquiry. Perhaps it was only her admittedly wild imagination that suggested his expression was a ploy, meant to relax her vigilance so he could draw specific information from her. Perhaps the tension stretching between them didn't mean he suspected her of some nefarious activity. Perhaps she was being a trifle oversensitive, what with the anger, pain and acute embarrassment that shot through her each time she recalled the touching domestic scene she'd witnessed on the walkway in front of Dave Johnson's house.

But Callie didn't want to think about that right now, let alone describe it to a stranger. She was way too tired to work up the energy required to tell the tale properly, to shape the day's events into a wild and funny story that would make these detectives laugh with her and not at her—and the stupidity that had brought her to this town.

However, she knew she had to come up with some kind of answer. Detective Scanlon's dark eyes gazed unwaveringly into hers in a way that seemed to say, "Talk to me. Trust me with all your secrets."

Impossible.

Not now, anyway. Not with the sense of betrayal filling her chest, rising to choke her. Not with the anger and sorrow burning behind her eyes, threatening to melt into a hot river of tears. Callie just knew if she tried to explain her reason for being in San Francisco, that her voice would falter, tears would trickle onto her cheeks, and the ache in her chest would rise in a hopeless sob.

She couldn't allow that to happen. Given the choice between lying and exposing herself to possible ridicule, or worse—pity—there was no question. She would go with the lie.

Chapter 2

"I came to visit a friend," Callie said.

True, so far. A bit of understatement, perhaps, but that was what she'd thought she was doing.

"I see," Scanlon replied. "And your friend picked you up at the airport and brought you here?"

Callie shook her head. She knew the motel manager could contradict that, so she took the basics of her story and told Detective Scanlon that she'd taken a cab to her *friend's* house, only to learn that this person had been suddenly called out of town on a family emergency. After that, Callie explained, she'd had no choice but to ask the taxi driver to recommend an inexpensive place to stay.

Callie finished with a small smile. This last part, at least, was the truth. And the rest was close enough to let her release a tiny breath of relief.

"How long will you be staying?"

The question caught Callie mid-sigh. "I...don't know."

I thought it might be forever.

Callie brushed away the self-pitying thought, blinking as she tried to come up with an answer that wouldn't lead the detective back to her *friend*. Scanlon saved her that effort by reaching into his breast pocket and handing her a small white rectangle.

"Here's my card. I might have more questions to ask you at a later date, so if you do change addresses, let me know."

Marcus chose his words and tone carefully so there would be no doubt in the woman's mind that this was not just a suggestion. He watched Callie take the card, glance at it then look up at him. When her pale eyes widened in comprehension, he gave her a brief nod, stood up and turned for the door.

Outside, he waited at the foot of the stairs leading to the third-floor balcony until Malone joined him.

"Let's see if forensics has come up with anything, then we can call it a night." As he started up the stairs, he said, "I got a memo from the D.A. today regarding the Gerraro shooting. I want you to stop at the gun shop at Mission and Ninth tomorrow morning before coming to the station. We've given that fellow enough time to locate that registration form he *misplaced*. And just in case you think I'm slacking, I'll be getting in early, too. I need to make some calls to the east coast."

He had lowered his voice as they reached the top step, aware that sound travelled easily down open staircases.

Malone turned to him. "Back east? Why?"

Marcus pulled his partner into room thirty-nine, where three men wearing suits and plastic gloves moved about, small brushes, tweezers and plastic baggies in hand.

"I need to do some checking on Miss Chance."

"On Calliope?" Malone frowned. "Why? I'm not any happier than you that our catnappers escaped, but her situation seems to be a rather clear-cut case of being in the wrong place at the wrong time. Which would appear like a run of rather rotten luck on the part of this particular young lady. First she loses her job, next the friend she's to stay with isn't here when she arrives, and then she ends up in the worst motel on a street full of far more decent ones."

Marcus stared at his partner. Malone was right. *Miss*

Chance did seem to be living up to her name. And she certainly presented the picture of injured innocence, with those large opalescent eyes and that wavy rust-tinted hair tangling in waiflike disarray to her shoulders.

But being good at his job required that Marcus look past things like thick-lashed eyes and wide mouths that curved suddenly into disarming smiles. It meant listening for changes of inflection, watching for hands to tighten, sensing when someone paused too often or too long. Marcus had taught himself to be aware of all these things, and more. His close observation of Callie Chance had made one thing abundantly clear.

"She's lying."

"Lying?" Malone gave a scoffing snort. "About what?"

"I'm not sure."

By ten o'clock the next morning, although Marcus knew quite a bit more about Callie Jane Chance, he still had no idea what she might have been lying about. And he wasn't sure he was going to get the opportunity to find out.

"Scanlon. I got your message when I arrived at the station. What brings us to the emergency room?"

Marcus turned to see the double doors shut behind Rick Malone. "Miss Chance," he replied.

Malone frowned. "Calliope? What about her?"

"She was the victim of a hit-and-run accident this morning. Paramedics brought her in about nine-thirty. A nurse found my card in the young woman's purse and telephoned me. According to the officers who were called to the scene, the only witness is the man who runs a flower stand near the motel. Seems that Miss Chance landed in a display set up as—you're not going to believe this—a bed of roses."

Malone's face broke into a wide grin. "You're kidding."

Marcus shook his head. "No. The flower stand owner couldn't give the car's make or model, just said it was dark blue. Or maybe gray. I was told that Miss Chance was barely semiconscious when she arrived, so no one has taken a statement from her yet. I told the uniforms we'd do the honors."

"She hurt bad?"

Marcus shrugged. "Apparently the flowers did a fair job of breaking her fall. The paramedics said she didn't appear to have any broken bones and her vital signs were good. The biggest concern is the possibility of a head injury. I've been told to wait here for someone to apprise me of her condition."

Malone glanced around the emergency room, where men and women in blue scrubs scuttled between the central desk area and various white curtained cubicles. "Looks like a madhouse in here."

"It was worse when I arrived. There was an accident involving a van load of preschoolers. A nurse just told me they've all been checked out and none of them are seriously hurt. I'm beginning to wonder, though, if Miss Chance has been forgotten in the shuffle."

Scanlon's stomach tightened at the thought of the young woman lying alone, untended behind one of those curtains. Like last night's strange desire to smile, this reaction was completely out of character for him. He prided himself on maintaining an emotional detachment, found that this made it easier to focus and extract the truth from a situation.

And that was what he needed to do now—focus on the case at hand. Turning to Malone, he recounted his conversation with Marie Wilson, Callie's former employer. The woman had explained that she and her husband, Stan, had recently received a surprise offer for their deli. Since Callie was living in an apartment above the business, and the new owners had their own staff and wanted immediate occupancy, Miss Chance became unemployed and homeless in one fell swoop.

"Is that so?" Malone narrowed his eyes and gave Marcus a wide smile. "Now tell me, just when are you going to give *her* your little lecture on not believing in bad luck?"

Marcus fought the temptation to smile, lifting one eyebrow instead as he replied. "I have to admit, that thought did occur to me this morning. According to the Wilson woman, before coming to Cape Cod, Callie had a rather checkered past, job-wise.''

Marcus paused as a nurse walked by, moving too fast for him to grab her and ask about Callie.

''Fired?'' Malone prodded.

''Not according to Mrs. Wilson. It seems something unfortunate inevitably happened. For example, Miss Chance worked as a doctor's receptionist for six months, until authorities arrested the man for practicing medicine without a license. A woman who owned a plant shop was training Callie as a florist, when her entire inventory was wiped out by an infestation of spider mites, forcing the woman into bankruptcy. And then there was the pillow factory, where a boiler exploded. No one was hurt, but several hundred pounds of feathers formed a mushroom cloud above a four-block area of Manhattan, creating a minor panic in the streets.''

Marcus allowed himself a small smile as he went on. ''It was apparently after the last fiasco that Miss Chance moved to the Cape. Mrs. Wilson was quick to inform me that absolutely nothing of an unfortunate nature happened while the young woman was working for her. On the contrary, she said, the deli expanded into catering shortly after Callie hired on, and the business thrived. On top of that, the recent offer for their place will provide the couple with a nice retirement.''

Malone cocked his head to one side. ''Still think Calliope's lying about something?''

Marcus frowned. ''*Lying* might not be the right word. More like holding something back. According to Mrs. Wilson, Callie worked and lived with her and her husband for a full year before she began talking much about her past jobs, making them into amusing tales that could have been scripts for Laurel and Hardy. Apparently, however, the young woman said very little about her personal life.''

''Whew.'' Malone made a big show of shuddering. ''Makes you wonder about those stories, doesn't it?''

Marcus frowned at the sarcastic grin twisting his partner's mouth, then shrugged. He *had* been wondering about that. As the Wilson woman answered his questions, he'd found himself recalling Callie's overly bright smile—a defense mechanism if he ever saw one—and the way she crossed her arms in a tight hug, as if accustomed to having sole responsibility for comforting herself.

After drawing in a slow breath, Marcus clamped his jaw tightly. He took pride in his ability to analyze the people he came in contact with. The skill had come at a great cost to him, after blindly trusting two of the people who'd been closest to him. That little miscalculation had cost him everything, and it was a mistake he'd vowed never to repeat.

"Can I help you two?"

The soft voice pulled Marcus's attention to the short, grayhaired woman in blue scrubs who stood on his left, gazing up at him expectantly.

"We're police detectives," Marcus replied, reaching into the breast pocket of his jacket, withdrawing a leather wallet and flashing his badge in one practiced move. "We're here about Callie Chance. How is she?"

"Been awake and alert for a half hour now. The doctor treating her is over there." She gestured to a tall man in green, scribbling on a clipboard. "The patient is in the curtained cubicle in the far right corner."

"Thank you." Marcus turned to Malone. "Why don't you check her status with the doctor? I'll get started with Miss Chance."

As Marcus reached the curtained-off area, he heard a female voice say, "You were incredibly lucky, you know."

Stopping at the edge of the foot-wide opening in the white drape, he stared past the blond nurse who had spoken. Callie reclined against the raised mattress of the narrow gurney, a sling holding her left arm across the front of her blue-on-white checked hospital gown. Her red-brown hair looked darker and almost as tangled as the night before, while the nearly insignificant freckles he'd noticed dotting her nose seemed now all too prominent against her pale complexion.

"Lucky?" Callie asked as she glanced at the nurse. She gave an odd, choked laugh before going on, "Well, I might be wrong, but I think if I'd been *truly* lucky, I wouldn't be in a hospital.''

The nurse smiled as she removed the blood pressure cuff from Callie's slender arm.

"Well, yes. But you have no broken bones, and even though you were unconscious for a bit, you don't seem to have a concussion. Just a sprained wrist, some lovely bruises, and surprisingly few scratches, considering.''

"Florists' roses rarely have thorns,'' Callie replied. "Unless someone orders the wrong ones, in which case—never mind. Do you suppose I could get dressed and leave now?''

Her expression, that of a winsome ten year old asking to go out and play, made Marcus smile in spite of himself. A moment later he firmed his lips into a compressed line.

Joking around with fellow officers was one thing, he reminded himself. Laughing with an outsider was a different matter altogether, especially when that outsider had so mysteriously and inexplicably thrown a perfectly good stakeout into total disarray.

"You *are* a persistent one, aren't you?'' The nurse was speaking again. "I told you, Miss Chance, we can't let you go until your paperwork is finished. And you shouldn't leave alone. Who can I call to come get you?''

Marcus took this as his cue. Stepping through the split in the curtain he said, "I think I can take care of that. My name is Detective Scanlon.'' Again the badge came out. "I'm here to question Miss Chance about her accident. And when she's ready to leave, I'll provide taxi service for her.''

The nurse nodded. "Perfect. I'll see how her release forms are coming.'' She turned to Callie. "The doctor will be in for one more look at you.''

With that, the woman stepped past Marcus. The swish of fabric marked her exit through the curtains behind him as he studied the combined surprise and suspicion in Callie Chance's light green eyes.

"How did you know I was here?'' she asked.

"The admitting clerk called me. They found my card in

your purse. Mine was the only San Francisco telephone number in there.''

Marcus watched carefully for her response. Her rust-colored eyebrows moved together, but her gaze didn't waver.

"Oh, that's right," she said. "I put your card in there last night, after you left.''

Marcus remained silent for another moment. As he'd told his partner, so far everything he'd learned about this woman matched the information she'd given him the night before, including her wildly improbable first name. What didn't mesh was the fact that the admitting clerk hadn't found any other San Francisco numbers, like one for the "friend" Callie claimed to be visiting.

He knew that this fact alone didn't mean Callie was lying about this friend—she might very well know this person's number by heart. Still, the instincts he'd developed over the last ten years told him that she was holding *something* back. Eventually he'd find out what this was and how it might apply to last night's debacle at the motel, but in the meantime he had to deal with this newest development.

"So, Miss Chance," he said softly as he stepped to the end of her bed. "What—"

He stopped speaking in response to the hand Callie lifted in an arresting motion.

"Would you mind not calling me that?" she asked.

Marcus frowned. "Calling you what?"

"*Mischance*. You know, as in accidents and mishaps. I've had more than enough of those commodities during the last twenty-four hours, thank you very much. In fact, most of my life—"

She broke off and glanced away. Marcus watched as she gave her head a small, almost imperceptible shake before she looked back at him with a smile and asked, "Would you just call me Callie?"

Marcus found himself staring at her mouth. It was wide, perhaps too much so for her long, slender face, but her smile had a way of lighting up her rather ordinary features, lending them an odd sort of beauty and tempting him to smile in return.

This time he gave in to the urge. It was good strategy, he told himself, a way to gain her confidence, to break down the wary expression darkening her eyes.

"All right, then, *Callie,*" he said. "What happened to you?"

"It seems I was hit by a car."

"I know that much." Marcus paused, letting his lips widen just a bit more. "Where and how did this happen?"

"I was going to the diner near the motel for some breakfast, crossing at the corner, and on a green light, like a good girl. I'd barely stepped off the curb when I heard brakes squealing, then someone shouting, *Look out!* I turned and saw a car coming for me. I tried to get out of the way, but I guess I zigged when I should have zagged because the left fender hit my hip as I moved. I remember flying into the air, and the next thing I knew, I was waking up here."

Marcus nodded slowly. It might only be a coincidence that this woman had become the victim of a hit-and-run the day after she'd caught a glimpse of two suspected felons. But he didn't like coincidences any more than he liked lies.

"What can you tell me about the car? Did you get a glimpse of the driver?"

"No, I—" She broke off, frowning as she continued. "I didn't see the driver. I do remember watching the car come at me, kind of like I imagine a deer would stare at approaching headlights. I think the car was some dark color, but I don't recall noticing the plate at all."

Marcus nodded. "Shock will do that to you. There's a chance you'll remember later. If it doesn't happen spontaneously, we might consider hypnosis. With your permission, of course."

Callie's eyes widened. Before either of them could speak, a male voice broke in.

"Well, *Miss Chance,* you certainly are living up to your name."

Scanlon turned to find his partner standing just inside the curtain, a slightly snide smile twisting Malone's thin lips.

The sudden desire to punch the man caught Marcus by complete surprise. Clenching his jaw instead of his fist, he glared at the man and grated out, "And we're to call her Callie for just that reason."

Malone's lips flattened out as his smile widened. Lifting his shoulders, he said, "Well then, I guess 'Calamity Jane' would be out of the question."

At the sound of that hated, dreaded nickname, Callie's mouth opened and air came rushing in, none too quietly, before the sound was drowned out by Scanlon's, "*Yes.* That would be out of the question. And you, Detective Malone, are out of order."

Callie blinked as she closed her mouth. No one, absolutely no one in her entire life had ever come to her defense like this. She turned to Scanlon, searching for the words to thank him, but before she could form one syllable, he spoke to his partner again.

"Now that we have that settled, we have a problem. I don't think it's a good idea for Callie to return to that motel. Her description of the occupants of room thirty-nine are pretty useless, but our catnappers would have no way of knowing that. I suppose that—"

"Wait a minute." Callie couldn't keep from interrupting. "Are you trying to say that someone ran me over today on *purpose?*"

Scanlon turned to her. She thought she saw something like concern in his hard-as-sapphire eyes as he replied, "It's a distinct possibility. Which means we'll have to find another place for you to stay. Some place you can't be traced to. Perhaps—" his eyes suddenly narrowed "—that friend of yours might be home now?"

So much for hero-worship.

The gratitude Callie had felt toward this man for defending her against his partner's barb completely faded in the face of this sneak attack. Oh, she knew Scanlon had a job to do. She might even admire the fact that he had obviously seen through her little lie. But she wasn't about to feel beholden to a man who was trying to strip her soul bare while she was stuck, helpless, in a hospital bed.

If she attempted to tell these two men about this so-called friend, she'd be forced to reveal the entire, sordid tale of her latest and most disastrous attempt at love. At this moment, she was far too angry and embarrassed to consider letting anyone know how foolish she'd been.

Especially with Detective Malone's thin lips just waiting to smirk again.

So, she stared directly into Scanlon's dark blue eyes as she replied, "I don't think that would be possible. I have no idea when my friend will return. Besides, I've told you everything I can recall. I've been thinking that perhaps I should just arrange to go back to Cape Cod, unless you're saying I have to stay in San Francisco."

Scanlon's gaze held hers for several seconds before he replied, "No, you don't have to, but I was hoping you might work with our sketch artist. The motel manager never saw the woman's face and his recollection of the male suspect is compromised by the fact that he saw the man's ID, which we now know to be fake. This makes you the only person who might identify either of these people."

"But I told you, I could barely make out the woman's features in the poor light, and I never saw the man's face at all."

"I know what you said, and what you think you did or didn't see. But my landlady is a hypnotherapist, who is quite skilled at helping witnesses access memories they aren't consciously aware of. If you agree to work with Zoe and the department's sketch artist, you might just provide us with a drawing of the suspects, not to mention help us find the hit-and-run driver who put you in here."

When Scanlon stopped speaking, he continued to hold Callie's gaze. Just as she began to fear that he could see right into her soul, the man smiled, a wide gorgeous smile just like the first one he'd flashed her in the motel, the one that had made her feel safe, warm and totally at ease.

"Hey," he murmured as he leaned toward her. "If you don't care about yourself, think about the missing cat. An innocent kitty is counting on you. Imagine what a *cat*astrophe it would be if he never got back to his owner? Think of his poor owner being deprived of his puddy-tat pal, just because you wouldn't take the time to search your subconscious and give us a usable description."

Callie shook her head slowly. What a rotten, *rotten* man this was, making her feel guilty about some *cat*. She fought off a shudder at the thought.

Her mother had warned her from the time she was little that felines were harbingers of bad luck, and the unfortunate experience with Ebony had taught her this was true. As much as she wanted to help this stolen cat and its owner, bad luck was a commodity she didn't need any more of at the moment.

"Look," she said. "This little accident of mine has changed things quite a bit. After paying my emergency room bill, I won't have a lot to live on while looking for a job in a strange city. So, I've decided that my best bet is to buy a bus ticket back to the East Coast, where I have contacts and some hope of getting a job."

"Well, Miss Chance, that is something you shouldn't do for at least a day or so."

Marcus swivelled toward this new voice. A thin, bespectacled doctor rounded the far end of the bed and placed his hand on Callie's forehead to gently urge her face toward his.

"The CAT scan showed no sign of internal bleeding, or head trauma," he said as he peered into her eyes. "But you were unconscious for a little over an hour. Someone should check on you every hour for the next twenty-four. How about we admit you into the hospital for observation?"

Marcus watched Callie closely as she looked up at the doctor. For one moment fear registered in her wide eyes. Then the bright smile appeared. "CAT-scan?" Callie asked. "That wouldn't be some sort of sick pun that Detective Scanlon here put you up to making, would it?"

When the doctor only frowned in reply, Callie shot a wry

glance toward Marcus before her expression sobered and she returned her attention to the physician.

"Look," she said. "I'm fine, really. I probably just passed out from hunger and shock. I don't even have a headache. Besides, I really can't afford a night here. I'm sure I'll be all right on my own. Just let me—"

"I know a place she can stay."

The words were out of Marcus's mouth before he had a chance to second-guess them.

For ten long years he'd been meticulous about keeping his professional and private lives separate. What he had in mind now was going to violate that principle—big time.

He had his reasons, of course. Callie Chance might very well hold the key to finding whoever had stolen Gerald Harding's championship Russian blue cat, a case he wanted solved and off his books as soon as possible.

Looking for an overpriced ball of fur might not have irritated him so, if he hadn't had several more compelling cases in his files. Or if Captain Bradford hadn't taken such obvious, unholy glee in assigning the case to Marcus, right on the heels of saddling him with Rick Malone.

He had no idea what had gotten the captain's back up this time. Could be the racquetball tournament Marcus had bested him in two weeks ago, or the fact that Marcus refused to play political ping-pong. Could just be that the man got up on the wrong side of his crypt.

The point was, the stakes had been raised. They didn't call him "Bulldog" Scanlon for nothing. Once he got his teeth into a case, he refused to let go. He needed to solve this crime, to show his boss who was…boss. It was time to return Bradford's serve, and at the moment, the only ball in Marcus's court was the pale woman lying in the bed in front of him.

"There's a vacant studio apartment in my building," he told Callie. "I'll get it listed as a temporary safe house and the department will pick up the rent."

Marcus was watching for Callie's response, when Malone spoke up. "You sure that will fly with Bradford?"

Marcus didn't take his eyes off the woman in the gurney. "Yes. That is, if Miss Chance agrees to work with the sketch artist."

Callie was no longer smiling. The frown lines above her eyes told him she was weighing her choices. Finally she nodded. "I can do that."

"Well, this all sounds well and good." The doctor spoke in clipped tones, as he consulted Callie's chart. "But if I'm going to release you from hospital, I need to know there will be someone available to watch over you for the next twenty-four hours."

Marcus shrugged. "Sure, doc. Me. Maybe my partner. *Someone* will be there tonight."

The expression on Callie's face when he'd suggested that Malone might watch over her had almost been too comical, Marcus decided as his vintage Karmann-Ghia pulled away from the motel an hour later. Of course, she wouldn't have had any way of knowing that he'd had no intention of foisting Rick Malone on her.

While Callie had settled up with the hospital, he'd sent his partner off to work on the other cases in their load. The young detective had been briefed on all of them and, who knew, maybe a pair of fresh eyes would pick up a new lead and clear one or two.

It would never occur to the highly competitive Larry Bradford that Marcus's first priority was to bring a case to a successful conclusion, with little regard for where the credit went. So, if Malone ended up solving any of the items in his files, Bradford might be so pleased at Marcus's "humiliation" that he wouldn't balk at all at springing for Callie's stay at Zoe's place.

Marcus really didn't need to see the dark circles under Callie's eyes to know she was tired. But after refusing his offer to pack her things up, she'd finally allowed him to carry her suitcase down to the car, while insisting on taking her bulging leather tote bag herself, which looked every bit as heavy.

When he held the door for her to slip into the passenger seat, Marcus had watched her gather the bag into her lap, then examine with a frown the tattered strap attached to a large metal ring by what looked like a thread. Again with a little shake of her head, she leaned back against the seat and closed her eyes with a resigned sigh that seemed to ask what else could go wrong.

"Is this going to be all right with your landlady?"

Marcus glanced at Callie. Now her eyes were wide-open and full of concern.

He gave in to the urge to offer some reassurance, smiled and said, "Odd. When I spoke to Marie Wilson today, she told me that you'd held quite a number of jobs in the past. I don't recall mind-reading being on the list."

Callie's confused expression widened his smile. "I was just thinking about my landlady when you asked about her. While you were finishing up at the hospital, I got hold of my captain and convinced him it would be less expensive to put you up in the studio rather than take up an entire safe house. Then I called Zoe. She said she hasn't found the right person to rent the place to yet, so a temporary tenant is just fine with her."

"You're sure?"

Marcus nodded. "You'll like Zoe. And you'll love the apartment, if you don't mind climbing stairs. The building has four levels, and the studio is on the fourth, but the hike is worth it. If you enjoy looking at that—" he nodded to the right as they turned onto Marina Drive "—you'll love the view from your window."

Turning in the direction Marcus had indicated, Callie found herself gazing at a wide swath of green grass flowing away from the nearby curb to the edge of the bay. A forest of masts rose from a harbor ahead of them, and beyond that, the graceful scallop of the Golden Gate Bridge rode between the pale blue sky and the deep turquoise water.

"I might never leave my window," she breathed.

"You will if you want to eat."

Callie shifted her attention to Marcus as he turned left into a neighborhood packed with homes built right next to each other, like a series of townhouses.

"What do you mean by that?" she asked.

"Zoe's place isn't an official apartment building, just a large house. Zoe decided after her husband's death ten years ago that it was too large for one person. So she rents out portions of it. You'll be in the attic studio. I have a bathroom, bedroom and living room on the floor below, and Zoe has a matching set of rooms on the same level, where she lives with her two cats."

"Cats?"

The question, and the hint of panic in her voice, slipped out before Callie had time to think. Scanlon negotiated another turn onto a side street, then glanced at her, one eyebrow cocked in query.

"You allergic? Don't worry. Zoe still sees a few clients— she's a semi-retired therapist—and uses the first level living room as an office, so she usually keeps the animals upstairs."

Callie wasn't allergic, but she had no intention of explaining her feelings about cats, so she turned her attention to the tightly packed houses lining the streets.

On the ground level, they all had some combination of garage door and entryway, or garage door and steps leading to a second level. Above that, however, each building was different, with heights running anywhere from two to four stories and styles alternating wildly. In one short block she saw an example of Victorian Gothic, a place that looked like an Italian villa, an English Tudor-style home and a Spanish hacienda.

"It was too much expense and hassle for Zoe to add kitchens to the apartments," Marcus was saying. "So the occupants all use the one on the main floor. We each have an assigned set of shelves, both in the fridge and in the cupboards."

The car pulled into a driveway as Marcus finished speaking. He switched the engine off, then turned to Callie. "Well, here you are. Home sweet home. For a while, anyway."

For a very short while, Callie thought. Her lips tightened

against the bitter taste in her mouth. Here today, gone tomorrow. How familiar, how like those years when she and her mother existed in a series of trailers, following the circus route, rarely in one place for more than a week.

Shrugging away the old, familiar sense of uncertainty, Callie opened her door. Once on her feet, she struggled to adjust her heavy brown shoulder bag, reminding herself to fix the strap as soon as she unpacked needle and thread, then glanced up to see just what sort of place she was going to be living in for the next few days.

The house sang of Paris. Looking up, past the shimmering black garage door and the wrought iron railing that curved up to a bright pink doorway, she saw that the stucco structure was a soft dove gray. On either side of the front door, two wide windows were framed with black shutters and ledged with window boxes overflowing with brilliant flowers. Above that, two more windows were enclosed by iron balconies. A mansard roof, tiled in dark blue slate and inset with a single dormered window, formed the fourth level.

"Marcus," a female voice called out. "What are you thinking?"

Callie turned toward the voice. A woman stood at the top of the steps. Her short gray hair matched the color of the house and framed a lean face, while the dress flowing down her slim body echoed the exuberant flowers at the windows.

Marcus's reply echoed off the building. "I'm only going to be parked here a moment."

"No, no. Not your car." The gray head shook. "I meant that you should not keep the young woman standing there. Bring her up to me immediately."

Marcus turned to Callie with a wide smile, one even wider than the first one that had made him appear so boyish.

"You may have heard the British refer to She Who Must Be Obeyed," he said. "Well, prepare yourself to meet the French version."

"Zoe is French?" Callie asked as she followed Marcus toward the stairs.

He signalled her to precede him, then replied as they

mounted, "French by birth, Italian by marriage, and San Franciscan by choice. Callie Chance, meet Zoe Zeffarelli," he finished as they reached the top step.

Zoe didn't look anywhere near the seventy years of age that Marcus had mentioned. Every inch of her lean, five-foot-eight frame looked spry and strong, and her skin showed few lines. When Callie stretched out her hand, Zoe enfolded it in long lean fingers. Her hazel eyes searched Callie's for several moments, until her bright red lips eased into a wide smile.

"I do not believe this," she said. "You are absolutely *perfect*."

Before Callie knew what was happening, the strong hand was tugging at hers, pulling her into an enthusiastic hug, leather tote and all. When the embrace was over, warm hazel eyes smiled into Callie's for one second before the woman turned and began leading her into the foyer, speaking to Marcus as she went.

"Oh, what wonderful luck. I had begun to despair of ever finding the right person to share my home. And, look, here is just the one. Marcus, go fetch her bags and bring them to her room. We shall meet you there."

Callie barely registered the last part of the woman's enthusiastic statement. Although the warmth of her greeting flowed through Callie like the sunlight streaming into the bright foyer, the glow was swallowed up in an icy shadow as her mind froze on the word "luck."

There was only one kind of luck in Callie's life right now, and it was most definitely not the good sort Zoe had mentioned. And though she might not know Marcus or Zoe very well, she was sure that neither of these people deserved the sort of disaster that would undoubtedly befall them if she should come to live under their roof.

Zoe had already begun to mount the stairs when Callie ordered her feet to stop moving, bringing herself to an abrupt halt as she said, "Wait."

The older woman turned toward her. Marcus halted his march toward the door. As Callie turned to meet his surprised look, her bag swung around, reached the apex of its arc, then kept moving until it crashed to the floor, spilling the entire contents across the creamy marble.

Callie just shook her head, stared numbly at the mess on the floor before looking up, and forced herself to speak. "I can't stay here. Detective Malone was right. I *am* a Calamity Jane."

Chapter 3

With Callie's words echoing in the light-filled foyer, Zoe Zeffarelli gazed at her quizzically. Marcus was staring at her as well. Finally he lifted one eyebrow and repeated, "A Calamity Jane."

"Yes," Callie replied as she hunkered down, towed the purse to her, and began stuffing items into the cavernous mouth, starting with her wallet, makeup case and checkbook. "You know, a jinx." She scooped up her rabbit's foot. "An albatross." A small horseshoe and clear acrylic circle holding a four-leaf clover disappeared into the leather maw. "An ill wind that blows nobody any good." She grabbed the salt shaker and piece of wood and dumped them in as well. "Bad luck," she finished as she fisted the mouth of her bag and stood to meet Marcus's gaze, her face flaming.

"I don't believe—"

"In luck," Callie finished. "So I've heard. But it doesn't matter if you believe or not. The fact of the matter is, I am a jinx. When I'm around—"

Zoe's fingers clamped suddenly around Callie's free hand, halting Callie's words.

A fierce frown etched two deep vertical lines between the older woman's black eyebrows. "Come. In here." As she spoke, Zoe moved into a long, narrow room, drawing Callie with her. The far end was filled with a large desk flanked by tall oak file cabinets. Closer to the French doors leading into the room, golden light spilled from a window draped in creamy gauze onto a tobacco-toned overstuffed couch. The woman pointed to it and said, "Sit."

Callie did as she was told. To her right, opposite the narrow wrought-iron-and-glass coffee table, Zoe sat in a comfortable-looking wing chair upholstered with a dark floral print. When the woman cast a pointed glance toward Marcus, he moved from the wide doorway to the wooden chair next to her and lowered himself to a cushion made of the same autumn-hued fabric.

"Now, we will talk," Zoe started. "Over the phone Marcus told me that you have encountered some unfortunate situations the last two days. And now you say that you are a jinx. I want to know what you mean by this. Not more definitions. I want you to tell me *why* you call yourself a Calamity Jane."

Callie was just getting over the embarrassment of having all her good-luck charms—her rather useless charms, it seemed—exposed. She really didn't want to get into this with these two strangers. The story was too long. Too ridiculous-sounding. But there was something about the firm but warm, expression in the woman's eyes that made her take a deep breath and begin.

"Because that was my mother's nickname for me. She didn't use it in a mean-spirited way, you understand. She always said it wasn't my fault that I was so unlucky. I was conceived on a Friday the thirteenth, on the night of a full moon. Also, I'm left-handed, and I have eyes the color of opals."

Zoe's dark eyebrows formed a skeptical frown. "Your mother knew the exact night you were conceived?"

Callie nodded. "My mom was only sixteen when she met the man who fathered me, and she only made love to him once. He was an aerial acrobat—you know, the daring young man on the flying trapeze? My mother said it was love at first sight. And it probably was, for her. My mom always did fall in love easily.''

Pausing to take a deep breath, Callie managed to urge a tiny smile to her weary lips.

''Anyway, the guy was long gone by the time my mother learned she was pregnant with me. My grandmother had died when my mom was little, so she only had her father to turn to. He was a preacher, of the fire-and-brimstone variety, from what Mom said, somewhere in the Midwest—she never would tell me what city. In fact, I have no idea what my mother's real name was. Shortly after she learned she was pregnant, she joined the next traveling carny that came through town. She got a job as a fortune-teller's assistant and started calling herself Bonnie Chance.''

Zoe was listening intently. Marcus was frowning. ''How did she manage the name change?'' he asked.

Callie allowed herself a small smile. Only a detective would ask that question. ''I don't know,'' she replied. ''Circus people are very independent, and protective of each other. I do know that Bonnie Chance is the name printed under ''mother'' on my birth certificate, and she had a driver's license with that name, as well.''

''And your father's name?'' Zoe asked.

Callie bit her lip as she turned to the woman. ''My birth certificate says 'unknown.' My mother only knew him by his circus name, the Great Gregorio. Mom said she ran away to keep her father's condemning lectures from *infecting* me.'' She paused, allowing one side of her mouth to curve slightly. ''But mainly she did it because she had this fantasy that somehow she'd catch up with my father along the circuit, that he'd marry her and the three of us would live happily ever after beneath the big top.''

When Callie stopped speaking, Zoe leaned forward and quietly asked, ''That never happened, did it?''

''No,'' Callie responded softly, then gave Zoe a rueful smile. ''At this point in the story, I usually tell people that I figure Mom never found my father because he must have *dropped out* of the flying trapeze business. Sick, huh?''

"It gets a laugh, does it not?" Zoe's gaze was holding Callie's with an expression that managed to include sympathy, understanding and encouragement. "I believe I see what has happened here. Your mother was young, impressionable, and worked with a fortune-teller. She came to believe, then passed on to you, endless superstitions."

Callie shook her head, this time more vehemently. "This isn't about superstitions, about not stepping on cracks or avoiding black cats, or any of that." She paused. "Well, maybe the cat thing. But it's not that I have bad luck, but that bad things happen to other people when I'm around."

She turned to Marcus. "You said you spoke to Marie Wilson, my employer at the deli. She must have told you some of the stories. About the pillow shop that went up in a puff of feathers when I was working there, for example."

Marcus nodded.

Callie tensed. Normally she didn't reveal this much about her past on such short acquaintance, but these two people needed to know the sort of danger that could come along with letting her into their home. Before either Zoe or Marcus could ask a question, she hurried on.

"This sort of thing has happened periodically all my life, but I didn't become aware of it until I was five. My mother had just been hired by a real circus, and had her very own fortune-telling wagon. Everything was fine until the black panther got loose less than a week after we arrived. Ebony ate ten chickens, three goats and five blueberry pies some farmer's wife had left on a windowsill to cool. The only thing that kept the townspeople from shooting Ebony was that he collapsed with indigestion, enabling his trainer to capture him. Then, two—"

"Oh, come on," Marcus interrupted. "You can't believe—"

Callie stopped his protest with an upraised hand and went on forcefully, "Two nights later, the Amazing Allende slipped from the high wire. He worked without a net, and only escaped death because he managed to grab the wire as he fell, giving some acrobats waiting to go on enough time to push their trampoline beneath him. A week after *that,* the doors to the clown car jammed. Ten clowns nearly suffocated before the wranglers arrived with crowbars to release them.''

Aware of the skeptical glint in Marcus's eyes, Callie paused, barely long enough to take a quick breath, then continued, ''I had been near Ebony's cage, watching some newborn tiger cubs not long before the panther escaped, *and* I was seated in the front row at the other two performances. After the clown situation, my mother sat me down and explained that her worst fears had come to pass. I was marked by ill-fated stars. She told me I was to stay away from the tent during rehearsals and performances, and to avoid the animals, warning me that if the circus people realized I was a jinx, they would force us to leave.''

Marcus saw Callie close her mouth quickly over the last words. As she lowered her gaze to stare at the coffee table, the look on her face expressed more than any words could the shame and fear she must have experienced while growing up.

''Hey,'' he said softly. ''Those things were *accidents.* Someone failed to inspect that boiler in the feather factory. As to the circus stuff, you hear about high wire performers falling all the time. Were you at all of *their* performances?''

Callie looked up. ''Of course not, but—''

''No buts,'' Marcus broke in. ''It's simple. Your mother fed you a bunch of hog-wash. There is no such thing as luck—good or bad. Life is what you make it.''

The look Callie shot him was distinctly mutinous. Marcus clenched his teeth. Great, he'd probably just stepped right into the middle of some sacred mother-daughter relationship. So much for trying to help, for trying to disabuse Callie of her rather odd, and to his mind, possibly harmful ideas. If he knew what was good for him, he wouldn't say another word.

But he couldn't get his first image of Callie Chance out of his mind, sitting in the middle of disaster, smiling brightly. His gut had told him then that she was hiding something.

And his intuition had been correct. She'd been hiding the fact that she felt responsible for everything that had led up to, then followed, the flood from the room above hers. That was far too heavy a burden to carry, especially when it was so uncalled for.

"Callie." Zoe's tone was infinitely more gentle than his had been. "The subject of luck is quite complex. Marcus is right on one point. The experiences that most people refer to as good or bad luck are normally the result of some action they have taken in the past. I believe that all things happen for a reason, and sometimes things that look unfortunate at first glance turn out to be beneficial. Your tightrope walker, for example, perhaps learned to focus more consciously after his close call."

Zoe paused to smile. "However, I have observed firsthand that sometimes things happen out of the blue. I believe in kismet, that someone or something can enter one's life at just the right moment, and change that life. But that change is always consciously made, by grasping or refusing the opportunity presented. It is not the result of some magical spell or supernatural curse."

"Besides," Marcus said, leaning forward, "Mrs. Wilson told me that she and her husband had nothing but *good* luck while you were living there. If you're such a jinx, how do you explain that?"

Callie seemed to freeze. The only thing that moved were her large eyes, which slid slowly toward him. She spoke so softly that her murmuring sounded something like, "I'll never tell."

"What did you say?"

Meeting Marcus's gaze, Callie replied, "I said, *I cast a spell.*" Straightening her shoulders, she went on quickly, "Not with circles drawn on the floor, or eye of newt, or anything weird. But when I came home after the pillow factory incident, unemployed once more, I found a note from the actor I was engaged to. In it, Joshua said that it was my fault he wasn't getting any parts, that my love was jinxing his career. He was leaving me and begged me not to attempt to contact him.''

Her lips twisted into a wry smile as she paused. ''It appeared that he didn't feel the curse extended to all the furnishings that I had paid for, because the apartment was stripped bare of everything except for my clothes. I was just about to pack, when I stared at the stuff hiding in the closet and decided to leave behind everything that I had ever worn or touched, and thus infected with bad-luck vibrations. I had just enough in savings to get some clothes and a used suitcase from a thrift store and buy a bus ticket to Cape Cod.''

''Good girl.'' Zoe stood as she spoke. ''Callie, I am certain your mother loved you, but she taught you some very harmful things. You must believe me when I say that there is no such thing as a curse, as you put it, that would make you affect another person's luck. Turning your back on such beliefs was a powerful move.''

The woman paused, her bright red lips curving into a smile as she extended a hand toward Callie. ''And that is what I expect you to do now. You will start by agreeing to stay here, under my roof, and know that no harm will come to me or to Marcus because of your presence.''

Marcus watched Callie closely. After a moment she grabbed her purse in her free hand and stepped around the coffee table to join Zoe. The two women had just started toward the door, when Zoe turned and once more ordered him to bring Callie's suitcase upstairs.

This he did quickly, anxious to get to the station. Along with the case of the catnapped cat, several other investigations needed his attention. Which was exactly what he informed Zoe and Callie as he delivered the young woman's luggage, before he turned and headed down the stairs.

Callie watched him depart, then returned to her study of the room that would be her home for the next few days.

The only straight wall was the one they'd entered. A row of white shuttered doors, that Zoe said formed the room's closet, extended to her right to butt up against the edge of a white curtain that ran the length of the room.

The other two walls angled in slightly to follow the line of the roof. They were painted a soft blue then sponged with white clouds, as was the flat ceiling above. Directly in front of her, a dormered window formed a sleeping alcove, where the mattress was draped in blue fabric and strewn with white, lacy pillows.

To her left a small wooden table was flanked by a wooden armchair and a wingback upholstered in faded blue velvet. Behind that a set of French doors led onto a dormered balcony with an iron railing. The white gauze on either side of the windowed doors emphasized the breathtaking view of the boats moored in the marina and the blue-green water of the bay beyond.

"This is my favorite room in the entire house."

Zoe's slightly wistful tone caught Callie's attention. She watched the woman gaze around the room. "I'd planned it to be a play room for the children I was to have. Unfortunately, no children arrived." She shrugged, then turned to Callie with a smile. "However, this house has been good to me. My husband and I were very happy, and now it allows special people to share it with me. The young lady who last occupied this room was an artist. It was she who painted the clouds. Very effective, are they not?"

"Yes, they are."

Zoe's smile widened as she walked toward the white curtains at the other end of the room. "Now, here is your bathing chamber."

Brass rings slid over a metal bar as she pulled the curtains back to reveal an area tiled in white. In the right corner, a porcelain sink had been set into an old white dresser with an elaborately carved mirror. The windowed alcove held a generously sized claw-foot bathtub.

"You will find the toilet behind that old folding screen in the other corner." Zoe began to cross the room. "I allow tenants to have a coffee pot and a microwave in their rooms, if they choose to purchase them. However, the kitchen downstairs is at your complete disposal. After you get settled, I'll show you which cupboards and refrigerator shelves are for your use.''

Callie could only nod. Her throat was too tight for words. If she had tried to imagine a more lovely place, she couldn't have come up with anything as perfect as this, nor could she have dreamed up anyone more warm and welcoming as Zoe Zeffarelli.

''Now,'' the woman in question spoke over her shoulder as she reached the door. ''I am expecting a client at any moment. I will be with her for an hour, which will give you time to unpack and settle in. Dress in something you will be comfortable sleeping in. When Marcus called me earlier, he mentioned that the doctor ordered that you be closely observed this first night. Although I'm sure the man means to do this himself, he often returns very late from work. These old bones are not accustomed to climbing the extra stairs to this room, especially not once an hour, so we will have dinner, then camp out in the living room.''

With these words, Zoe stepped through the door and closed it behind her.

Old bones? Callie shook her head. The woman certainly demonstrated more energy than Callie felt at the moment. Weariness pulled at each muscle as she lifted her suitcase and dragged it toward the bed. Frowning at the elastic bandage encasing her left wrist and hand, she made an awkward business of unzipping the case and transferring her clothes to the closet and drawers.

A waste of time, she supposed. Once she'd spoken to the police sketch artist, there would be no reason for the police department to pay for her board here. And she had heard horror stories about the exorbitant rent in San Francisco, so she figured she would be leaving in a day, maybe two. However, for that brief time she could at least pretend that this room was her home.

Leaving out a pair of blue pajamas, she walked over to the deep old tub and turned on the faucet. Bathing in hot water up to her neck, while staring at the row of Victorian homes perched on the distant hill, would go a long way toward soothing the various aches and pains she was suddenly becoming aware of, courtesy of that hit-and-run driver.

The tightening knot in the center of her stomach was another thing altogether. She was still concerned that her presence might cause something bad to happen to Zoe or Marcus. But as her body began to relax in the warmth of her bath, Callie remembered what Marcus had said about Marie and Stan Wilson.

It was true that in the two years she lived with them, neither of those people had suffered any sort of bad luck. Maybe certain people had a built-in immunity to bad luck, Callie mused, some special gene that protected them against ''Calamity Janes.'' Or maybe misfortune was like voodoo—you had to believe in it to be affected by it.

And maybe Zoe was right, she thought hopefully. Maybe there never had been any curse, just a mistaken belief she'd inherited from her mother. Maybe there *was* some logical explanation for the disasters that seemed to follow her like rats after the Pied Piper.

By the time Callie pulled herself out of the bathtub, she was too tired to think anymore. She barely had enough energy to pull on her pajamas and thin pink robe before Zoe arrived to take her down to the kitchen, where a hearty bowl of minestrone and some crusty bread waited on the large, scarred pine table.

Callie felt no hunger, yet she ate to show her gratitude, then followed Zoe to the living room. The moment Callie slipped between the sheets that had been drawn over the cushions and beneath the warm quilts, the last thin thread of energy unravelled. After murmuring her thanks to Zoe, Callie closed her eyes and fell asleep.

It was much later than Marcus had expected when he finally pulled into Zoe's driveway. Frowning, he set his parking brake and let the Ghia idle as he got out to open the garage door.

His afternoon and evening hadn't produced any helpful information, just more aggravation. The florist who had witnessed Callie's accident really could not remember whether the car that had hit her had been black or dark blue, only that it was some mid-size foreign model and that it had appeared to swerve before making contact.

Shaking his head, Marcus pulled into the garage.

When he got back to the station, forensics had informed him that room thirty-nine had been wiped down pretty thoroughly before the occupants left. They felt that the few fingerprints they did discover would most likely prove to belong to motel employees. They had, however, uncovered several medium-length strands of dark hair, along with much shorter, finer ones. Gerald Harding had provided some hairs from his cat's bed and the lab was already attempting to match them with the small ones found at the motel.

Marcus sighed as he closed the garage door and started up the curving front steps. Nice to know that Harding was cooperating with *someone,* since the man had made it clear last night that he was less than pleased with the police in general, and Marcus in particular. Forget the fact that the man had known his cat had been stolen two days earlier, and only informed the authorities at the last minute, making the stakeout at the motel a tossed-together affair using rookie cops who'd been too easily distracted by the arrival of the fire department.

Gerald P. Harding was a former dock worker, who through a combination of hard work and shrewd investments had amassed the fortune that enabled him to dabble in the arts, and own pets that possessed the blue blood he lacked. He also contributed heavily to various political campaigns, which most likely explained why the police commissioner himself called Marcus and Malone into Chief Bradford's office this evening, demanding to know just how the catnappers had managed to escape and what they were going to do to rectify the situation.

Marcus had ignored the first part of the question. He had no doubt that Justin Hall had read the report he'd filed last night. To the second part of the question, he replied that the case would be solved like all others, with solid police work.

He would continue to interview witnesses, especially one Callie Chance, and check out any leads the forensics lab might produce, while maintaining the tap on Harding's phone in hopes that the catnappers would make another ransom attempt. He would also alert all veterinaries, animal shelters and pet stores to watch for a gray cat with bright green eyes.

Marcus's frown became a scowl as he entered the door and began to cross the entryway. The commissioner's departure hadn't been the end of the evening's inquisition, just the jumping-off point for Captain Bradford.

Although Gerald Harding's cat was a political priority, Bradford said with a smile, the city of San Francisco had far more important problems to deal with. Marcus had been ready to agree with the man, when the captain informed him that, aside from the men assigned to Harding's phone tap, Marcus was to be the sole detective on the cat case. The rest of his load would be handled by Malone and Detective Rodriguez, whose partner was out on medical leave.

The meaning behind all this maneuvering was perfectly clear. Harding had influence. Marcus's future on this city's force rested on his ability to return the man's pampered puss not only unharmed, but in time for the creature to compete in some all-important cat show that was to be held in three weeks' time.

The perfect end to the perfect day.

Marcus was preparing to mount the stairs to his apartment when a soft mewing caught his attention. He paused and heard it again, floating through the French doors from Zoe's office.

It sounded like a kitten.

Marcus knew it couldn't be that. Zoe's cats rarely left her suite of rooms, one level up.

Then he remembered Callie, and the fact that someone was supposed to keep an eye on her tonight.

A weary sigh slid past his lips. By all rights, that someone should be him. Not only had he brought Callie into the building, there was a fair chance that she'd been injured because he hadn't stopped to think that her run-in with the suspects might put her in danger. With a sigh, he tapped gently at the glass-paned door, then, after a moment, opened it and stepped onto the buff-colored carpet, words of apology on his lips.

The floral armchair had been moved over to the left-hand side of the couch. The pillow and blanket draped over the chair told him that was the spot his landlady had chosen to stand, or rather sit, sentry over Miss Chance. However, Zoe was nowhere to be seen.

The couch, on the other hand, was *not* empty. A small lamp on the end table next to Zoe's chair cast a muted glow onto a lumpy layer of blankets. Beneath them, Marcus could make out a slender form wedged against the rear cushions. He heard that soft whimpering sound again and let it draw him slowly, reluctantly across the room.

Callie was lying on her right side, leaving only the left portion of her face visible. A soft beam of light glimmered off a thin, damp streak that coursed from the corner of the young woman's eye, down her cheek, over her jaw and onto her slender neck.

During the daylight hours, Marcus was immune to tears. In order to do his job properly, he closed himself off, remained dispassionate as he studied the one doing the crying to determine if their sorrow was real, or a ruse to hide their guilt.

But tears in the night, especially nearly silent ones, pulled at the heartstrings he thought he'd long ago clipped.

"Callie," he said softly as he bent forward. The soft scent of musk and flowers rose as his hand brushed over a soft, waving tendril of rust-colored hair. When he received no response to his whisper, he moved his hand to her shoulder and gently shook her. She neither moved nor opened her eyes.

"Is she crying again?"

Marcus turned with a jerk at Zoe's whispered question. Dressed in a rainbow-hued caftan, the woman stood next to him.

"Again?" he asked.

Zoe nodded. "This is something she has done several times since falling asleep. I wait until the tears dry to wake her. I believe that Miss Callie Chance prefers that strangers not see her pain.''

Marcus didn't argue with Zoe on this point. Although he'd had his share of lively adversarial discussions with his landlady on a variety of subjects, he'd learned shortly after taking the apartment opposite Zoe's just how accurate the woman was when it came to what she called her "people sense."

"I'm sorry to have saddled you with this," he said. "You go on to bed now. I'll sleep on the recliner, and set my watch to beep each hour."

"No. You appear to be exhausted."

Marcus shook his head. "Nah. I'm fine. I have to do some more thinking on this case, anyway, so I doubt I'll get much sleep. When is she to be woken next?"

Zoe glanced at the round black alarm clock on the coffee table. "In about twenty minutes. I will warn you, she wakes slowly, even though she refused to take any pain pills. I wait until her eyes focus, make sure the pupils are of even size, get her to tell me her name, then let her go back to sleep. She drops off quickly."

Marcus nodded. "I can handle that."

When Zoe turned to leave the room, he stopped her with a question.

"Do you think she would be up to a session of hypnosis tomorrow?"

"Why hypnosis?"

"Because she caught a glimpse of two suspects last night. She didn't get a very good look at them, but you're always telling me that the subconscious records more than we're aware of. I thought if you put her under, and questioned her in the presence of a sketch artist, we might get an image that will further our investigation."

"I see." Zoe paused. "Well, I would say this would depend on how Callie feels when she wakes up. And, more important, if she is comfortable enough with me to relax and respond to my attempts to place her in a trance."

Marcus nodded. He'd learned quite a bit about hypnosis since coming to live under this roof, enough to know that he would not be a good subject. He was far too attached to his sense of control. It was one of those things he and Zoe bantered about. She seemed to believe that he would benefit from relaxing a bit, letting down his guard. He, of course, knew only too well just how disastrous that could be.

"All we can do is ask her," Zoe said softly. "Good night."

The hourly wake-up scenario that Zoe described repeated itself until seven o'clock the following morning. That was when Zoe entered the room again, dressed in a loose turquoise jacket and black pants, to relieve him.

In his room, Marcus filled his coffeemaker with water and freshly ground beans, then undressed for his shower. After drying off, he threw on his bathrobe and staggered to the pot, where he poured himself a cup, then drank it down in three gulps.

Now he was awake. Awake and ready to start another day.

He shaved and dressed with practiced speed, consuming two more cups of coffee as he went. Grabbing the collar of his suit jacket, he tossed it over his shoulder, stepped out into the hall and started down the stairs, his mind racing ahead toward all he had to do today. As he neared the foyer, he heard Zoe's voice.

"...if you feel it's too soon to trust me, I'm sure Marcus will understand."

Marcus reached the bottom step and stood between the open French doors to see Callie sitting on the couch, winding a strand of hair slowly around her finger as she spoke. "Well, if hypnosis can help me provide a useful description, I should do it today."

He noted the look of doubt on Zoe's face, then watched Callie flash the woman a quick smile as she rose from the couch and said, "I'd like to go up to my room now, though, take a shower and get into some clothes. I really appreciate the way you—"

Callie had taken two steps toward the door when both her words and her feet came to a sudden halt. Marcus saw her sway. He noticed Zoe take a step toward the young woman, but he moved faster, crossing the floor to reach for her.

Callie was aware that she'd gotten to her feet far too quickly. As she stood perfectly still, hoping that the room would quit swaying beneath her feet, her blurred vision told her that a figure was approaching. The face came into focus, and she recognized the dark eyes, saw the arms stretched toward her.

A part of her sighed with relief. Someone—Marcus Scanlon—was going to catch her, was going to keep her from falling. Even as she realized it had been his deep voice waking her in the night, his warm hand gently shaking her shoulder, another part of her stiffened.

The most recent person to promise her a safety net had turned out to be a liar and trickster. And because of that, she had taken a fall that she wasn't sure she would ever recover from.

She wasn't going to make the same mistake again.

Chapter 4

Callie drew in a deep breath and raised her right hand, palm up in an arresting motion as Marcus neared. He stopped inches from her.

"I'm all right," she forced herself to say as she lowered her arm.

And she found that the dizzy spell had, indeed, vanished. Her left hip was sore, probably from where the car hit her the day before, and her knees still felt slightly wobbly, but they were certainly no longer threatening to collapse beneath her weight. Which meant there was no reason for this man to touch her, to hold her. No reason for her to justify even one moment of weakness.

It was a shame really. But although she'd found a great deal of comfort in Zoe Zeffarelli's assurances that there was no such thing as a jinx, she wasn't completely convinced. Not that it mattered. Whether she'd been born a jinx, as her mother insisted, or whether Marcus was right when he stated that life was simply what you made of it, the fact of the matter was that she'd made a mess of hers. And she wasn't about to compound the situation by looking for someone else to bear the weight of it.

Even if that someone was as strong and self-assured as Marcus Scanlon. Because if it turned out that her mother was right, the streak of bad luck that had caught up with her two days ago could whisk him to disaster as easily as Dorothy's house had been twisted into Oz.

"You sure you're okay?" Scanlon's question drew her gaze to his dark eyes. "The doctor said a concussion can take a while to show up."

Callie managed a small, tight smile. "Well, it seems I dodged that particular bullet. I was dizzy there for a moment, but I think that just came from standing too quickly. Other than that, my head's fine. I'm a bit stiff, as the nurse said I'd be, but the only thing that really hurts is my wrist."

And *it* hurt like the dickens, throbbing with a constant, dull ache until she moved it, when pain shot from the tips of her fingers to her elbow. But since this was information that Callie had intended to keep to herself, it seemed that it was once again time to smile and make light of the situation.

"I was just telling Zoe that I'd be glad to try hypnosis," she said. "I take it you'd like to do this today."

Before replying, Scanlon silently stared into her eyes, his gaze intense. "If possible," he said at last. "It'll probably be an hour or two before I can get to the station, set things up and get back here. Do you have some schedule I need to work around?"

In the unmistakably sharp note in Scanlon's voice and the narrowing of his dark eyes, Callie recognized suspicion. She couldn't imagine what he might be suspicious of, but as diversions went, this would do. At least the man no longer looked as if he was about to sweep her into his arms in some gallant and protective motion.

Under other circumstances, she might not have minded that. If the firm curves beneath his white shirt meant anything, Marcus Scanlon had an athletic body. And towering over her as he did, she was sure he was more than capable of lifting all five-foot-ten of her without doing any damage to himself.

The only damage might be to her, to her determination to control any attraction she felt for Marcus Scanlon, or any other man.

Two nights ago, as she bathed in the motel room, it had occurred to her that the worst of her "Calamity Jane" periods had come whenever she was particularly attached to someone or something. As a little girl she'd fallen in love with the big cats the moment she saw them, Ebony in particular, drawn by the panther's sinuous grace, beauty and strength. She'd watched the Amazing Allende dance on the wire seventy feet above the ground with all the hero-worshiping awe a five year old could possess, and had adored the antics of the clowns.

Her teen years were littered with crushes, all short-lived. Most of the time this was because she moved so often, but more than one object of her affection had suffered some sort of accident, like Jeff Tisdale, who threw his arm out pitching while a talent scout from a major league team watched. Then there had been her two-year engagement to Joshua Michaels and her unshakable faith that the actor would marry her, as promised, once he finally hit "the big time," an event that never came to pass.

It seemed to follow that if she allowed herself to respond to the lure of Marcus Scanlon's dark eyes and quiet strength, it might not bode too well for the man. Besides, she had no business being attracted to anyone right now. Two days ago, she'd been rudely reminded just how unlucky in love she was. Until she had time to deal with her feelings of anger and betrayal, it seemed best to maintain emotional distance.

"Well, Detective Scanlon," she replied evenly. "I hadn't actually gotten around to making any plans for the day. I just thought I'd like to shower and perhaps have a bite to eat before I have my subconscious probed by a group of strangers."

"Callie," Zoe spoke softly as she stepped forward. "You don't have to worry that any of us will ask you about anything private. I will only work with buried memories pertaining to the two people you saw the night before last."

The compassion in the woman's voice eased some of the

tension that had been stretching Callie's nerves tight, enabling her to dredge up one of the lighthearted smiles she'd perfected for moments like this.

"Glad to hear it," she said. "Not that I have any national secrets hidden there, you understand. Just stuff I haven't sorted through. I'd hate to think of anyone wandering into my mind and getting lost in all the clutter."

Zoe smiled at that, and when Callie shifted her attention to Scanlon, she saw that the tightness had eased from his lips and his frown had disappeared. The intense expression in his eyes was still there, however, suggesting he could see through her defenses without the aid of hypnosis. Fearing he could sense all the old pain hidden behind her smile, Callie felt it waver.

"Well, then," she said quickly. "If I only have a couple of hours to get ready, I guess I'd better get moving. Something tells me that working around this wrist is going to take me a while. Now, if I were right-handed, like most people, spraining a left wrist wouldn't be such a handicap, but it's just my luck…"

Letting her words trail off, she twisted her face into a rueful expression as she moved forward, planning to step between Zoe and Scanlon for a quick exit.

Zoe placed a gentle hand on Callie's uninjured arm. "Do you need some help?" she asked. "I could—"

Interrupting the woman with a decided shake of her head, Callie replied through suddenly tight lips. "No. I'm sure I can manage on my own."

Callie *did* manage to bathe and dress on her own, but just barely. Free of the elastic bandage, her injured arm hung throbbing at her side in the shower as she washed her body and hair with her right hand.

That was the easy part.

After slipping into her bathrobe, she rewrapped her arm and replaced it in the sling, then sat on the bed, waiting for the worst of the pain to ease as she stared at her makeup bag in despair.

The doctor had given her a prescription for painkillers, but once she saw her ER bill, she'd decided it would be more painful to part with the extra money. At the moment, she seriously questioned that choice.

The sprain apparently involved the muscles of her hand, leaving her fingers too aching and weak to grasp anything. It would be impossible to line her eyes with her unschooled right hand, unless she wanted to look like Rocky Raccoon, or worse, Rocky Balboa after the big fight. And as much as she wanted to cover the hated freckles that had refused to fade as her mother promised, she didn't feel up to her normal camouflage job. It required a delicate touch to keep her makeup base from looking like an uneven application of plaster, a skill her right hand lacked completely.

In the end she managed a swipe of mascara to her eyelashes and a hint of blush to her cheeks. Knowing that she needed two hands to control her hair while using a blow-dryer, she decided to let it air dry in loose ringlets as she had the day before.

From her closet she drew forth a pink sleeveless V-necked dress made of some travel-friendly knit that slipped over her head easily. Recalling the biting breeze of the day before, Callie tossed a black cardigan over her shoulders, then stepped into a pair of beige flats before heading downstairs.

"Perfect timing."

Zoe turned to face Callie as she reached the bottom of the stairs. "One of my clients," Zoe said, inclining her head in the direction of a gray-suited man Callie had seen step out the front door. "I have another one due in a little over an hour. Marcus just called to say that he and the sketch artist are on their way, so you have time to eat breakfast while I make some notes on my last session. Help yourself to anything you find in the refrigerator, or the pantry."

Callie had barely noticed the kitchen the night before. As she entered the room she saw that the walls and cabinets were a soft yellow, the counter had been tiled in medium blue, and the floor was a checkerboard of blue and white. In the refrigerator Callie found plenty of eggs and some wonderful-looking whole-grain bread for toast, but when she considered the logistics of making eggs not only one-handed but wrong-handed, even scrambled ones, she opted for a large bowl of milk-soaked cold cereal.

She then discovered that someone, most likely Zoe, had left the coffeemaker on, and that it still held a generous cup of the fragrant brew. If ever she'd needed a cup of caffeine, it was this particular moment. After pouring herself a cup, she sat at the pine table in the center of the room, sipping coffee that was pleasantly strong, promising to deliver the energy she so needed.

The simple acts of showering, dressing and eating had left her drained. And she still had the worst of the day to get through, allowing herself to be placed in a trance where she might reveal who-knew-what about herself to a set of perfect strangers.

"Hey, it won't be that bad."

The deep voice made Callie jump, then look up. Marcus Scanlon stood in the doorway, leaning against the jamb, his mouth twisted into a lopsided grin, his dark eyes grabbing hers with that intense gaze of his. Feeling a shiver race up her arms and her right hand go suddenly numb, Callie lowered her cup to the table and managed a smile.

"Probably not," she replied. "Zoe promises me that going under is as easy as falling asleep at the beach—totally painless, with nothing to fear."

"Well, we're ready if you are."

Callie took a quick gulp of coffee to warm her suddenly chilled and quivering insides, then got to her feet and forced a smile to her lips. Marcus's eyes narrowed as she approached. He reached out and placed a hand on her shoulder.

"You do know that you have to relax for this to work, don't you?"

His grip was gentle but firm, his hand warm. Callie dredged up another bright smile, nodded and forced herself to meet the man's gaze as he frowned into her eyes, searching, she supposed, for signs of fear. She battled to keep her expression pleasant, lighthearted. Just when she thought the muscles in her face were about to give out, he pushed himself away from the door, dropped his hand from her shoulder, then turned and led her down the hall toward Zoe's office.

Callie released some of the air trapped in her chest as she followed. He wanted her to relax, did he? Right. Just how was she supposed to do that, when despite his scoffing and Zoe's reassurances, she was still very much afraid that her presence in this house might bring down a plague of locusts, or some equally horrendous bit of bad luck, onto anyone who lived there?

The only answer was to leave, she told herself as she entered the office. And once she'd allowed herself to be hypnotized, and her subconscious came up with a description that enabled the sketch artist to produce a useful image of the man and woman in room thirty-nine, she would be free to do just that.

Where she would go, and *how* she would afford to get there, were questions she'd have to settle later. Right now she had to smile at the young man who turned to her as she stepped into the room.

"Callie, this is Detective Wong," Marcus said. "He'll be the one doing the sketch."

Detective Wong was dressed in a crisp navy blue suit. He stood perhaps an inch taller than Callie. In one arm he cradled a sketch pad and his fist held several pencils.

"Call me George," he said as he extended his free hand. "Since I've been informed that you prefer to be addressed as Callie."

The statement confused her a moment, until Callie recalled begging Scanlon not to call her "Miss Chance." Sending him a quick grateful glance, she took the officer's hand and replied, "Yes, I do. Thank you."

"No, thank *you*, Miss—Callie. I understand that you've had a rough couple of days. I do have a lot of questions for you, but once you've gone under, the answers will come easy."

At this point, Zoe stepped forward. "Callie, would you be more comfortable on the couch, or in the chair?"

Callie was aware that the couch was very comfortable, but she also knew that lying flat on her back would make her feel far too vulnerable.

"I'd like to sit, I think."

Callie moved toward the dark floral chair as she spoke. By the time she'd seated herself, Zoe had moved over to sit on the corner of the couch closest to Callie, and Detective Wong was in the wooden chair. Marcus had positioned himself at the far end of the couch, still standing, his eyes dark as he met her gaze.

"Callie?" She turned in response to Zoe's soft tone. "How are you feeling?"

Paranoid, she wanted to answer. *Nearly petrified at the thought that my presence in your life might somehow threaten it.*

She couldn't say those words, though. She knew that Zoe would only try to explain away her fears, as she had yesterday, and she didn't have the energy to counter with more horror stories from her past. So until she could explain things as she made her hasty exit, she simply answered, "I feel fine."

"Good."

Zoe nodded, but her hazel eyes were shadowed by a slight look of doubt. Callie managed a bright smile to offer the woman some reassurance, but Zoe's expression did not soften.

"There's no hocus-pocus to anything I do, you understand? You will slip into a state much like dreaming, but you will be alert at all times. First off, I want you to pull the lever on the side of the chair, and recline it to a position in which you feel relaxed and at ease."

After Callie had followed these instructions, Zoe went on in a soothing tone. "Now, you will see a small, round crystal hanging from the ceiling. I want you to stare at that while you listen to my voice."

Callie nodded, then gazed at the crystal globe, noting the rainbow dots it threw onto the cream ceiling.

"I would like you to take a big breath," Zoe said. "Draw

it deep into your lungs—that's right—then hold it, hold it, hold it. Now release it slowly, Callie, slowly. Imagine the air coming from the tips of your toes and your fingers, easing away all tightness from your muscles.''

Callie followed each direction. As the air slowly left her chest, she did feel some of her tension slip away. Then Zoe repeated the instructions, and again Callie followed them. The procedure was followed several more times, and with each repetition, Zoe spoke softer and more slowly, until she said, "Callie, the room is warm. You feel safe and secure and totally at ease. Your eyelids feel heavy.''

Yes, they did.

"You can close them.''

Good, I will.

"Now, Callie, I would like for you to recall the day you arrived in San Francisco. You're getting off the plane. Do you have baggage to collect?''

Callie nodded.

"All right. You have collected your luggage and you need to catch a cab into the city.''

Callie frowned. Something was missing, but she did remember the taxi. "Yes.''

"Can you see the cab driver?''

A dark face beneath curly black hair appeared in Callie's mind. Large eyes, nearly black, smiled at her.

"Yes,'' she replied. "His name is Raj. He's from Pakistan, and he's very helpful.''

"Helpful, how?''

This question sparked the image of a blond man zooming past in a red convertible. Following this came blurred images of the cab attempting to follow the Porsche, then a huge Victorian house rising behind the blond man, who gazed in shock over the heads of the woman and child he was embracing.

One final image flitted into Callie's mind. She was in the cab again, staring at the ring encircling the third finger of her left hand. A large diamond winked in the sun, the diamond that promised everything she'd ever dreamed of—having

someone to love, someone who would risk loving her for all
time.

"Callie? Where is the cab taking you?"

Zoe's voice, soft as it was, jolted Callie out of those memories, out of the dreamy state in which she'd been floating,
into the realization that she couldn't answer this question—
not truthfully, anyway.

When the police had asked her about this part of her trip
from the airport to the motel, she'd made up a story about a
friend she'd come to see. A friend who didn't exist. And
since she was aware of that, she knew she must no longer be
hypnotized.

She wasn't sure that she'd completely gone into a trance
at all, only that she'd been relaxed enough to slip into the
nightmare she wasn't yet ready to publicly relive.

But she couldn't lie anymore. She just didn't have the
strength. So she opened her eyes and looked across at Zoe.

"It's not working," she said.

Zoe reached out and took Callie's hand in hers. The
woman's fingers were quite warm, as was her smile.

"I am not at all surprised by this. I could feel the tension
in you. So. We will simply try again, after you have had time
to absorb all that has happened to you and become a little
more accustomed to your surroundings."

The kindness in Zoe's eyes was almost Callie's downfall.
Although her mother had always insisted that she loved her
daughter, jinx or no jinx, Callie had always seen a faint
shadow of fear in her eyes. Zoe's gaze held no such darkness,
only confidence and faith.

It was almost enough to make Callie break down and cry.
And she never cried. Not in public, at least.

Yet she was tempted in this case. Somehow she knew that
this woman would offer support and comfort without judg-
ment, soothe the aches and fears that never truly left her heart.

But, of course, Callie couldn't let Zoe do such a dangerous
thing. So she blinked the warning prickle from her eyes,
cleared her throat of the treacherous lump that had formed

there, then forced lips still threatening to tremble to form a smile.

"Yes," she replied. "I think that would be a good idea."

As Callie rose from the chair, she became aware that Detective Wong was now standing next to Scanlon. When Marcus stepped toward her, Callie looked into his dark eyes and said, "I'm sorry, Detective Scanlon."

He shrugged and shook his head. "Hey, you did your best."

Callie knew that wasn't true. She'd held back. Worse, she was sure she wouldn't be able to relax deeply enough for hypnosis as long as she still feared that her presence in this house might bring some kind of disaster to Marcus and his landlady. The one good thing that had come out of this aborted session was that she now had an idea how to get hold of the money that would help her get another place to stay.

"I'd like to go to my room now." Callie abruptly got to her feet, then addressed Detective Wong. "I'm sorry you came all the way here for nothing."

The man shrugged. "No problem. When you get ready to try again, just give me a call and I'll come back, pad and pencils in hand."

Callie managed a small smile, then turned and left the room. Hurrying up the stairs, her mind raced ahead to the telephone and directory sitting atop the small table. Yesterday Zoe had mentioned that she had arranged to have the telephone left on in her name to save any new tenant the cost of hook-up.

By the time she reached her room, Callie was breathless from her rush up the stairs, but she didn't pause to rest. Grabbing her huge purse, she pulled out the card that Raj had given her two days ago and dialed the number of the cab company. As she waited for a dispatcher to answer, she flipped through the yellow pages to pawn shops.

Downstairs, Marcus spoke to Zoe for several moments. After assuring him that the delay wouldn't blunt Callie's subconscious memories of the suspected catnappers, Zoe opened the door to admit her eleven o'clock client. Marcus and Wong were just about to leave when Marcus's cell phone rang. He stepped into the kitchen to take the call and ten minutes later, returned to the foyer.

"That was Rick Malone," Marcus told Wong. "He needed to check some facts on a few cases I started with my former partner before Samuels retired. Malone also told me that the captain has requested my presence in his office at, and I quote, 'my earliest convenience.'"

Wong gave him a wry grin. "Head-on-the-platter time again?"

Marcus shrugged as he opened the front door. "Who knows? Bradford already busted my chops over the catnapping case last night. But some people just can't get enough fun, ya know?"

At the bottom of the stairs, Marcus turned left. He and Zoe had agreed that he wouldn't use the driveway during the day, leaving a place for her clients to park. When he'd arrived with Wong, he'd been forced to circle the block three times before he snagged a minuscule spot a good hike down the street.

As he and Wong walked past the neighboring houses, Marcus found himself mulling over the scene he'd witnessed between Zoe and Miss Callie Chance. Once again he was struck by the feeling that something about her was off-kilter, like a song sung just slightly out of tune. Still deep in thought, Marcus crossed the street and unlocked his car door. Getting in, he reached over to open the passenger door, his mind on Callie even as Detective Wong slid into his seat.

Two nights ago, he'd been convinced that Callie had something to hide. He'd received a similar impression at the hospital, but he decided he must be picking up on her efforts to minimize the pain she was in. Now he wondered if he'd allowed his concern for the wounded woman, along with the fact that he found her both attractive and fascinating, to blunt the suspicions he'd formed upon first meeting her.

Turning his attention to the practical matter of San Francisco traffic, Marcus waited for a cab to go by, then pulled out. As he drove back down the familiar street, he let his mind wander along its earlier path, the one that began and ended with Callie Chance.

Today, the young woman's bright smile and little jokes had reminded him of the misdirection tricks used by magicians or con men, meant to keep the observer from seeing the truth. There had been something about the way—

"Hey, isn't that Miss Chance?"

Wong had barely finished speaking when Marcus stepped on the brake, pulling to a stop two houses from Zoe's.

Indeed, it was Miss Chance, in the black sweater and rose dress that skimmed her slender form so nicely, rushing down the steps and into the waiting cab.

Marcus let the taxi glide to the end of the block and turn left before easing his car forward and following.

Wong shot him a surprised look. "You're going to tail her?"

"Yep. There's a couple of things that don't add up with this young woman." Marcus paused. "I know. You're expected back at the station, and Bradford is on the rampage. So we'll flag down the next black-and-white we see and have the officer drive you in."

This turned out to be unnecessary. The cab led Marcus through the heart of downtown San Francisco, allowing him to drop Wong off three blocks from the station, before continuing his tail.

It was in the area south of Market Street, a rather bohemian mix of factory outlets, artists' lofts and manufacturing plants known as the SOMA district, that the cab pulled over and let Callie out. As Marcus cruised slowly by, he saw her enter a pawn shop. Frowning, he searched furiously for a parking space.

He was just beginning to think he was going to be forced to park illegally and risk a ticket, when an ancient VW that was more rust than bug pulled out in front of him, leaving a spot. After maneuvering his car into the tight opening, Marcus rushed the block and a half to the pawn shop. He drew to a stop in front of the large front window, slightly out of breath. Peering in, he caught sight of a head of reddish-brown hair.

On the other side of a counter littered with cameras, binoculars and glittering displays of jewelry in Lucite cases, stood a thin dark-haired man. Even through the smoke-stained window Marcus had no problem recognizing Joe Larson, recently back on the street after serving time for dealing in stolen goods.

Marcus stood well to the side of the window, where he had a clear view but could duck out of sight in an instant. Normally felons like Larson dealt in jewelry, appliances or some sort of art. But thieves were thieves. It was entirely possible that one of Larson's associates had decided to steal something different, an expensive, prize-winning cat, for instance.

Which brought Marcus to the question of why Callie Jane Chance might be talking to a known fence.

A scenario began to build in his mind. Perhaps this mysterious "friend" she was supposed to stay with had learned that Callie was about to lose her job and apartment. Perhaps, anticipating trouble at the ransom scene, the friend had offered Callie a plane ticket to San Francisco in return for acting as a decoy, if things appeared to get sticky.

Marcus knew that this was probably pushing things past the limits of logic. But he also knew that his gut had been sending him mixed messages about this young woman since the very first moment he laid eyes on her. The attraction had been immediate. Insane, of course, given that she looked rather like a half-drowned kitten at the time. But there had been that brave smile, not to mention the slender body beneath the damp nightgown.

Marcus's eyes narrowed as he continued to peer through the grimy window. Hell. He knew better than this. Had learned his lesson about women long ago—from the first one he'd been serious about, a woman who'd captured his heart with her fragile beauty and the sort of needy vulnerability that had him promising the whole picket-fence package.

Considering the disaster *that* had led to, he thought he'd

learned to keep his physical desires separate from what might be called a heart connection. And yet, if he was going to be honest with himself, he had to admit that somehow Callie Chance had gotten to that part of his anatomy, along with several others, in record time.

That was okay, he told himself. He was damned good at the art of hardening his heart. Once he had the truth from Callie Chance, he would have no feelings for her at all. Being lied to by a woman had a way of doing that to him.

A bright yellow reflection flashed on the window, yanking Marcus's attention back to his surroundings. He turned to his right, to see a cab pull up in front of the pawn shop; it stopped and double parked. A narrow sign advertising the motel that had been the scene of the botched ransom attempt sat atop the roof, the same sign that had helped him tail Callie's cab to this spot.

So, she had asked the driver to circle, to wait for her. Not a bad idea, given the somewhat seedy block the pawn shop was located in. It probably meant that Miss Chance planned on coming back out again sometime soon.

Now, actually.

The shop door was opening. Marcus stepped forward quickly, intending to intercept Callie before she could reach the cab. This turned out not to be much of a challenge. As the door shut behind her, Callie came to a stop. She stood completely still, staring straight ahead, blinking, almost as if she couldn't see the bright yellow cab only eight feet away.

Marcus reached Callie's side just as she started toward the waiting vehicle. Grabbing both her shoulders, he turned her toward him.

"Just where are you going, Miss Chance?" he asked. "Or, more to the point, just what have you been up to?"

Chapter 5

Marcus figured that Callie would respond to his words with either embarrassment or anger. He also figured she would attempt to disguise her reaction with one of her quick, disarming smiles, so he watched closely as she raised her head.

Her lips were thin and tight, and her eyes didn't quite meet his. For several seconds she seemed to stare blankly at the center of his blue-and-gray tie. When her heavily lashed lids finally lifted, she gazed vacantly at him, her opal-green eyes glassy with moisture. Marcus watched, helpless panic whirling in his stomach, as Callie blinked and a single tear rolled out of each eye onto her cheeks.

"I came to sell my...my r-ring," she said, then swallowed and blinked again.

"Your ring?" Marcus didn't make any attempt to keep the doubt from his tone. He refused to be swayed by the tears, regardless of the tension that had moved from his stomach to his chest. He had a job to do, after all. "Would you mind telling me exactly what *ring* might this be?"

Her soft mouth opened, only to close again as her eyes filled with more moisture. She blinked furiously, then used the heel of her right hand to scrub the wet streaks from each side of her face. Her features tightened as she took a deep breath that shuddered slightly as it was drawn in.

"It was my en—"

The rest of the word seemed to get caught in her throat. Again she blinked the film from her eyes, took one more breath then forced out, "My en*gagement* ring," before clamping tremulous lips together.

"I see," Marcus said slowly.

He didn't see at all, of course. She hadn't been wearing any rings when he met her at the motel. It was one of those things he automatically checked, both from a personal and detecting point of view. The woman hadn't mentioned one word about an engagement, or wedding plans, either. Not that he'd asked. It was hardly part of the case.

Or was it?

"That friend," Marcus said slowly. "The one you were supposed to stay with when you arrived in San Francisco. Might this person have been more than a friend? A fiancé, perhaps?"

Callie opened her mouth to reply, but the only sound that came out was a sob, a sound she quickly closed quivering lips to mute.

Marcus knew he was in trouble even before he heard the second choking sound. Despite continued vigorous blinking, more tears began to flow. Callie lifted her one free hand to her eyes in an obvious attempt to hide them, but even without the tears and the poorly muffled sobs, her pain and defeat would have been clear in the slump of her shoulders.

For one moment Marcus froze, watching her draw a deep breath and hold it, no doubt a valiant attempt to stop the sobs that shuddered through her. Valiant, but ineffectual.

He couldn't just stand there, hands on her shoulders, dispassionately observing this struggle, so he did the only thing he could think of. Pulling her forward, he encircled her waist with one arm and lifted his other hand to awkwardly pat her back. Then he let her cry on his shoulder while he frowned

and asked himself just what he thought he was doing holding
a suspect—okay, a *potential* suspect—in his arms.

Enjoying the hell out of it, came the mental reply.

Well, not the sobbing part, nor the still-smoldering doubts
he had about this young woman's reasons for visiting this
particular pawnshop. But he couldn't deny the fact that holding Callie Chance's slenderly curved body was one of the
most pleasurable sensations he'd experienced.

His arm fit easily around her waist. As he tightened his
hold ever so slightly, her breasts pressed warm and pliant
against his chest. The heat of her thighs against his woke
another, deeper heat that invoked sudden images of burying
his fingers in her hair, gently easing her head back, then kissing her long and hard, until her sobs of anguish became gasps
of longing.

"Excuse me, Miss Callie, is something wrong?"

The question brought an abrupt end to Marcus's fantasy.
He looked up to find a man with black hair and mahogany
eyes standing next to them. Before he could ask the new-
comer's name, Callie lifted her head from his shoulder, turned
to the man and choked out, "No, Raj." She stopped, then
said, "Well, yes, something *is* wrong, but—"

"This man—" the stranger broke in. Stepping forward, he
drew himself up to his full height of perhaps five foot three
to scowl at Marcus. "Is he bothering you?"

Callie pulled away from Marcus's grasp, running her hand
over each eye in a swiping movement as she spoke. "No,
Raj. He's a fr—a police detective. He's investigating that
situation at your cousin's motel the other night." She reached
into her oversize shoulder bag as she said, "I don't know
how long I'll be, so let me pay you for bringing me down
here. What's the fare?"

The man glanced from Callie to Marcus, as she fumbled
in her cavernous purse, then back to the woman. "Are you
sure?" he asked, then, at Callie's nod, he told her, "The
meter says thirteen dollars and forty-seven cents."

After Callie fished out her wallet, handed over twenty dollars and instructed him to keep the change, the man she'd

called "Raj" turned to go. Marcus stopped him with one word.

"Wait."

When Raj pivoted, eyebrows lifted in inquiry, Marcus asked, "You took Callie from the airport to the motel on Lombard Street the other day?"

Raj nodded.

"Would you mind telling me where you took her before that?"

The taxi driver's dark eyes darted toward Callie.

Marcus, looking impatient at the delay, said, "Your cab *is* illegally parked, you know."

Callie drew in a deep breath and stiffened as she quickly turned to Marcus. "There's no need for you to question Raj. I'll tell you all about it."

Marcus gazed impassively into her green eyes. "The *truth* this time?"

Callie's lips were no longer trembling. They compressed into a white line before she replied, "I told you the truth, just not all of it. But that's not Raj's fault. Let him go."

Callie's features had tightened into a fierce expression that brought to mind a mother tiger protecting her young. Marcus found himself battling the urge to laugh out loud. Instead, he allowed one side of his mouth to curl into a half smile.

"No problem," he said. "As long I get the *whole* truth, I don't care who I get it from."

Callie continued to glare at him for a moment further, before turning to the cab driver. "It's okay, Raj. You can go now. And thanks for arriving so quickly after I called."

"Of course, Miss Callie. And you remember what I told you about that ointment. It will help your arm heal most quickly."

He bent forward in an action that was halfway between a nod and a bow, then pivoted and walked toward his car.

Marcus turned to Callie. "Okay. I'm ready to hear your story."

Callie looked at him before glancing away. When her eyes once more met his, he saw resignation mixed with reluctance.

"It's a rather long tale. Do you think we could go somewhere…" She paused to look away again.

Marcus followed the direction of her gaze. Not five feet away a small crowd had gathered, consisting of a few street people along with men and women in business clothes who'd apparently left the safety of the nearby financial district for a lunchtime stroll.

When they all suddenly swung away and began to disperse, Callie finished, "Somewhere less public?"

Marcus took in the tears staining her cheeks and the slight slump to her shoulders before replying. "I think we could both use something to eat. I know a place we can grab some sandwiches and find some privacy." After glancing at the traffic, he said, "This place is a fairly healthy hike from here, but it would take forever to find another parking space. Do you mind walking?"

Callie drew in a shuddering breath and gave a jerky shake of her head. "No. I think a good hike is just what I need."

Marcus started toward Market Street, Callie's long legs easily matching his stride. As they walked, he found himself glancing at her from time to time. Her delicate features wore the same mixture of fear and resignation he'd seen more than once on the face of a suspect during interrogation.

At some point in the last ten minutes, perhaps when he was holding Callie's sobbing form in his arms, he had begun to doubt his earlier suspicions regarding this woman. Perhaps she *had* only been guilty of being in the wrong place at the wrong time. Now, as he considered the look of dread on her face, his earlier doubts about her once again gnawed at the emptiness in his stomach.

As they reached the end of the block, he reached out to place a hand on Callie's arm. "We go right here," he said.

Callie turned as directed, then bit back a curse as she saw that the light was red. She didn't want to stand still. She wanted to continue walking, wanted to maintain the quick pace Scanlon had set, wanted to keep moving until she'd pushed all the emotion down and was sure she wouldn't burst into tears again.

She had never felt so stupid in her life. Blinking back tears and swallowing pain had become second nature to her. The few times she'd allowed herself to cry, she'd made sure she was alone, in some dark, private spot where her emotions couldn't affect any of those around her.

Glancing at the surrounding crowd, she saw an equal mix of casual dress and business suits. The modern granite structures rising in the midst of older brick structures, the cars rushing past, bumper to bumper to bumper, and the clutch of people poised at the edge of the corner reminded her of New York City. She remembered what it was like to be lost in a sea of people anxious to be about their lunchtime errands. People who didn't know her, who had no knowledge of the little scene she'd made three blocks back. People who didn't care anything about her past, present or future. It was a scene that offered its own sort of privacy.

It also brought a whiff of danger. Despite the events of the past few days, Callie's life had been so calm during the last two years that she'd almost forgotten the trouble she seemed to bring to people. Trouble that, according to her mother, was triggered by strong emotion.

The thought had barely slipped through her mind when the light turned green. The first row of people stepped off the curb. Brakes screamed and a collective gasp rose from the crowd. Callie reached out to grab Marcus's hand as a small black car swerved, barely missing a short man dressed in a brown suit, as the vehicle finished running the red light.

Then the herd was surging forward again, as if nothing had happened.

When Marcus turned to her, his eyes dark with alarm, Callie released his hand and let the mass of people sweep her forward. On the other side of the street, she slowed her steps, allowing the others to move past. Aware that Scanlon kept glancing toward her, she knew he was about to ask her about that little scene at the light.

She didn't want to get into that now. If she told him she was afraid that her little emotional breakdown in front of the pawnshop had attracted that near accident, he'd only scoff.

He was going to ask her about the pawnshop anyway, so she might as well get it over with. Turning to him, without missing a step, she said, "Your guess was right."

Marcus met her gaze. When he lifted one eyebrow, she went on, "That *friend* I said I'd come to see *was* my fiancé."

Marcus stared ahead as they took a couple more steps, then he glanced at Callie again. "The engagement is over?"

"Oh, yeah." Feeling her throat close over the last word, Callie swallowed and forced herself to speak again. "Somehow the idea of being part of a harem doesn't appeal to me."

Marcus stopped walking and turned to Callie. "Excuse me?"

Callie drew in a long, shuddering breath as she came to a standstill and lifted her eyes to his. "As I mentioned earlier, it's a long story. But the short of it is that this man didn't know I was coming to town." She paused. "Actually, *I* didn't know I was coming here until a couple of days ago. After I learned about the sale of the Wilsons' deli, I sort of panicked. I had this feeling that things might be starting to go wrong, so I tried to call him. But—"

"Wait." Marcus held up one hand. "I specifically asked Marie Wilson about your social life. She didn't say anything about a fiancé. And I didn't notice you wearing any engagement ring."

"Well, that's because I wasn't wearing the ring at the motel. And Mrs. Wilson didn't know about him or the engagement."

"How long did you know this guy?"

"Eight months."

"And you didn't tell Mrs. Wilson about him? I got the impression the two of you were quite close."

"We were. I didn't say anything because..." Callie paused, then finished softly, "Because I didn't want to jinx anything."

Marcus cocked his head to one side. As Callie met the blatant skepticism in his dark eyes, every muscle in her body tensed. She knew, just *knew,* that he was cataloguing her in his brain under some heading like "Total Kook."

"Okay," she said. "I know that you don't believe in luck, but—"

Again Marcus held up a hand to halt her. "Hey," he said. "I don't want to attack anyone's *belief* system."

"Good. Because it makes up a significant part of my story. It so happens that this man shared my beliefs. Not only did Dave accept what I told him about being a jinx, he promised we would stay…"

Callie's voice trailed off as she found herself looking at Dave's promise in a very new light.

"You're losing me."

She met Marcus's dark, impatient eyes. Tension crept into her shoulders, her lips tightened, and anger formed itself into words before she had time to stop them.

"Look, Detective Scanlon," she said. "Quite a lot has happened to me in the last couple of days, and I really haven't had the time to work through all of it. So you'll have to *excuse* me if I ramble on just a little."

She turned and began walking again, even faster than before. In a matter of seconds, Marcus was striding alongside her.

"Do you ramble better when you walk?"

"Yes, Detective Scanlon," she replied. "As a matter of fact, sometimes I do."

"Well then, ramble on. And cut out the 'Detective Scanlon' stuff. My name is Marcus."

Callie glanced at him again. Unexpected amusement crinkled the corners of his eyes. And he was smiling. That wide smile she'd first noticed the night they met. The one that made him look almost boyish. The one that made her feel so safe, so at ease.

A one-man good cop–bad cop.

"Okay," she said. "Here're the facts, as bare as I can make them. About eight months ago, I ferried over to Nantucket on my day off, to visit an artist friend of mine. I met a man who was looking at some of her work. He and I got into an enthusiastic discussion about my friend's work, and after he ordered several for the West Coast gallery he represented, he asked me if I'd accompany him to a few other artists' lofts. Dave was so easy to talk to, I found myself telling him all about my past, the jobs I'd left, the disasters I believed I'd caused. He didn't even blink. While waiting for my ferry to the Cape, he asked if he could see me again.''

"And you said yes."

Callie nodded. "I returned to Nantucket for dinner with him the next night, and he came to the Cape the following day, and met me at a gallery in a town not far from the one the deli was located in. We saw each other every day for a week, and then he had to leave. After that, he managed to get back to the East Coast at least once a month. When he was gone, he called every night. When he was in town, we'd meet on Nantucket, Martha's Vineyard or one of the other towns on the Cape.''

A breath of wind blew up the street, bringing the slightest scent of salt from the bay. The muted cry of a seagull recalled the memory of those days so very clearly that Callie's footsteps faltered, then stopped. Marcus came to a halt a few inches in front of her. He turned and bent his head toward her as she softly continued, her mind racing ahead of her words.

"Even though Dave claimed he led a charmed life, I was the one who insisted on keeping our romance a secret, and once we were engaged, it was my choice to wear the ring on a chain around my neck. I suppose I should have been suspicious that he was content to go along with this, but it seemed so right at the time, a way to insure that nothing bad could—''

Callie stopped. She was veering into emotional waters. Not at all where she wanted to go. Forcing a smile to her lips as she squared her shoulders, she went on more quickly.

"I had come to see Cape Cod as some sort of good luck sanctuary, where nothing bad could touch the people I cared about. When Dave not only seemed to understand, but encouraged my beliefs, I fell in love. When he handed me a ring with a big diamond, I agreed to marry him. He told me he would be out of the country, purchasing native work in

Africa. Before he left, we put a down payment on an old house with a huge kitchen, with the idea that I would start my own catering business once we were married. One week after he left, the Wilsons' business sold and I was told I would have to be out of my studio in two weeks. I called to see how soon our escrow would close, only to learn that our real estate agent had skipped town without ever giving the bank our money. Of course, my first instinct was to call Dave.''

Callie paused, tightening her jaw as she swallowed the ache rising in her throat. She shook her head, then giving her smile a rueful twist, she went on.

''There was just one small problem. The only number I had was his cell phone, since he said he was rarely at his warehouse in San Francisco. Was I suspicious? Nah. I called my artist friend and got the warehouse number off his business card. When I called, a secretary told me he wouldn't be back in the country for another three days. That was when I decided to come here and surprise him, telling myself that all the bad luck I'd suddenly found myself facing was fate's way of telling me that we should live *here,* close to his business.''

Callie paused again, shaking her head as it occurred to her how very stupid and naive—even laughable—this all must sound to a person who made his living as a detective. She was aware that Marcus Scanlon's complete attention was upon her. His eyes were dark, unreadable as always, as he gazed at her.

He didn't seem amused, though. There was no hint of laughter at the corners of his lips. She wasn't sure if this was good or bad. She preferred her stories of woe to come out funny, but she had the sinking feeling that if *this* man were to laugh at her right now, she would once again disgrace herself and burst into tears.

''So, the secretary gave you this guy's home address?''

Callie shook her head. ''No, but I was able to get her to tell me what date and time he would be arriving from Kenya, and with that info it was easy to learn his flight number. I loaded everything I couldn't stuff into my suitcase or tote into a large box and shipped it to his warehouse, then made reservations on a flight that would arrive just before his plane was due. I'd planned on meeting him at his gate, but my flight was delayed in Chicago, and when I finally got in, his plane had been on the ground for over a half hour. That's where Raj, the taxi driver, comes into the story. He'd just finished loading my suitcase into the trunk of his cab, when Dave shot out of the parking lot and past the passenger loading area in his little red Porsche."

Callie paused to take a deep breath. She was getting into it. She could feel the storyteller rise out of her soul, preparing to make this into a tale that would "amuse and astound," as the circus ringleader used to say. Turning, she began walking quickly. With Marcus at her side, she matched her words to their pace.

"So it became a race. Raj and his lumbering taxi against Dave and his little Porsche. Raj was magnificent. Unable to match the convertible's speed, he managed to keep it in view and maneuver through traffic to gain on it. Until, that is, Dave crossed three lanes of traffic in one fell swoop, and made a quick left turn to race up a hill. Refusing to be beaten, Raj shouldered his way to the same left turn lane, only to come up against an *interminable* line of traffic that kept us imprisoned for what seemed like an hour. I was afraid we'd lost Dave for sure. We crawled up the hill, Raj looking to the left, me checking each street that jutted off to the right, and luck of lucks, I saw the Porsche turn into a driveway. Raj stepped on the gas, hurried up the long block, turned one corner, then another and rushed back toward the spot I'd seen the Porsche."

Callie's heart was racing now, her breath coming fast. She paused to take in a gulp of air, aware that the story was reaching its climax.

"At this point, Raj was still under the impression we were looking for the red convertible, so he drove right past Dave, who was now walking past a row of houses. At my order, Raj pulled to a stop, I leapt out of the taxi and hurried back toward Dave, imagining the look of joy that would light his face.''

Another corner loomed in front of Callie, but the light was green. She took another breath, preparing to go on, when Marcus placed a restraining hand on her right arm.

"We have to cross to the left here."

Callie nodded, standing next to him impatiently, her mind rushing ahead with her story. The light turned, they crossed and as the crowd had surged ahead Marcus spoke.

"I take it that look of joy you'd been hoping to see didn't appear.''

Callie sent him a bright smirk. "Well, yes and no. Dave certainly looked happy as he watched the woman who ran out of the house to meet him, preceded by a small child squealing, 'Mommy! Mommy! Daddy's home!' This was followed by a touching domestic scene, where Dave kissed the woman, then tossed the child in the air. All of which happened while I was still moving forward, as if on autopilot. It wasn't until I was five feet away from these people that Dave looked up and saw me. And, no, there wasn't any joy in his eyes at that moment.''

She paused, searching for the right metaphor. "It was like he'd found a large spider in his salad, a mixture of fear, anger and revulsion. That expression stopped me in my tracks, turned me around and had me running back to the cab, where I told Raj to take me to an affordable motel.''

"Raj. The last name of the motel manager is Rajustani. Didn't you say they were related?''

Marcus's observation was so calm, so matter-of-fact, that Callie turned to gaze at him in stunned surprise. It was as if she'd just told him that the Dow Jones average had dropped two points that morning, instead of spinning a story with every ounce of skill she possessed, baring her very soul in the process.

She rather liked that. It made it all so much easier to maintain her equilibrium.

"Yes," she replied. "They're cousins."

"Well, that explains how you ended up at that particular

motel at that particular time. I still have some questions, but first, I think we *both* need some lunch. Do you like sub sandwiches, or are you one of those turkey-on-whole-wheat-hold-the-mayo types?''

Marcus opened a door as he spoke. The scents of salami, garlic and vinegar drew Callie into a tiny deli. After informing him that a sub sounded just right, she followed Marcus to the counter. He ordered the sandwiches to go, along with a cup of coffee, while she eyed the cookies displayed in a plastic container, feeling a combination of longing and revulsion as she noticed the large chunks of chocolate in the goodies on the right.

When the clerk asked for her beverage choice, she ordered coffee also and asked him to add an oatmeal raisin cookie. Marcus shrugged off her attempt to pay for her food, took the large white bag from the clerk and directed Callie to the door. Once outside, he turned toward the clock-topped structure at the end of the block and began walking.

''That's the Ferry Building,'' he told her. ''There are a couple of benches in an area just to the left of it where I used to eat lunch when I first started on the force. It might not be elegant, but it has a good view of the Bay Bridge and the water. I find it rather soothing.''

Soothing, Callie thought. That would be nice.

After crossing a very busy street, Callie found that the large cement area overlooking the water did offer a welcome respite from the hustle and bustle they'd left behind. White and gray seagulls wheeled overhead, issuing loud cries every so often as she followed Marcus to a pair of benches perched on the edge of the bay.

A ferry was just pulling away as Callie began her sandwich. She watched the white wake curl away to form gentle waves that rose and fell as they moved toward her. Eating slowly, she gazed at the silver double-deck bridge that arched over the water toward the eastern section of the bay, then turned to look behind her, where the city of San Francisco rose in a breathtaking series of towers and spires, punctuated by a slender pyramid and round, fluted turret.

"It's a good-looking city."

Callie turned to see that Marcus was taking in the same view.

"It's beautiful, actually," she replied.

He gave her a quick smile. "Yes. But like any big city, you have to watch where you go, and although the area south of Market Street is turning around, pockets of it are less than savory. You should know that sort of thing, before you go off on your own."

Seeing his eyes narrow pointedly as he finished speaking, Callie glanced at the second half of her sandwich. Her stomach suddenly needed something lighter, something sweet, to settle it. She reached for her cookie, glancing at Marcus as she began to remove the clear cellophane it was wrapped in.

"Question time again, I see," she said. "I must say, it was nice of you to get some food into me before you resumed your interrogation."

Marcus lifted his eyebrows, then smiled. Another of those wide smiles that made Callie's knees feel suddenly rubbery.

"Well," he said. "I've done this sort of thing once or twice before. It's amazing what you can do with a little food and coffee. Keeping it back will shake some people into revealing their hand, while others respond better on a full stomach. I sensed you were getting near the end of your reserves. And if you need some more fueling, I can wait a little longer."

Callie took a big bite of her cookie, savoring the sweetness before washing it down with the soothing warmth of the very strong coffee.

"Okay. That should do it," she said. "Now, what do you want to know?"

"I want to know exactly what you were doing at that pawnshop?"

Oh, Callie thought. The pawnshop.

Again she glanced at her cookie, then took another bite. The scene at the pawnshop wasn't really something she was ready to talk about. Just thinking about those moments outside the place brought back all the anger and embarrassment of the moment.

She sipped her coffee slowly, staring over the rim, into Marcus's dark intent eyes. She was going to have to answer. Forget trying to be funny, she told herself as she lowered the paper cup. Think of it as ripping off a bandage. Make it quick.

"I told you," she said evenly. "My engagement ring. The one with the big diamond I mentioned earlier—I went in to pawn it."

"Really. How much did you get for it?"

Callie glanced away, stared at a gull that was inching its way toward the second half of her sandwich. Callie pulled her food into her lap, then turned back to Marcus.

"All of forty-six dollars and eighty-nine cents."

She saw the question in his eyes, but before he could voice it, she spoke again.

"It seems that the diamond wasn't real. It wasn't even a good fake. If the setting hadn't been a little unusual, the pawn-dealer said he wouldn't have been able to offer that much." Callie paused, shook her head, and went on. "I don't know why I was surprised. I already knew that Dave had misrepresented himself. Why shouldn't the diamond be as fake as he was, as fake as the real estate agent who took our money, as fake as the love he claimed—"

Callie clamped her mouth shut. Her eyes had begun to burn again, her throat to tighten in anger. But she wasn't going to let the tears win this time. Turning to one side, she stared at the green ripples on the bay, willing the rhythmic rise and fall of the water to soothe her agitation.

"Look." Marcus's voice was low. "You're hardly the first person to be fooled by a con man."

Callie turned slowly. His eyes were dark, his features drawn into tight lines. The official face of a police detective, studying her, assessing her words and her motives. No doubt judging her.

"Oh, of course not," she replied. "I'm sure you've dealt with hundreds of people who've let themselves be fooled by this sort of person. It must drive you police crazy when people like me not only fall for charming lies and smooth reassurances, we actually go out of our way to help the…creep get what he wants. Actually, it's probably amusing for you, like watching Wile E. Coyote engineer his own disasters.''

Ending with her normal self-deprecating humor, Callie fully expected to see the corners of Marcus's mouth twitch, at least a little. Instead his frown tightened to a scowl, and his lips firmed to a thin line as his eyes held hers.

''And what did this creep get from you?''

Callie gazed back at him before she replied. ''Most of my savings. My dreams. My heart.'' She shrugged. ''Basically all I had.''

Marcus gazed into her eyes a few moments longer before he nodded. ''Well, you're right on one point,'' he said slowly. ''I *have* investigated my share of fraud cases. And I'll admit to thinking that a few of the victims ended up in that position out of their own greed. But most of the people I've dealt with were drawn in because they trusted, or loved, too much. And I don't find anything about that in the least amusing. You see, I've been there myself, and I know just how painful and devastating that can be.''

Chapter 6

Marcus watched Callie closely for her reaction to his statement.

It was true. She wasn't the first victim he'd watched struggle with disbelief, a sense of betrayal, and anger, at themselves most of all, when they realized just how easy they'd made things for the perpetrator. The response was similar whether they'd been conned by a stranger over the phone or they'd been exploited by someone near and dear. Seeing this always made him angry, but in the interest of bringing the case to justice, he always maintained an air of detachment.

Never before had his chest ached, twisting with the pain of betrayal that was nearly as sharp as it had been ten years earlier. He felt that pain now. Perhaps somehow, as he'd held Callie in his arms, her shuddering sobs of grief and anger had woken a sympathetic vibration in him.

He could see that she had no idea what effect her story had on him. In fact, Callie's gaze said clearly that she doubted his words. Her wide mouth was drawn into a tight line that told him she'd said all she was going to say, her body was visibly tense, her shoulders hunched as if to protect her vulnerability. She was withdrawing, pulling into herself, drawing a cloak of control about her. After all, that was what he'd done himself, all those years ago.

Much as he would have liked to allow Callie that comfort, he couldn't. He had a case to solve—a stupid catnapping, which would normally have been treated as a minor felony, if it weren't for the wealth and political influence of the animal's owner, and the fact that his captain, with all *his* political aspirations, was insisting on immediate results.

Callie Chance just might hold the key to those results somewhere in her subconscious. The wary look in her green eyes made it clear that she was on the verge of shutting down, making it impossible for even Zoe to get her to relax. It was up to him to reassure her, to convince her that she had someone on her side, someone who knew exactly how she felt, someone who wasn't judging her actions.

Even if it meant opening a chapter of his life he'd long ago closed the book on.

"You don't believe a cop can be fooled?"

Callie's features remained tight for a moment after he asked the question. When her face softened with uncertainty, he said, "It happened before I joined the force. I put all my faith in two people I loved and trusted, and they turned around and destroyed everything I cared for."

Marcus could see that these words weren't enough. He was going to have to tell her the entire story, in all its foolish glory.

"You want details?" he asked. "Okay. I was twenty-one, attending college in Chicago, working like hell to get my business administration degree. I had a fiancée at home—a small town in Iowa. She was from a wealthy family, and I was determined to take my father's small furniture company and make it into a huge chain store, so that I could, quote, 'support Miranda in the style to which she was accustomed.'"

Marcus paused, his lips twisting bitterly at the memory. "My best friend, a guy who'd been like a brother to me from the day we met in the kindergarten sandbox, was *helping* my father while I was in college. Helping himself, it turned out, to every penny of the company profits and to Miranda as well. I had no clue, of course. During my weekly telephone conversations with Miranda, she whispered words of love, and on my visits home she returned my kisses, showed me *Bride's Magazine* clippings of the wedding dresses she liked. I was totally secure in the knowledge that she loved me until the night my father called to tell me that both Ron and Miranda had left town, and the business was completely bankrupt. I arrived home the next day to learn that my father had suffered a heart attack and was in the hospital. He died that night.''

As Marcus spoke, those days came back to him with a vividness that nearly took his breath away. When a vision of his father's coffin appeared before his eyes, a jolt of pain, unblunted by time, ripped through his chest, tightened his throat and blurred his vision in less than a heartbeat.

Swallowing quickly, Marcus blinked. When his vision cleared, he found Callie staring at him, her eyes dry but full of sympathy. For him.

The last thing he wanted or needed.

Forcing his suddenly tight muscles to relax, Marcus reminded himself that this was *just* what he needed, if it meant gaining her trust.

''I felt every bit of the anger at myself that you're feeling now,'' he said quietly. ''I felt I should have suspected something.''

''Why should you have?'' Callie countered. ''Your situation was totally different. I only knew Dave eight months, less if you figure we only had a face-to-face relationship a quarter of that time. I should have been much more cautious about trusting someone I barely knew. But you'd known both of these people for years.''

Marcus shook his head. ''The length of time doesn't matter. Con men are totally convincing because they believe their own lies. Also, they are masters at creating sympathy. I knew Ron had a juvenile record, for example, but I let it slide, because I knew how difficult his home life had been. And Miranda...well, she was the prettiest girl in town. I was so bowled over by the fact that she'd chosen *me* that I ignored the little ways she went about trying to 'fix' me.''

Callie nodded slowly. ''Just like I let Dave's nearly nightly phone calls filled with plans for our future keep me from asking more about his life in San Francisco.''

Her gaze shifted to the water once more. Marcus watched Callie stare into the distance for several moments. As she turned to meet his gaze again, he noticed the dark smudges rimming her eyes.

''So, what did you do about Ron and Miranda?'' she asked.

Marcus's lips twisted angrily as he replied. ''I fought back. When the local police claimed they couldn't locate them, I took up the chase myself. And when I found Ron and Miranda, I turned them over to the authorities, then saw to it that they were prosecuted to the fullest extent of the law.''

He paused to sigh. ''It didn't get me much, of course. They'd spent most of the money already. So I sold my father's house to pay off the business debts, moved out here and figured I might as well put those detecting talents I had developed to good use, and became a cop.''

When Marcus finished speaking, he almost laughed. The story sounded all so cut-and-dried when he left out the fact that he'd never released any of the bitterness, that he'd stubbornly held on to his own reluctance to trust. And now here he was, telling this story to Callie to keep her from closing herself off the way he had.

Of course, this deep-seated suspicion was one of the things that made him so good at his job. And his job was all he had. All he cared to have. After all, he was very good at it. Already he could see that listening to his tale had made Callie relax. He could also see the compassion in her soft green eyes. Stiffening against the sympathetic words he feared might be coming his way, he refocused the conversation on her.

''So, do I have your full story now?''

Callie blinked. ''My full story?''

''Yes. Was there any other reason you flew out here so

suddenly? Like, perhaps, discovering that you were carrying this man's child?''

This time Callie's eyes flashed wide. She gazed at him for several heartbeats before she issued a harsh laugh and shook her head.

''No. Believe it or not, that was one direction in which I didn't allow myself to be led. After giving everything to that actor I'd been engaged to, this time I was determined to wait for my wedding night to make love.''

Noting the soft blush staining her cheeks, Marcus nodded. ''Look, why don't I take you back to Zoe's. We can stop in at the station and you can fill out a complaint on this fiancé of yours.''

''*Former* fiancé,'' Callie corrected. ''And what would I be charging him with—attempted bigamy?''

''No. As an accessory to grand larceny. He may have been involved with the real estate agent who ran off with your money.''

Marcus watched as Callie's eyes narrowed to consider this possibility. Her reply came out slowly. ''I really can't see him being involved in that setup. Of course, I couldn't imagine that he had a wife and kid, either.''

Callie paused to stuff the remains of her sandwich into her large purse, then released a sigh and stood. Once she was on her feet, she turned to meet his eyes. ''I want to talk to Dave before I make any official complaint. Besides, right now I have more important things to attend to, like helping you catch a catnapper. Do you think Zoe and Officer Wong might have the time to try hypnotizing me again today?''

Marcus allowed himself the tiniest of smiles. His good-cop routine had panned out better than he'd hoped. Dredging up those almost buried memories of his hadn't been exactly comfortable, but the pain had been worth it when he considered the results. His conscience did prick him, however. He should at least suggest that she take some time to absorb what happened to her.

''Look, this can wait another day,'' he found himself saying as he stood. "You might need some more time to rest up."

"No." Callie shook her head. "I want to do it today."

Placing a hand on her right shoulder, Marcus gave it a gentle shake and said softly, "Let's get going, then."

As they walked back to the car, Marcus pulled out his cell phone. By the time they reached the car, he'd cleared things with Zoe and made arrangements to pick up Officer Wong at the station. He held the car door open for Callie. After she slid into the passenger seat, he saw her draw a deep breath, close her eyes and rest her head against the high-backed seat. As her right hand shifted to cradle the arm in the sling, her smile disappeared.

Marcus shut the door quietly, an action that took every ounce of his self-control. What he really wanted to do was slam it, to help release the mixture of anger and frustration suddenly coursing through his veins.

Feeling sympathy for a victim was one thing, he told himself, but the almost tender, protective response that this woman drew from him was *not* an acceptable reaction. *Acceptable* was the sort of relationship he normally had with the women he met, simple and straightforward, perhaps a little on the superficial side.

After sliding behind the wheel and automatically buckling his shoulder harness, Marcus glanced at Callie. There was nothing superficial about this woman. Her strange belief that she was some sort of albatross might be completely silly, but it was obvious that her convictions ran deep. It was also obvious that she was exhausted. Her eyes were still closed, her good arm still cradling the other. But some of the tightness had eased from her face. She looked so peaceful that he considered just sitting there a few moments longer.

A loud *honk* took the decision away from him.

Callie's eyes flew open and she turned toward the sound. A second later, her eyes shifted to his. Marcus noted that they were dry, and though they were still rimmed with the dark smudges he'd noticed earlier, they appeared free of apprehension.

"I think someone would like your parking space," she said quietly.

Marcus let his mouth relax into a twisted grin. "That's San Francisco for you in a nutshell. The city motto ought to be, My Kingdom for a Parking Space."

Glancing behind him, Marcus gave a brief nod and wave to the car idling just off his back bumper, then turned to Callie.

"Your seat belt, please."

Callie nodded, then reached up to fumble with the shoulder harness hanging above her right arm. Seeing that the angle was too sharp to make for easy gripping, and knowing that her left arm wasn't available to assist, Marcus reached across to grab the buckle.

Callie was already holding it. When his hand closed over hers, Callie turned wide eyes to his. Their faces were only inches apart. Marcus heard Callie draw in a soft breath at the same moment that he breathed in that intoxicating scent of hers. He felt her fingers stiffen beneath his. Various parts of his own body tightened in response, first the muscles in his chest, then an area much lower.

These were involuntary movements, things Marcus had no control over. He did, however, have enough control to draw back slightly as he said, "Let me get the belt. It'll be quicker."

He made damned sure it was quick. The moment Callie slid her hand from beneath his, he grasped the buckle, pulled the shoulder harness across her body, clicked it into its metal clasp, then turned to switch on the ignition.

Just as the engine hummed to life, another honk came from behind. Marcus glanced back at the driver as he began to pull out and growled softly, "Have some patience, guy. I'm going."

He waited until he was safely out of the parking space and heading down the street before he glanced at Callie again, half afraid she'd still be wearing that stunned, half-expectant gaze that had tempted him to place a kiss on those soft lips of hers. Instead, he saw that she was rooting in her large shoulder bag. Noticing the large safety pin holding the broken strap to the metal ring, he recalled the odd assortment of things that had fallen out the day before, and decided he'd had enough explanations for one day.

A block later, stopped at a red light, he noticed that Callie had pulled out a small mirror and was dabbing at her eyes with a handkerchief. Muttered words floated his way, so softly spoken he could only catch something about "make-up," "waste of time," and, oddly enough, "raccoon." Again deciding it was probably best not to ask, Marcus concentrated on maneuvering through the downtown traffic.

Callie released a relieved sigh when she saw that Marcus was focusing on the cars in front of them, and no longer looking her way. Now that she had the tear-and-mascara stains removed from her eyes and some blush back on her cheeks, she felt a little more in control. Ridiculous what a little makeup could do.

And what it couldn't.

She doubted even her freckle-covering foundation would have been able to disguise the breathless sense of expectation that had gripped her when Marcus's hand had closed over her fingers and his gaze held hers for those endless moments.

Of course, he'd probably just added her reaction to the list of odd things she'd revealed today, such as realizing that she'd fallen in love with a married man, but never thinking that the ring he'd given her might be fake.

And now she was on the way to be hypnotized again, put in a trance where she might reveal some other bit of foolishness. Not a pleasant thought at all, but she had given her word to try this again.

In an attempt to relax and ready herself to trust her sub-conscious to a woman she hardly knew, Callie said little on the way to Zoe's, other than a brief hello to Detective Wong when Marcus pulled over to let the man get into the back seat. As the car moved back into traffic, a lethargic weariness spread through Callie, some sort of fallout, she imagined, from the emotional storm that had whipped through her in front of the pawnshop.

As if she was in some sort of waking dream, she only half understood the conversation between Marcus and Detective Wong. Laughing, Wong was saying that the captain was on a rampage because Marcus hadn't yet appeared in his office. His words seemed to come from some distance away, as did Marcus's harsh answering laugh. Several moments later, as Marcus slowed for a red light, a black pickup truck with giant tires shot past them on the right. As it barrelled through the signal, Callie saw a gray minivan enter the intersection. She felt as if she was watching a movie, aware of the threat to the driver and the children in the rear passenger seats, but observing dispassionately as the truck swerved just in time to avoid broadsiding the smaller vehicle.

By the time Marcus pulled into a parking space a block from Zoe's, Callie decided that she was already halfway into a trance, only peripherally aware of the surroundings. In Zoe's office she sat in the same comfortable chair that had cushioned her that morning, noting that the others reproduced their seating arrangement as well. After assuring Zoe that, yes, she did want to try this again, she turned herself over to the older woman's soothing words. After her eyes drifted shut, she heard Zoe's voice asking questions and another voice, her own, describing the images that floated to mind.

"Callie, open your eyes now."

Callie responded immediately to Zoe's command, to find Marcus standing next to her chair, smiling down at her so broadly that she couldn't help smiling in response.

"I did okay?" she asked.

"No." His grin grew even wider. "You did better than okay. You did damned good."

"Really?" A silly flush rose to her cheeks. "I was able to describe both of them?"

Marcus's smile faded a notch or two. "Well, you did really great with the woman. Look."

Detective Wong handed Callie the drawing. As she gazed at a detailed sketch of soft, round features beneath a dark helmet of hair, Marcus went on.

"As for the male suspect, apparently you only did see the

lower half of his face. You were able to describe his jaw and his mouth, *and* you were able to tell us that the cap he was wearing had the insignia of the Oakland A's. The motel manager had said it was a Giants cap.''

Callie nodded slowly as she gazed at the partial sketch Marcus had just handed her.

''You also remembered the object that the man dropped on the stairs.''

An image leapt to Callie's mind. ''A box of Benadryl,'' she said as she looked up.

Marcus nodded. ''Yep. That first night, do you remember telling us that the woman in room thirty-nine stopped speaking to sneeze? Benadryl is for allergies. And Wong tells me that forensics matched the cat hairs they found in the motel room to some gathered from the stolen animal's bed.''

Callie stared at Marcus's sudden wickedly amused smile. Then it hit her.

''Ohmygosh. One of the catnappers is allergic to *cats*.''

''Right. Which gives them a compelling motive to set up another ransom exchange soon, something Captain Bradshaw will be happy to hear, not to mention the cat's owner. Also, you've given me another clue to follow up. Mr. Oakland A most likely bought that Benadryl somewhere near the motel. I'm taking Wong with me right now. If we can find the clerk who sold the medicine, we might be able to fill out the upper portion of the male suspect's face.''

Marcus took one step away, paused then moved back and placed a hand on Callie's shoulder. The warmth permeated right into her flesh and down her entire left side as he gave her a glittering wide smile and said, ''Thanks. I know this wasn't easy for you.''

With that, he turned. Callie watched him depart with the sketch artist, feeling suddenly as though the parade had moved on without her.

''It's their job to find this stealer of cats,'' Zoe said softly. ''Your part is over.''

When Callie turned to the woman, Zoe smiled. ''No, I am not some mind reader. Your face is very expressive.''

"I know." Callie released a huge sigh.

"You do a good job of hiding your thoughts with that wide smile of yours, however." Zoe got to her feet. "But that sort of thing requires energy to maintain, and I don't think you have much of that commodity to spare right now. How does a nap sound?"

It sounded like heaven.

If only she could get up to her bed. As soon as Callie tried to get out of the chair, she discovered that each and every muscle in her body protested even the slightest motion.

"Feeling the results of your fall?"

Callie looked at the woman. If she wasn't a mind reader, she must be some kind of a witch.

Zoe grinned. "Something similar happened to me last year when I tripped over a rug. So, while you were in a trance, I took the liberty of giving you a post-hypnotic suggestion to encourage you to relax and rest. Normally hypnosis leaves patients energized, but I think it best if you take a hot bath, then climb into bed for a couple of hours. Do you have an alarm clock?"

Callie nodded.

"Good. I have one more client, and then I plan to prepare a spaghetti dinner. The sauce should be done by six. Would you care to join me?"

Callie woke from her long nap considerably less sore. After dressing in black leggings topped with an oversize blue sweater, Callie followed the scent of simmering spice-scented tomatoes down the stairs.

Hearing voices in the kitchen, she wondered if perhaps Marcus had returned. The sudden memory of his arms around her as they stood in front of the pawnshop, followed by the heated moment in the car, made her feel just a little shy. She entered the room slowly, only to discover that Zoe was alone, standing at the sink, tearing lettuce leaves into a bowl. A voice announced the beginning of the evening news from a small television set mounted in a cabinet above.

"The sauce smells great," Callie said. "Can I help you with anything?"

Zoe turned with a smile. "Yes. You can pull down one of those bottles of wine from the rack in the corner, pour a glass for me, and another for yourself. The one on the bottom right-hand corner of the rack is a very nice Merlot from a marvelous little winery up in Sonoma."

Callie pulled down the bottle, along with an opener that hung conveniently on the rack. Faced with the logistics of having only one usable hand, she wedged the bottle between her left arm and chest as she forced her right hand to twist the corkscrew in. She had just set the bottle on the counter, proud that her shaky "wrong" hand had managed to pour two glasses of wine without spilling, when a deep voice asked, "Hey, is that homemade spaghetti sauce I smell?"

Callie turned to see Marcus standing in the doorway.

"Yes, it is," Zoe replied. "And you are, of course, invited to join us in the partaking of it. Bring another plate to me, if you would, and put out the salad bowls and silverware. Callie, while he's doing that, please pour this overworked servant of the people a glass of wine."

It was a moment before Callie could move. Marcus was still leaning against the doorjamb. His tie was loosened and the top button of his white shirt undone, his jacket slung over his left shoulder. His mouth was twisted into that half grin she found so blessedly attractive. When his smiling eyes met hers, however, she quickly turned to the counter and picked up the wine bottle.

What was wrong with her? She couldn't—*couldn't*—be falling for this guy. She wasn't even over Dave yet.

Or was she?

Callie paused, the mouth of the bottle poised over the rim of the wineglass, searching within for the feelings she normally associated with Dave. And found nothing.

This made no sense at all. For months she'd been obsessed with the man, eagerly anticipating his every phone call when he was gone, and obsessed with spending every free moment with him when he was back on the East Coast, planning their future. She had been madly in love with him.

Hadn't she?

Slowly, Callie tipped the wine bottle, letting the dark liquid flow as she looked deep into her heart. When she'd first met Dave, she'd been nervous about trusting the feelings that seemed to spark so suddenly between them. After warning him about the less-than-fortunate effect she'd had on those she cared about in the past, Dave had assured her that he lived a charmed life, that things always went the way he wanted. He wanted Callie in that life with him, he'd whispered, wanted to share a home with her on the Cape, where only wonderful things happened.

And just like every little old lady who'd ever lost her life savings to a con man who promised impossibly huge returns on some investment, Callie had been willing to exchange everything she had, most of her money, her mind, her heart, to a man who had ferreted out her fears and dreams, then used them to control her.

Just like her mother, she'd been chasing a dream.

And perhaps some part of her knew that. Maybe she'd never made love to Dave because part of her never truly trusted him. But instead of recognizing the red flags that cautioned against promising her life to a man she knew so very little about, she blamed any fear on her concern that *she* might jinx things.

"Whoa! Hold it right there. My day hasn't been *that* bad."

Callie blinked and saw that the wine had almost reached the rim of the glass. With a start, she righted the bottle, at exactly the same moment Marcus's hand closed over hers. The world skittered to a halt, just as it had in the car, when they'd both reached for the seat belt. Again her hand felt the heat of his. In seconds her entire body was engulfed—hot, shaky, intensely aware of how close he stood, of the pleasant, barely-there scent of musk, of the warmth of his breath as it feathered past her hair.

"I'm afraid that Callie's having a little trouble managing things today," Zoe said.

In response to this statement a small, hysterical giggle gathered in Callie's throat. She kept it from bubbling to the surface by watching Marcus's fingers guide the bottle she held upright and safely back onto the counter.

Callie felt she should say something, preferably something light and amusing that would ease the strange tension stretching between them. Nothing came to mind. The silence was only broken by the final notes of a familiar and highly annoying commercial jingle, followed by the news anchor's booming voice.

"It seems that we have a rather different *cat*egory of crime to report tonight. For the story, we go to Simon Winslow."

Callie watched Marcus's gaze shift toward the television as he lifted his glass and took a long, slow sip of wine. Finding that she was once again able to breathe, Callie also turned to the small set.

The reporter, microphone in hand, had dark hair and a lean, bluntly angled face. The other man on screen was older, with thick silvery hair and a square face that managed to look hard despite the many lines time had placed there.

"I'm at the home of Gerald Harding," the reporter was saying. "CEO of Harding Enterprises, local philanthropist and owner of the prize-winning cat, Gerald's Electra. Three days ago, Electra was stolen. Mr. Harding was contacted by the catnappers, and arrangements were made for him to pay a ransom and recover the animal. I understand there was a problem with this, sir."

The reporter angled the microphone toward the older gentleman. Harding nodded and replied, "There most certainly was. When I informed the police of this extortion attempt, they convinced me to allow them to position men near the spot the exchange was to take place, promising they would nab the thieves and recover Electra. I cooperated fully with the authorities, and they bungled the entire operation. The catnappers got away—with my cat."

"As I understand it, this is a very valuable animal. A Russian Blue, is that correct?"

"Yes. She's a two-time champion, and registered to compete in a show next month, where she has every chance to gaining grand champion status.''

''I can imagine you're quite anxious to get her back. Do the police have a new plan?''

''They're no longer involved. I spoke with the chief of police today and lodged a complaint against Detective Scanlon, whose incompetence bungled the job, and informed the authorities I would no longer need their *assistance.* I can only hope that the people who took my cat will contact me again, so we can come to some arrangement that will return Electra safely to me.''

As the reporter turned to the camera to end the segment, Marcus walked over to the television and switched it off. Leaning against the counter, he took a long swig of wine. Callie took a tiny sip herself, then aware of how very numb her fingers were, carefully placed the glass on the tile surface.

''This is all my fault,'' she said.

Marcus lowered his glass and met her gaze. ''Hey—wrong place, wrong time. Nothing you could do anything about. Harding's complaint about me is no big deal. In fact—''

''No,'' Callie broke in. ''You don't understand. Of course it's my fault that you're in trouble. You laughed at me last night—said there was no such thing as a jinx. Well, now you know there is one—me. And before anything worse happens to you or to Zoe, I'm going to leave.''

Chapter 7

Marcus almost laughed. But the fear that tightened Callie's features stopped him, made him frown instead.

"I thought we cleared all that up yesterday," he said slowly. "I thought you agreed that this bad luck nonsense was just that—nonsense."

Callie shook her head. "No, I let myself be bullied by your arrogant doubts and soothed by Zoe's assurances that all I had to do was turn my back on my fears and everything would be all right. But it's clear that I'm still bringing bad luck to those around me."

Marcus glared down at her. "Can I have a 'for instance'?"

"Sure. For instance, we witnessed not one, but two near-accidents today. The man crossing the street and the minivan were both almost hit by cars running red lights."

"Right, Callie. And those were the only two vehicles that ran red lights today in the entire city of San Francisco. Get real."

He thought he'd gotten her with that bit of sarcasm. She stared up at him for several moments, her mouth pursed slightly, her eyes acknowledging the truth of his words. Then she gave her head a slow, almost weary shake.

"Perhaps not. But I didn't hear Mr. Harding mention any *other* detective in his complaint to the reporter just now. What about the fact that you've been taken off the catnapping case? Are you going to insist *that* is good luck?"

Again Marcus almost laughed. Actually, had he been taken off the case yesterday, he would have considered being removed from that particular investigation the best luck imaginable.

If, that is, he believed in luck.

However, after listening to his captain deliver a sneering repetition of Harding's pigheaded comments regarding Marcus's attempts to locate the man's damned cat, the case had gone from a nuisance to a challenge. And there was nothing Bulldog Scanlon enjoyed more than sinking his teeth into a challenge—like Callie's insistence that she was the bearer of some sort of ridiculous curse.

"Look, Callie. In the first place, I have not—"

"Stop!"

Zoe's command silenced Marcus immediately. He turned to the woman as she announced, "Dinner is on the table. The food I have prepared deserves to be savored, enjoyed. Therefore, there is to be no further discussion of this matter until dinner is over. Agreed?"

Marcus nodded, and saw Callie do the same. Stepping to the table, he pulled out a chair for Callie, did the same for Zoe, then took his own seat. The meal proceeded in silence for several minutes until Callie said, "This is truly delicious."

Marcus sent Zoe a quick glance and nodded his agreement while continuing to savor the pasta and sauce in his mouth.

"I'm glad you are enjoying it," Zoe replied. "The sauce is my mother-in-law's recipe."

A tiny, wistful smile curved Callie's lips. "How lovely of her to have shared it with you."

Zoe shook her head. "Oh, that was not exactly the situation, I'm afraid."

Marcus turned to his landlady just in time to see the woman's wide mouth twist into a wry smile. "My husband's mother did not approve of our marriage," she said. "The woman was determined that I would never learn the secret of her sauce. I was just as determined to have it."

Over the years, Marcus and Zoe had shared many a meal, often this same pasta and sauce, and had exchanged several tales. But this was one he'd never heard.

"Are you going to tell us that you stole it from the woman?" he asked.

Zoe took a sip of wine. While placing her glass on the table, she pursed her lips, then shrugged. "In a manner of speaking. You see, Giuseppe's mother had horrible headaches. She refused to believe that hypnosis could help, but one day the pain became so bad that she called me up and dared me to bring her some relief. I went to her home, and did as she asked. When I brought her out of the trance, it was obvious that her pain was gone. However, instead of being grateful, the woman insisted that this was because her medication had finally taken effect. A week later, she was again in pain. Again she asked me to hypnotize her, and again I complied. But this time, while she was in a trance state, I extracted from her the recipe for the sauce."

Marcus was grinning widely as Zoe finished speaking. Seeing the slight embarrassed color in her cheeks, he reached over and took her hand. "Good for you."

Zoe frowned. "You do not see this as a mental form of breaking and entering?"

"No. Haven't you always told me that a hypnotized person can't be forced to do something they don't really want to? Mama Zeffarelli probably planned on giving the recipe to you some day."

Zoe's features eased into a thoughtful expression as she said, "Perhaps. I suppose, then, that the sauce is not to be considered stolen merchandise. So—" a wicked smile lit her face as she gestured toward the bowl "—you can feel free to have another serving."

Laughing, Marcus did exactly that. When he offered a second helping to Callie, she shook her head. "It's delicious, but I couldn't eat another bite."

When she stood, lifting her plate as she drifted toward the sink, Zoe placed her hand on the young woman's arm. "Would you switch the coffee machine on while you are up? Then return to the table, if you please."

Though this last was politely worded, it was obviously not a request. Marcus fought another smile at the look of dismay that colored Callie's features before she turned to the counter. Suddenly reluctant to discuss this jinx situation, was she? Had he failed to tell her that Zoe's expertise lay in the field of phobias and fears? Perhaps he had. Well, it appeared Callie was about to learn just that, along with the fact that Dr. Zoe Zeffarelli wasn't the sort to let a challenge to her skills slip by.

He was right. The dishes had been cleared from the table, and all three of them had mugs of hot, fragrant coffee in front of them when Zoe turned to Callie and started in.

"Now, I want to speak to you about this reputed jinx business."

Callie met the woman's serious gaze, and sighed. "Look, I'm sure I must seem crazy to you, but you have to believe me. This is serious. Not all the things that have happened to people around me have been near-misses that make for amusing stories. I worked as a photographer's assistant once. He was hurt very badly when he fell from a ladder. A bike messenger was hit by a car right after delivering a package to me when I was working as a receptionist in a Manhattan office building. Then there was the time—"

Zoe's upheld hand halted Callie's recitation. "Tell me, if you would, did you set up this photographer's ladder?"

Callie nodded.

"And did you do so correctly? Made sure that it was level, that it was locked in place?"

Again she answered with a nod.

"Then how did the man come to fall?"

"Well, he climbed up to the very top to get a particular shot. I was across the room, holding a reflecting panel, when he started to lean forward. I told him to let me hold the ladder, but he ordered me to stay where I was. A moment later, he toppled over.''

Zoe looked into Callie's eyes for several minutes before she spoke again. ''You know, do you not, that this accident was the result of the man's own negligent actions.''

After a moment of silence, Callie responded. ''Yes. But—''

''No, there are no buts.'' Zoe shook her head. ''You know that this is true, as you know that the bicycle messenger probably darted into traffic as so many of them do, with barely a glance at oncoming cars. You must be aware that you do not possess, nor are you possessed by some *force* that could cause such things to happen to the people you come in contact with. You must know that you are not the center of the universe.''

Zoe's tone softened as she made this last statement. As she continued, the woman once again reached across to take Callie's hand.

''I want to apologize to you. When we spoke of this yesterday, I was not aware of how deep-seated your fears are in this area. I indicated that turning your back on these beliefs would be sufficient. I was wrong. You must examine these harmful beliefs and fears, one at a time, face them down and eradicate them from your life. I would like to help you do this. Would you let me?''

Marcus watched Callie's face intently. Hesitation was clearly evident in her soft green eyes, fear in the taut line of her wide mouth. He could almost feel the tension in her slender form, had to fight the temptation to place his hand over hers and urge her to trust—to trust Zoe, to trust him, if not herself.

Right, Scanlon, he thought. Big of you to expect her to begin trusting someone, when *you've* never learned that lesson.

Other than Zoe, he allowed no one to get close enough to truly get to know him. Hell, he hadn't even told Zoe all of the story that he'd shared with Callie today.

As if Callie had somehow picked up on his thoughts regarding that ten-year-old betrayal, her eyes shifted to his before she turned to Zoe with a decisive nod.

"All right. Tell me what to do."

"First, I wish for you to examine your past. Then I want you to make a list of all the things you fear the most, down to the least little thing. I am free after three tomorrow. We will meet in my office at that time and begin our work together. As for now, I think you need to get some sleep." She turned to Marcus. "You, too, young man. I'll see to the dishes. The activity of washing up relaxes me."

Feeling a little like a kid who'd been sent to bed early, Marcus followed Callie up the stairs. At the landing in front of his apartment, she turned to start up the flight leading to her room. Before she could begin climbing, he reached out and grabbed her hand. The eyes that met his were shadowed with doubt.

"Hey," he said softly. "Zoe knows what she's doing."

Callie frowned. "I hope so. If not…"

Her voice trailed off on an uncertain note. Marcus lifted one corner of his mouth in a smile meant to offer both comfort and challenge. "If not, what? The house will fall in on us? I don't believe that for one moment. In fact, just to show you how *seriously* I take your jinx status—"

He stopped speaking to stare down into Callie's large, darkly lashed eyes and saw a hint of anger mixed with the fear and doubt. This made him smile wider. But when she made no response, he lifted his hand to slide his fingers along her jaw and brush his thumb softly over her mouth.

Her lips were incredibly soft. And responsive. They parted instantly in answer to his touch. The shadows in her eyes faded as her eyebrows lifted, in surprise or perhaps question. Where his thumb rested, mere millimeters from the corner of her mouth, he became aware that her lips were easing out of their tight line, softening further.

Lowering his gaze to those lips, he leaned forward and touched them with his.

He'd intended the kiss to be a simple gesture, an act of defiance to show he didn't believe she represented any kind of danger. He certainly hadn't imagined that such a slight touch of flesh against flesh could have the power to call so deeply to his soul, arouse such instant desire in his body.

Make him want to kiss her again.

With a quick indrawn breath, Marcus drew back, dropping his hand to his side. Callie blinked up at him, surprised, he supposed. And perhaps a little offended.

"What was—" she began.

"It was a kiss," he broke in. "A kiss for luck—to set you on your way to facing down your demons."

"But you don't—"

"Believe in luck," he finished. "You're right. So, call it tempting fate, then."

Callie nodded. She knew she should probably spout something light and breezy to show him that she was totally unaffected by that kiss. But there was no way she could convincingly tell that lie. The best thing would be to escape his presence.

"Okay," she said at last, then turned and started up the stairs leading to her room. As she reached the top step, she heard a door click shut below. For some reason this made it suddenly easier for her to breathe as she entered her own apartment.

She had a lot to think about, she told herself. But she was suddenly far too weary to consider strategy. Besides, her mind didn't seem to want to wander too far from the memory of that oh-so-brief kiss. Foolish mind. No doubt a simply over-weary mind. A good night's sleep would no doubt put those moments on the landing in perspective.

So much for perspective.

The feel of Marcus Scanlon's lips touching hers was the first thing that Callie was aware of when she woke the next morning. She continued to lie in bed several moments, holding on to the memory of that kiss, smiling as she imagined Marcus Scanlon, knight in shining armor, proving his worth by conquering her shadowy fears.

Knight in shining armor?

Callie sat bolt upright, those words echoing in her mind. That was how she'd once thought of Dave. After she'd warned him about her curse, he had also claimed a desire to "tempt fate." And look how that had ended.

With a shudder, Callie forced herself to rise. Light streaming in the window to her right drew her to the French doors. Pushing aside the filmy curtains, her gaze skimmed over the boats in the marina, past the blue-green waters to focus on the magnificent double towers of the Golden Gate Bridge, lit to a brilliant shade of orange by the morning sun, etched against a cloudless blue, blue sky.

A new day.

The first day of the rest of your life.

Callie frowned. Her mother used to say that, every time something awful would happen—like the time the woman's crystal ball rolled off the table and shattered into a million pieces, or when their motor home broke down, or her mother's latest lover suddenly left. And each time her mother had intoned those words, the woman had glanced at Callie, as if to reassure her child while at the same time blaming her.

The memory brought quick tears, blurring the view before Callie into a shimmer of blue, green and orange, like some abstract painting. She blinked furiously, to clear both the scene in front of her as well as the way she viewed the past.

Almost immediately she realized what Zoe would say about these stories. Her *mother* was the one who'd forgotten to put the crystal sphere in its velvet-lined box. That motor home had been twelve years old and had almost two hundred thousand miles on the speedometer. As far as her mother's lack of luck with love, it had been Bonnie Chance's need that attracted one man after another, and just as quickly repelled them.

And if Callie didn't want to end up like her mother, running from unacknowledged pain all her life, she was going to have to do as Zoe suggested—face her fears.

Suddenly Callie didn't want to wait until three o'clock this afternoon to begin exorcising her ghosts. Not only did she want to start now, she needed to do something more forceful than making a list of her fears.

And she knew just the thing.

Pivoting quickly, Callie sank into the armchair, picked up the telephone and quickly dialed the number etched in her mind. After two rings, she received the cell phone's "not in service" message. Undaunted, Callie reached for the directory, looked up the business number she'd called before, and dialed again.

"Art Associates," a female voice responded.

"Hello. I'd like to speak with Dave Johnson."

Pleased at how calm and assured she'd managed to sound, Callie waited while the secretary hesitated.

"Um. Mr. Johnson isn't in the office right now."

Callie knew that the "office" was primarily a warehouse, where incoming pieces of art were received and stored before being shipped to the various galleries in the chain he represented. Dave had told her he was rarely there, which was why he preferred her to call him on the cell phone.

Coincidentally, where no secretary could get suspicious of a woman who called once too often.

"All right, then," Callie said evenly. "The moment he checks in, please have him call Callie Chance."

Callie rattled off the number printed on the strip beneath her phone's number pad, then hung up.

Feeling some of the air easing out of her sails, she forced herself to get busy. Filling the old tub only half full so she wouldn't be tempted to linger in the warm water, she took a quick bath. After a vigorous rubdown with a towel from the dresser in the corner, Callie discovered that the pain in her wrist had eased some, and enough strength had returned to her left hand to allow her to carefully pull on a pair of jeans. She topped those with a short sweater knitted in pink cotton. She then sat down, pad of paper on the little table, a pen held loosely in her freshly wrapped left hand and began her list of Fears and Superstitions to Be Faced Down.

It was quite a lengthy inventory. To make the undertaking

a little less intimidating, she broke it down to categories, the first one being Dave Johnson.

Under Step 1, she listed the action she'd just taken—call him.

Step 2: meet with the man and recover the box of personal effects she'd shipped to his warehouse before leaving Cape Cod.

Step 3: tell him about the real estate agent and watch for signs of guilt.

Step 4: tell him what a piece of slime he is.

Step 5: walk away and never think of him again.

With that list completed, she went on to more minor items. Under the heading of "superstitions and aversions," she wrote down: black cats, birds of all sorts, broken mirrors, chocolate—and then stopped. There were too many things to list, between the superstitions she'd picked up from her mother and the paranoia resulting from the various disasters she'd witnessed over the course of her life. The only way she could deal with these was one at a time, as they came up.

She turned to the heading, "fears," and gave that subject long, hard consideration.

The thing she dreaded most was that her presence might cause real harm to someone else. If she chose to believe Zoe, she had to learn to do her best and trust others to take care of their lives. Far easier said than done.

So she turned to her next concern—money. She had enough to feed herself and even pay for a month's rent—here, after her status as rent-free guest changed, and if the cost was reasonable. But she needed a job. Prior to working for the Wilsons' deli, her longest employment had lasted six months. However, she did have lots of varied experience to draw upon, which gave her a wide range of options should she decide to stay in San Francisco.

Her final fear, she realized, was that she'd end up like her mother, doomed to fall in love again and again with the wrong sort of man, never to have the stable home life she'd always longed for.

Callie took a deep breath as she stared at the lists spread

out before her, then released the air slowly. One thing at a time, she told herself as she patted the pages into a neat stack. Rising, she crossed the room to place them under her pillow. Her stomach growled as she straightened. She glanced at her watch. Nine-thirty. She would have to eat, and soon. But she didn't want to miss Dave's call.

After only one second of hesitation, she returned to the table, picked up the receiver and dialed. When she once again had the secretary on the phone, she coolly informed the woman that she wouldn't be available to receive Dave's call until eleven-thirty. However, she went on to say far more calmly than she felt, she *expected* to hear from him no later than noon.

So much for spending her valuable time waiting around for his call. Those days were over.

"Oh, Zoe, do you have a minute?"

Callie practically ran into the woman as she clattered down the last few steps to the foyer at the same moment that Zoe entered from her office.

"Of course. My first patient isn't due for a half hour. Would you like me to make you some breakfast while we talk?"

"No." Callie smiled as she shook her head. "I *am* hungry, but I'd prefer to provide my meals for myself today. I was wondering if there's a market nearby, so I can stock the refrigerator."

Zoe glanced at Callie's sling. "The closest market is several blocks away, on Chestnut Street. Are you sure you are up to the walk?"

"Yes. I'm still wearing the sling because my wrist throbs when I let it hang, but other than that, it's feeling much better. And my muscles are a little sore and tight, but I think a walk will loosen them up."

"Good. Follow me to the kitchen, then. I have a small wire cart you can take along to help you bring the groceries back."

It was a beautiful day. Once Callie was outside, with the sun on her face and the slight breeze cooling her cheeks, she wished she could take her time, wander along slowly while studying the different styles of the houses that rose on either side of her, investigate the shops she passed once she started up Chestnut Street, perhaps linger over the enticing display of fresh fruits and vegetables arranged in front of the market.

But she didn't want to miss that phone call. More important, she didn't want to take the edge off her determination to face Dave and reclaim at least the portion of her spirit that he'd stolen.

So she shopped quickly, then munched on an apple and a slice of cheese as she hurried back to the house. After lugging the cart up the front steps and into the kitchen, she placed her purchases on the shelves in the fridge and cupboard that Zoe had designated as hers, then ran up to her room.

It was eleven thirty-five. And the telephone was ringing. Callie took a deep breath as she closed the door behind her, then crossed the room with determined steps. She immediately recognized the voice that responded to her "Hello." Dave instantly went on the offensive, asking just why she'd come to San Francisco without speaking to him first. Callie refused to take the bait.

"I'll be more than happy to discuss that with you when I come for the box that I shipped to your warehouse. I'm sure you are aware of it, since I addressed it to your attention. Now, I can be there in a half hour or so, depending on how quickly the taxi—"

She blinked at Dave's vehement interruption, refusing that meeting place.

"Fine," she replied. "You can bring the box to me, then. I'm in an apartment in the Marina district."

After a moment of silence on Dave's part, that suggestion also met with refusal.

"All right, how about the Ferry Building? There's an area with benches to the left of it. Yes. In half an hour."

Chapter 8

The square of asphalt next to the Ferry Building was empty. As Callie sat on a bench watching the street, she was aware of a stream of people entering and exiting a gated area to her right, coming from and going to the boat docked behind her.

Her sling and elastic bandage were stashed in her large purse, a last-minute decision she'd made just before exiting Raj's cab. She didn't want anything about her to appear weak. At first, her wrist hadn't missed the support, but as the wait for Dave's arrival stretched on, her hand began to ache.

Just as Callie began to believe that Dave wasn't going to show, he appeared, rounding the Ferry Building on her left, carrying her large box. The sun's reflection made his hair a halo of pale and dark gold as he strode toward her, casual in jeans and a tan sweater. When he drew closer, she saw that the handsome features she'd once found so charming and disarming were tight and wary.

He dropped the box onto the bench next to Callie. "Here's your stuff. What else do you want?"

Callie got to her feet. Dave was only an inch taller, making it easy for her to hold his gaze. "How about an explanation or two," she said. "We can start with why you asked me to marry you when you already had a wife."

Dave's light blue eyes narrowed into hers for several moments. "I fell in love with you, okay?" he said at last. His words held just the right note of reluctance and regret. "You were so open, so free-spirited, so different from my so sophisticated, proper—never mind. It was wrong of me, I know. But it happened, and once I'd fallen under your spell, I had to find a way to stay there."

He stopped speaking, lifted his gaze to stare at the water behind Callie, raking his fingers through his hair. It was a gesture she'd once found endearing. Now it irritated her.

"You know, I don't believe a word you're saying," she replied evenly. "But on the off chance that even one-tenth of it is the truth, did it ever occur to you to be honest? With me? With her? A marriage is a serious commitment. If there is a problem with it, you don't just turn to someone else. You talk to your partner—work it out. And if that's not possible, you end it—up front. You certainly don't marry someone else before the first one is legally over."

Dave's eyes narrowed as he met Callie's gaze. "You have no idea what you're talking about, what my life is like. I'm not just married to a woman, I'm married to a family business, owned by my father-in-law. I've put in seven long years building it up from one tiny gallery to a chain, located in over twenty cities in the country. I would lose all of that in a divorce."

Pausing briefly, he shook his head. "I know. That's the cost of doing business. But I had my daughter to think about. Losing my income would have been bad enough, but the thought of losing Chrissy was unacceptable. I thought that maybe, just maybe, I could have it all. The business, my daughter, and eventually, you, and the life we planned on the Cape. But you made it clear I couldn't have you without marriage. So…"

His words trailed off as his eyes once again shifted away. Callie watched him stare past her shoulder for several beats of her heart. Each pulsation came stronger than the next, fueled by growing anger, till her fury exploded into words.

"So it's *my* fault that you attempted bigamy? Because you wanted, what, sex? You knew I'd been strung along with a false promise of marriage, that I refused to allow that to happen again. Having my heart wasn't enough for you, you wanted me in your bed, too, is that it? And if marrying me would bring that about, who cared about the little matter of the wife and child living in ignorance on the other side of the country."

She watched closely as Dave's eyebrows moved together a tiny fraction before they lifted, his eyes widening to blue-eyed wounded innocence as he stared at her, his golden hair ruffling in the rising breeze.

Callie took a good long look at the man she thought she had loved enough to marry. He had the kind of good looks that lured women to the movie matinees, where they could watch and sigh in the dark. Pure masculine beauty. Even now, knowing the sort of deception this man was capable of, the expression of injured honesty in his eyes would make him totally believable as one of the "good guys"—the sheriff in a Western or the leader of a rebel star colony in a science fiction epic.

And, suddenly, she knew why. Marcus had mentioned something about con men having the ability to believe their own lies. Dave was one of those people. He'd been able to convince her that he loved her, that he was free to offer his love, because he'd justified this in his own mind and heart. Which was why, careful as she'd been about trusting again, she'd fallen in love with him, or rather, with the illusion he'd so skillfully presented.

Well, the mask of charm was off now. And she wasn't about to be taken in by his new pose of misunderstood victim.

"Callie," he said. "I understand why you suspect me of having less than honorable intentions, considering that—"

"*Considering,*" Callie broke in, "that the diamond in the engagement ring you gave me was as fake as your proposal of marriage, an institution which I believe suggests an exclusive, one-on-one relationship.''

Dave stared at her for a moment. Slowly he began to shake his head. ''I don't believe it. This is about *money?* You thought that you were getting some rich husband, who would shower you with gifts and fancy houses? And now you're angry to learn that I'm just a poor working stiff, who was trying his best to figure a way through a difficult situation?''

Callie didn't know whether to laugh at this, or slap his face. The laugh won. It came out as a short, sharp bark.

''I don't believe *you,*'' she countered. ''I'm not the one who lied, who set up a deal with a Realtor, an apparently *phony* realtor, who disappeared with every cent of the down payment on the house that was supposed to be our home, our business.''

''Wait.'' Dave frowned as he shook his head. ''What are you talking about?''

''I'm talking about Mr. Henry Robinson, the real estate agent you picked out. Seems he decided to take a vacation with the money that was supposed to be the down payment on our house.''

''You don't think that I—'' Dave shook his head. ''You can't really believe I had anything to do with this guy taking off?''

''I have my suspicions. For instance, after you saw me in front of your house the other day, didn't it occur to you that I might be just a little peeved? That I might no longer want to buy a house with you and, therefore, you might want to call and cancel our offer on the house? Or had you already pocketed your portion of your take from the phony agent's scam?''

''Callie, don't be ridiculous. I didn't call about the house, because I wanted to speak to you first. To explain. To see if, somehow, we couldn't work something out. As for the money, remember *I* put down five thousand myself.''

Callie knew that. She also knew that the money wasn't the point.

"Why *shouldn't* I wonder about this? You lied to me, you cheated on your wife, you—"

"Not officially," Dave broke in. "You and I never went to bed. Therefore, I never cheated on Sunny."

Callie was fast losing her patience. "Look, call it whatever you want. It doesn't matter to me. I have what I came for."

She was turning toward the box on the bench when Dave's sarcastic "Really?" pivoted her back to him.

"You don't want money?" he asked. "A little something to soothe your *wounded* heart?"

Staring into his light blue eyes, Callie finally understood the angry wariness she'd seen there when Dave had first arrived. He was afraid she had blackmail on her mind.

"No, Dave, I don't want a thing," she said evenly. "Except to forget that I ever met you."

Frown lines formed over his eyes. The wary expression was replaced with doubt, which then eased into a look of relief.

"Then you're leaving San Francisco?"

Callie started to nod, then shrugged. "Probably. Eventually."

Dave's expression once again became guarded. "Eventually? Why not now?"

"I…" Callie hesitated as she considered telling him about her part in the catnapping case. Marcus had told her that if they found the suspects, they would want her to pick them out of a lineup.

A *fe*lineup.

Just the thought of that silly pun was enough to make her want to smile. Instead, she shrugged and answered lightly. "There isn't anything for me back on the Cape, but I have some thinking to do before I go running off somewhere new. Not that I could afford to. So, I've decided to get a job of some sort and do my thinking here."

"Look, Callie, I lied when I told you I didn't believe in your jinx. I don't want my life here ruined. If you give me a few days, I can get you some money. Maybe not the full five thousand. That would raise too many suspicions. But perhaps two? Tell me where you're staying, and I'll get it to you later today.''

The wary look in his eyes once more verged on panic. Callie shook her head.

''Look. I have no desire to mess up your little life here. I'm sure that, given enough time, you'll manage that quite nicely on your own. *Or* you can figure a way to deal honestly with your situation. It's totally unimportant to me. Just understand this. I don't want your money. I don't want *anything* from you, other than to never see you again.''

Callie had meant every word she'd said. And yet the very next evening, the moment she stepped into the Sutherland Gallery, she found herself staring in mute, stunned horror across the well-dressed crowd at Dave Johnson, standing arm in arm with his beautiful honey-blond wife.

She never should have come here tonight.

But it had seemed like such a good idea when Zoe suggested it. During their first session, after she returned from her meeting with Dave the previous afternoon, Zoe had been surprised and pleased with the decisive action that Callie had taken to confront her past. They'd then discussed other items on Callie's fear list and ways they could be addressed. Callie had spent the rest of that evening, and much of today, trying to implement Zoe's suggestions, which ran from various forms of meditation meant to help her ''get in touch'' with the origin of her fears, to the creation of affirmations to reinforce positive actions.

Since most of her fears involved being the catalyst for some sort of public disaster, the opening of this new exhibit tonight was supposed to help her confront and overcome that particular apprehension. She'd been nervous enough at that prospect, but now she faced an encounter with the woman who, only four days earlier, had looked up from Dave's embrace, brown eyes slowly filling with questions and suspicion.

''See? You have stepped into the room, and still the roof is safely above our heads.''

Zoe's gently teasing words made Callie blink.

The roof might be where it belonged, but Callie sincerely wished that the floor would suddenly open and swallow her up. Or that sometime during the last eight months she'd thought to ask the name of the galleries that Art Associates supplied.

She'd been sincere when she told Dave she didn't want to cause him any trouble. Now all it would take was for his wife to recognize her from that brief encounter and begin to ask questions. The cat would be out of the bag, so to speak, and the poop would hit the fan.

Somehow she had to keep that from happening.

Taking a deep breath, she returned Zoe's warm smile as the woman went on, "It is wonderful, is it not, that I was able to get an extra ticket for you?"

Oh, sure.

Callie forced herself to nod. Her silent response wasn't a complete lie, she told herself. Despite her disastrous relationship with Mr. Art Broker, the chance to view paintings and sculptures remained a joy. The fact that Marcus had escorted the two women to the gallery, and that the three of them would be dining together at the top of the Hyatt later, added to the allure.

However, twenty-twenty hindsight suggested tonight was too soon for all of this. Her wrist hurt from the struggle to pull her hair up into a French twist, and vanity had refused to let her mar the elegance of her simple outfit with a bulky Ace bandage. And now, she'd barely been in the gallery long enough to be handed a brochure describing the various artists' work being displayed, and already she was facing imminent disaster.

"Hey, I don't like these things all that much, either."

Marcus's voice pulled Callie's attention to her left. The black suit he wore had crisp, clean lines that emphasized the width of his shoulders. When Marcus gave her a world-weary half smile, she suddenly felt lighter, less anxious.

"What do you mean, *either?*"

"Well." He paused, glanced around, then bent his head to hers. "The way you're standing there, shoulders slumped, eyes staring blindly ahead, you remind me a little of someone who has just been convicted of a crime and is preparing to step into a jail cell.''

Callie stifled a groan. Yesterday she had planned on telling Marcus about her confrontation with Dave, but with the long hours he'd been keeping, this was the first time they'd been together for more than a few moments. Now, however, wasn't the time to go into that. Not in the same room with the man in question, his wife and who knew how many of their friends.

Shaking her head, Callie smiled. ''You're imagining things. I love to see artists' work honored like this. I've dabbled at drawing and painting just enough to really appreciate the kind of dedication and discipline it takes to get a piece displayed.''

Marcus noted the sudden brightness of Callie's smile as she finished speaking, and immediately suspicion broke through the fatigue caused by two days of endless, fruitless work on a case that he wasn't ''officially'' working on.

Some of his exhaustion had lifted when he'd watched Callie walk down the stairs to the foyer, where he'd been waiting with Zoe. He liked the way her long-sleeved crocheted sweater snugged along her slender form and the way her wine-red velvet skirt caressed her hips gently before flowing down to the floor. What had attracted the bulk of his attention was the tangle of loose curls atop her head, and the sudden mental image of burying his fingers in the silken mass until they tumbled down around her shoulders once more.

But now, as he looked into Callie's eyes, he saw a glint of some emotion very close to panic. He found himself wondering about that, until a large man in a dark gray suit moved past, jostling Callie. Marcus saw her right hand reach over her left wrist in a defensive gesture, and Marcus felt some of his suspicions relax, along with his protective response to Callie's look of fear.

Perhaps, he told himself, the skittishness he sensed in her came from the number of people milling about near the entrance to the gallery, emphasizing the fact that she was in a strange city, surrounded by strangers.

He was reluctant to examine his heightened sensitivity to Callie's emotional state. He'd done more than enough wondering and questioning in the course of his job over the last two days. When he'd arrived at Zoe's, he'd planned on spending his off time on his balcony, staring through his telescope at the stars, or maybe working on that chair he'd started to build down in the garage. Something—anything— to take his mind off the fact that his life had suddenly become all about cats and the people who steal them. Not to mention attempting to convince a beautiful woman she wasn't a jinx.

He'd totally forgotten that, in a weak moment a month earlier, he'd let Zoe bribe him with the promise of a fantastic dinner in exchange for accompanying her to this opening. How the woman had managed to get an extra ticket for Callie was a mystery to him, but although Zoe underplayed her involvement in society and politics, he knew she had her "sources."

"The gallery is donating a portion of tonight's profits to a favorite charity of mine."

Zoe's voice broke into Marcus's thoughts. He watched Callie nod in response and noted that it was a rather distracted nod. Her gaze seemed to stray from Zoe's several times, glancing repeatedly toward the end of the room. When Marcus looked in that direction, the only thing of interest he saw were a couple of tables laid out with hors d'oeuvres.

"...will contribute to the renovation of a building that will provide homes for over fifty homeless people," Zoe was saying. "All of whom help with the construction of their own apartments."

"That sounds like a wonderful project."

Zoe gave a sharp nod of her head. "I like to support organizations which encourage people to take charge of their lives. Now, I see a few people I need to speak to. They would bore you senseless." The woman paused to smile, a smile that included Marcus as well as Callie, before she went on, "So, why don't the two of you circulate, look at the lovely paintings and sculptures, have a little champagne and get some of those canapés from the table at the end of the room. I shall make the connections required of me and take a peek at the art as I can. We can meet back here in, say, forty-five minutes, then go for dinner.''

With that, Zoe moved away, slipping through the people clustered just inside the entrance to the gallery. Marcus glanced around again, frowning. All this art might be a feast for the eyes, but his stomach was grumbling a warning that it needed a little bit of feeding before he could truly enjoy the visual treats.

He turned to Callie. ''I think the canapé table sounds like a good idea. What do you say we head that way now, before the other vultures descend on the goodies.''

He smiled at his own little joke, a reference to the fact that almost everyone in the room seemed to be dressed in black, himself included. He was wearing his only good suit, a garment he reserved for weddings, funerals, and the rare times he really wanted to impress a date. Rare because he made a point of keeping his relationships casual, at least on an emotional level.

This had been rather easy to accomplish, considering the type of woman he normally associated with—female officers on the fast track to promotion, lawyers obsessed with their caseload, a judge with political aspirations, and a few idle-rich charity types he'd met through Zoe. Sooner or later, they'd all bored Marcus to tears.

Unlike the woman next to him.

Marcus glanced at Callie. From the moment he'd met her, he'd been alternately perturbed, confused, and fascinated. He was never sure what she'd say or do. Like now. Most women he knew would at least pretend to be more interested in the art than in food. But Callie seemed to have immediately taken to his suggestion that they eat, her eyes darting to the food tables, then sweeping over the room, as if gauging the quickest way to get there.

Placing his hand on the small of her back, he began to

steer her toward the right, saying, "The crowd seems to be thinner this way."

Callie took one step in that direction, then froze. Marcus glanced over to see her eyes widen with the sort of panic he'd once seen in a horse getting ready to bolt. Before he could ask what was wrong, she pivoted to step toward a painting on the wall, then stood there as still as the small bronze statue of a fisherman on her left.

Before Marcus could join her, he noticed a slender blond woman approach, accompanied by a man with sun-streaked hair. The man's light blue eyes were narrowed and practically boring a hole in Callie's back. When his escort tugged on his hand, the man pulled his eyes away, turned and disappeared into the crowd.

Callie hadn't moved. Marcus glanced at the picture she stood before, an oil painting of a white clapboard building set against a bank of dark gray clouds. A sign over the structure's multipaned window announced that it was the Nantucket Fish Market.

When he reached Callie's side, Marcus asked, "Familiar?"

She jumped and turned toward him. "Is who familiar?"

Marcus lifted his eyebrows. "Not who. Where."

"What do you mean, where?"

Callie stared up at him, a confused frown on her face. Marcus pointed to the painting. "There. The fish shop. I thought maybe you recognized it."

Callie turned toward the wall again. "Oh," she said a moment later. "Yeah. I've been there. In fact…"

Her voice trailed off. "Yes?" Marcus prompted.

Callie's smile was bright as she turned to him, once more rousing Marcus's suspicions.

"I know the artist. I mentioned her the other day. She was the one who gave me—" she glanced around "—who gave me the telephone number off the business card of that man…."

Her voice trailed off as she continued to peruse the room. Marcus's detecting antennae began twitching. "I see," he said. "Is there a problem I should know about?"

Callie jerked back to face him. "No. Of course not. I'm…" She paused, then shook her head slowly. "I'm not sure it's a *problem,* exactly. Just something I don't want to explain about *here.*"

"Here, in front of this painting?" Marcus cocked one eyebrow. "What? You think it's bugged or something?"

"No. By here I mean—this gallery."

Marcus studied her face a moment. The overbright smile was gone. Her complexion was a shade paler, her eyes silently pleading.

"I see," he found himself saying once more. "Another of your long stories?"

"Not all that long. But not something I care to discuss here…now. Later," she said. "At dinner."

Dinner. Marcus's stomach growled.

"Agreed. I can wait to hear the story, but I didn't get lunch today, so if I'm going to exercise that kind of patience, I'm going to need some food now. Will you join me?"

Callie turned once again to survey the tables at the end of the room before giving him a wide smile.

"Don't mind if I do," she replied. "I sort of combined breakfast and lunch myself, and I'm starving."

It took several moments to work their way across the room, past clutches of people gathered around various paintings, people who could be heard to mutter things like, "I just don't see it," or "Wonderful use of light." As Marcus led Callie, holding her right hand in his, he noticed that the works of art all had a nautical theme, from the paintings of Nantucket's quaint stores, like the one Callie had been studying so intently, to scenes depicting deep-sea fishing in Alaska. But Marcus only gave the artwork a cursory glance, keeping his primary attention on his goal.

"What a beautiful layout." Callie spoke softly as she stood in front of the table laden with various appetizers. "Oh. Look at these." She picked up a small ball of something nestled in white fluted paper. "They look just like the little crab puffs that Mrs. Wilson taught me to make. I wonder…"

Her voice trailed off as she opened her mouth to pop the

bite-size morsel in. She chewed slowly, then nodded as she swallowed.

"That's it. The exact taste. I wonder how—"

When Callie broke off with a gasp, Marcus turned to see that her eyes were wide, staring ahead with what could be surprise, or might reflect the sudden inability to breathe. He didn't waste time wondering which, just reached over and gave her a hard whack between the shoulder blades.

A little too hard, perhaps.

The force of his blow propelled Callie forward. Her hips hit the edge of the table with enough force to make it and everything on it shudder as her upper body bent forward at the waist. Seeing that her breasts were headed toward a three-tiered display of shrimp, Marcus closed his fingers over her right elbow and pulled her back from the brink of disaster.

Once righted, Callie pivoted to him, eyes wide. "You hit me."

"I know. I guess I got a little carried away. I should have done the Heimlich maneuver, but when I saw you were choking, I acted on reflex."

Callie shook her head and said, "I wasn't choking, I was wondering if—"

"What are you doing, Scanlon?" A deep, forceful voice interrupted. "Taking your anger at your own incompetence out on this young woman?"

Marcus slowly turned toward the familiar voice to find himself staring into gray eyes narrowed in a scowling face. The man's thick hair shimmered pale silver beneath the lights, in sharp contrast to his black silk suit.

Marcus didn't know whether to laugh out loud or roar with frustration. This was the last person he wanted to run into tonight, for more than one reason. And the last person he wanted a public altercation with.

"Callie," he said quietly. "I want you to meet Gerald Harding. Harding, this is Callie Chance, who I was attempting to save from choking on a crab puff."

The older man's lips twisted into a snide smile as he extended his hand.

"Pleased to meet you, Miss Chance. If I might be excused for giving advice on such short acquaintance, I'd suggest that you not accept any sort of *help* from this man. It will likely only end in disaster. Take tonight, for example."

Harding's voice sharpened as he turned to Marcus. "You've managed to muck things up again, Scanlon. I was contacted earlier today and told that someone would meet me here tonight, someone who would tell me how to get my cat back. Now, I'm willing to bet that this someone has seen *you* here, and won't dare to approach me." The man paused, his eyes narrowing. "Just what *are* you doing here anyway? I thought that you, and the rest of your department, had been ordered to leave me alone."

Actually, no, Marcus wanted to reply. He was still very much on the case. In fact, he'd been doing quite a bit of extensive, though quiet, investigating the last couple of days. And not without some results.

However, the fact that the department was still pursuing the case was not for public consumption, which was why he hadn't told Callie or Zoe about it after Harding's complaints about him on the news the other night. It was vital that it appear that the police had indeed backed off, and the fewer people who knew about it, the better.

Running into this man here, tonight, was *not* part of the plan. But this also wasn't something that Marcus could explain to Harding, especially when the surrounding crowd contained a familiar member of the print media, the very sharp-eyed redhead he'd noticed just before Callie started to choke. He didn't need to glance at Shirley McIntyre to know that the woman was finding the confrontation between Marcus and Harding far more appetizing than any of the food on the table.

He did need to say *something,* however, loud enough to be heard. "Look, Harding, my world doesn't revolve around you and your cat, okay? I'm off the clock. I came here with a couple of friends and—"

"And," Callie broke in, stepping forward. "If you want to blame anyone for the fiasco that allowed the catnappers to escape, you can blame me. I was the one who knocked on the door to their room—by mistake, mind you—which apparently spooked them into running. So, if you aren't approached tonight with new ransom directions, that will also be my fault. Both of the catnappers can recognize me, so it would be seeing *me* standing around that would frighten them off, not Detective Scanlon. *Who,* by the way, was doing his level best to chase down every lead. You should have thanked him instead of getting him tossed off the case.''

Marcus scowled a bit over the way Callie's voice had risen with obvious anger, then grabbed the exit line she'd provided.

''Forget that last part,'' he said. ''Being off the case is just where I want to be. Good night, Mr. Harding.''

As he finished speaking, Marcus took Callie's arm and began leading her away, then glanced over his shoulder and added, ''Oh, and give the crab puffs a try, why don't you?''

Callie looked back to see Harding's scowl deepen and his face take on a dark red color. She could feel her own face growing warm as she turned her attention to the frowning man next to her.

''I'm sorry,'' she said.

He said nothing as he stepped to one side, pulling her past a group of people clustered around a driftwood sculpture of a leaping whale. Reaching a pocket of space between clusters of chattering art lovers, he turned to her and said, ''I need to talk to you. Outside. Away from all these people.''

Callie stared into his dark blue eyes and sighed. Of course he wanted to talk to her. He probably wanted to know what had possessed her to verbally come to his defense with that Harding guy, probably wanted to tell her he could fight his own battles and all that macho cop stuff. Either that or he wanted to know why she'd been acting so distracted and downright weird ever since they stepped into the gallery.

Though she dreaded it, she'd have to tell him the truth, that the man she'd been engaged to was right here, in this room, with his loving wife. Marcus did know the story, after all, as did Zoe. But somehow she felt a little less foolish with

Dave being an anonymous, faceless stranger to these two people.

Callie was aware of Marcus's strong fingers holding her hand as he forged a meandering path between works of art and clumps of patrons. Beneath his firm grip, her fingers were beginning to ache, but the din of conversation would mean she'd have to shout for him to hear her, and she'd been the center of attention enough for one evening.

By the time they were within sight of the entrance, Callie didn't think she could feel more miserable. Until they reached the spot where they were to meet Zoe. The older woman was already there, deep in conversation with two others. The tall woman with the short spiky platinum hair was a complete stranger to Callie, but the tiny one with soft, honey-colored tresses pulled into a neat chignon at the base of her skull was all too familiar.

Marcus walked right past the trio, as if he didn't even see them, pulling Callie in his wake. However, as Callie followed, Zoe grabbed Callie's right hand, tugging her free of Marcus's grasp. She saw him glance back, hesitate a minute as his eyes swept the group of women, then turn and continue his escape.

"Just the person I was looking for." Zoe's voice drew Callie's attention to the group of women. "Callie, I want you to meet Pia Blanchard and Sunny Sutherland-Johnson. Sunny's family owns this gallery."

As the petite woman put out her hand, Callie almost found herself saying, "We've met."

They hadn't, of course, unless she wanted to count those few moments when the woman's eyes met hers over a black wrought iron fence, while Sunny stood in Dave's arms.

"Do I know you from somewhere?"

Sunny's voice was soft, but Callie couldn't have been more startled if the woman had shouted in her ear. Taking a quick breath, Callie shook her head.

"No. I—I don't think so. I only arrived in town a couple of days ago."

Tiny frown lines marred Sunny's smooth brow. "Well, I

used to travel a lot, buying for the gallery, until my daughter was born. Perhaps we met somewhere in art circles. New York, maybe, or—''

''Oh, New York,'' Callie broke in, grasping that straw before the woman could move on to someplace closer to the truth. The painting of Nantucket, with its proximity to Cape Cod, was far too close for comfort.

''You know,'' Callie continued, ''I did work in a gallery in Soho for a little while.'' Until the owner absconded with an entire exhibit of valuable primitive art. ''We might have run into each other there.''

Sunny was still frowning. ''I don't know. I think it was much more recent. Perhaps—''

''Sunny, dear,'' Zoe interrupted, placing a hand on the woman's arm. ''My friends and I are running late for a dinner appointment. I think we need to get back to the matter at hand.''

''Yes,'' a slightly nasal voice interjected. ''Are you *sure* that Monique can't make some time for us?''

The platinum blonde leaned forward as she spoke, her eyes pleading, the low-cut neckline of her black jacket revealing amazingly ample breasts for someone so thin. Or perhaps they were the result of an industrial-strength Wonderbra. Callie guessed the woman was somewhere in her late thirties, despite her spiky hair and short, short skirt.

''Yes, Pia,'' Sunny replied with a sigh. ''I am sure. Monique is booked up months in advance, something I warned you about when you agreed to organize this benefit.''

The woman named Pia took a sip from her fluted glass, then frowned. ''Well, *I* understood you to say that you'd handle that part of it for me. *You* are her best friend.''

Sunny shook her head. ''Pia, I never said any such thing. I had this opening to arrange, and—never mind. The fact of the matter is that you are just going to have to find someone else.''

''At this late date?'' Pia shook her head. ''Impossible. We'll have to cancel.''

''No.'' This came from Zoe. ''I just ran into Greg Laramie.

He was telling me that the animal shelter counts on this fundraiser taking place in May. They work their budget around the amount we raise. Besides, I think I have the answer for you.'' She paused and turned to Callie. ''Callie assisted the owner of a catering business for two years, did you not?''

Callie nodded.

''Well, my dear, Pia has a problem. In a little less than a week, she is hosting a wine-and-food fest at her home, and she needs someone to arrange the food for the affair. This is for charity, so your fee would be nominal. But if you can pull it off, this would be a wonderful way to establish yourself here.''

Callie couldn't think of anything she'd like better, if it weren't for the fact that this would very likely mean running into Sunny and Dave Johnson again.

Even if Callie had been counting how many times her luck had moved from good to bad since stepping into this room, she knew she would have lost track by this point. Was this opportunity beneficial, or only another door to disaster?

The slight narrowing of Zoe's gray eyes suggested that the woman knew just what Callie was thinking, and was warning Callie not to go there, to think positive and take charge of her attitude and her life. So, she did just that.

''I'll be happy to do it.''

''You *will?*'' Pia reached across and clasped Callie's left hand between her palms. A shaft of pain shot up Callie's arm as the woman shook her hand violently and gushed, ''Oh, that is really terrific. The shelter does *such* important work, you know, and I do so want everything to go right. When can you get to work on it?''

''Tomorrow,'' Callie replied as she began the task of extricating her hand slowly, trying to pull it back without causing any more pain to her wrist.

''When can you get to work on *what?*''

At the sound of Dave's voice Callie jumped, freeing her hand of Pia's grasp with a jerk. She looked up to find him standing behind Sunny, his hands resting on his wife's shoulders, his lips curved in a wide smile, while he glared across the small circle at Callie.

She couldn't say a word. Fortunately, Pia was more than capable of explaining the deal that had just been struck. When the woman paused in the middle of her recitation, Callie broke in.

"I'm sorry. It's getting a little stuffy in here for me. Pia, Zoe has your number, doesn't she? I'll call you first thing in the morning and set up a meeting. Zoe, I'll wait for you out front. Take your time."

The night air was cool and slightly damp. Callie felt better the moment she stepped outside, free of the suffocating crowd, free to fill her chest with the first full breath she'd been able to draw since stepping into the gallery and spying Dave across the room.

"Took you long enough."

Marcus's voice. Callie jerked around to stare up at him. Before she could utter a word of explanation, he hooked his hand into her arm and guided her to the end of the building, out of the path of people entering and leaving. When he came to a stop near a concrete column, he turned her toward him, looked down into her eyes and said, "You know, waiting out here has given me lots of time to think, but I still haven't decided whether I want to throttle you, or kiss you."

Chapter 9

I'd much prefer to be kissed.

The thought formed slowly as, dazed, Callie stared up into Marcus's dark eyes. His hands were firm and warm on her shoulders, holding her mere inches away from him. The space between their bodies radiated heat, a heat that seemed to surround her like a magnetic embrace, urging her to sway toward him. Some force apparently pulled at him as well, making his head bend toward hers.

"Oh, there you are." Zoe's voice broke the spell. Callie turned from Marcus as the woman continued to approach, still talking. "I'm so sorry to keep you waiting. Pia needed all sorts of reassurances that you..."

Zoe's thought trailed off as she drew closer. She glanced from Callie to Marcus and back, then smiled. "Assurances that you can do the job. I promised you could. I hope I haven't overstepped my bounds by offering your services."

Callie took a deep steadying breath. "No, not at all. It's perfect. A way to earn some money, but nothing permanent, just in case I decide San Francisco isn't the place for me. It's going to be a challenge to get everything together in time, however.''

''Get what together in time for what?''

Marcus stepped from behind Callie to place himself to one side between the two women.

''The wine-tasting at Pia's, for the Cat Connection,'' Zoe responded. ''The foolish woman dropped the ball, as usual, and has left the catering, and who knows what else to the last moment. So, Callie is going to have to rescue the affair.''

Or turn it into a complete disaster.

Once again, Callie's thoughts moved too fast for her to control them. Her sudden fear must have been reflected on her face, for Zoe turned to her with a motherly scowl.

''Young lady, what did I tell you about *expecting* trouble? The only way to get past all this jinx nonsense is to put good, positive thoughts in your mind, tell yourself repeatedly that all will go well, and then act accordingly, no matter what fears might assail you.''

Callie managed a smile for Zoe. The woman was right, of course. No point borrowing trouble from the future. Especially when she had more than enough to deal with in the present.

Glancing at Marcus, she saw he was still frowning deeply, reminding her of the threat he'd issued earlier. Throttle, or kiss. What was it to be?

She didn't have to ask why he wanted to throttle her. She was painfully aware that she should have stayed out of his altercation with Gerald Harding.

But why would he want to kiss her?

That particular question haunted her, off and on, all through dinner at the revolving restaurant atop the Hyatt Hotel. Off, when her attention was captured by the glittering dark beauty of San Francisco at night. On again, when she caught Marcus staring at her as Zoe explained about the fundraiser Callie was to cater. Things came to a head as their empty dinner plates were swept away.

''While we wait for our dessert,'' Marcus said, turning to

her. "Now would be a good time for you to tell me what was making you so jumpy at the art gallery."

Oh, darn.

Callie knew he deserved an explanation. But before she mentioned seeing Dave tonight, and Marcus started talking about pressing charges, she decided she needed to start with the fact that she'd seen the man, and decided that Dave had been just as much a victim as she in the real-estate scam.

"You met with him alone?" Marcus demanded as she finished.

Callie pulled her eyes from the sight of Coit Tower, rising like a huge fluted column atop a steep hill, to meet his disapproving look. She gave him a weak shrug and said, "Yes."

"Callie. That could have been dangerous."

His last word echoed in Callie's mind for several moments as she stared across the table, then said it aloud.

"Dangerous? The man is guilty of attempted bigamy. He's not suspected of being a serial murderer, or anything."

"How do you know? You admitted that you never checked his background."

Callie stared at him for several more seconds. "Look, I'm supposed to be taking charge of my life. I have enough trouble dealing with my own fears, without you adding yours."

"Yes, but mine are based on reality, on the sorts of things I see every day."

"Oh, and *my* fears are simply figments of my imagination? You tell that to the Good Night Pillow Company. I'm sure they're *still* picking feathers out of the bricks."

"No negativity while we eat." Zoe spoke in a very low voice. Callie turned to find the woman frowning at both of them. "It isn't good at all for the digestion. Marcus, Callie and I discussed this matter yesterday. She was very careful to meet the man in a public place."

"That's right," Callie said. "And I'd arranged for Raj to bring the cab around to pick me up at a certain time. If anything had gone wrong, I wouldn't have been alone."

"Raj is all of five foot three," Marcus broke in. "If a problem had arisen, what could he have done?"

Callie turned to him, eyes narrowed. "He could have called a cop—a big, burly policeman—to come to my rescue. So instead of simply feeling like a jinx, I could have felt like a victim. Some improvement."

Marcus crossed his upper arms on the edge of the table and leaned forward. "If it keeps you alive."

"Marcus!"

Zoe's sharp voice prevented Callie from responding to his last retort.

"Callie is trying to overcome years of expecting the worst. She did her best to protect herself, but facing this man was something she had to do alone. I would think that you, of all people, could accept and understand that."

Marcus was still glaring at Callie. But after several moments, his severe expression eased, and he nodded.

Well, so much for the kiss, Callie thought as the waiter placed a plate of cheesecake in front of each of them, then refilled their coffee cups. A throttle was as good as guaranteed now.

The moment the waiter stepped away, Marcus caught her gaze again. "Since my question about your behavior at the gallery brought up the subject of Dave, can I deduce he was there tonight?"

Something about the arch, oh-so-certain tone of Marcus's voice stiffened Callie's spine. "Yes, Sherlock," she replied. "You have deduced correctly."

Marcus stared at her for several moments, eyes narrowing in concentration. One eyebrow rose as he asked, "Might that be David *Johnson?*"

Callie nodded.

The silence that followed was broken by Zoe's acerbic comment. "Well, I for one am not surprised. That man has almost everyone fooled, except for me, of course. From the moment I met him, I thought he was just a bit too smooth. Sunny's father doesn't trust him either, which is why Joseph Sutherland keeps the art gallery in his name."

Meeting Zoe's eyes, Callie was aware of the woman's unspoken message. Painful as it had been, Callie knew she was very lucky to have learned about Dave's lies before she became trapped, like his wife.

Little more was said as Marcus drove them back to the house. While he put his car in the garage, Callie followed Zoe up the stairs and into the house, then waited while the woman entered her office to get Pia Blanchard's telephone number. Once she had the slip of paper in her hand, she started up the stairs, hoping to reach the sanctuary of her room before Marcus saw her.

"Callie."

His voice stopped her at the landing, right in front of his door. Without turning to look at him, she rounded the corner and hurried up the last flight of stairs, aware of the pounding of his feet following her as she reached the door to her apartment. She had the key in her lock and thought she heard it click, when Marcus's hands closed over her shoulders, and he was turning her to face him.

The tiny rectangle in front of her door suddenly felt so very small, so very cramped, so very warm, the air highly charged. She wanted to turn away, to escape into her room and quickly lock the door behind her. But, nooo. She was under orders to face her fears.

So she stood her ground, met Marcus's dark gaze and said, "Okay. Go ahead."

His frown took on a puzzled tilt. "Go ahead and what?"

"Throttle me. That's what you want to do. And you have every right to do it. I shouldn't have said anything to that Harding man."

Marcus's frown didn't abate one bit, but the corners of his mouth *did* twitch ever so slightly before he spoke. "You're right. Aside from the fact that I didn't need you stepping in to take a bullet on my behalf over the debacle at the motel, my confrontation with Harding came under the heading of police business. Especially when a newspaper reporter with sharp eyes and even sharper ears was standing only ten feet away."

"Oh, no."

Marcus cocked one eyebrow. "Oh, yes. Captain Bradford

made it very clear that he didn't want any more press on this subject. However..." As he paused, his lips twisted into the same wide, lopsided smile that had grabbed her attention the moment she'd first seen him. The one that made her heart beat more quickly and her knees grow soft. "As far as I'm concerned," he continued, "the scenario couldn't have played out any better if it had been scripted. I have no doubt that tomorrow's paper will carry a colorful article recounting my exchange of words with Harding. It will undoubtedly tick Bradford off, but it just might convince the catnappers that my appearance at the art gallery wasn't part of some police conspiracy to trap them."

As Marcus spoke, Callie found she couldn't take her eyes off his mouth. It was so very near to hers now, a very present reminder of how firm and warm that one brief kiss they'd shared had been. It also reminded her of Marcus's threat to repeat that procedure, if he didn't throttle her.

His last words indicated that he'd decided against the throttle. That was good, in more ways than one. She decided that she very much wanted to reexperience the shock and heat that had surged through her the other night, just one flight from where they now stood.

At least she *thought* that was what she wanted.

After her meeting with Dave the day before, it was clear that she'd had her own part in the game of deception he'd played. Like a skilled con man, he'd assessed her needs and molded himself to fit them. And like the perfect con victim, she had wanted that version of happily-ever-after so badly that she'd ignored the intuitive voice warning that something wasn't quite right.

So now, with her mind free of the illusions that had drawn her to Dave, she was safe to trust her instincts again, safe to let her heart guide her. Or was she? Was it the beginning of love she felt for Marcus, or was the undeniable physical attraction just a distraction created by her mind to make her forget her past mistakes?

The last thing she wanted to do was jump from the frying pan into the fire, and the heat building between her body and

Marcus's was definitely reaching the spark point. *Talk,* a voice in her mind ordered. *Make him talk. Ask him to explain his last statement.*

"I'm confused," she managed to blurt out. "I thought the police had been ordered off the catnapping case. You make it sound as if you're still investigating it."

"I am," he replied. "Until that cat is recovered, I'm afraid I'm stuck with the assignment."

All the glorious heat Callie had felt surging from Marcus's body to hers suddenly chilled.

"Oh," she said. "Like you're stuck with me, your only witness."

Callie tried to step away from him, only to find herself pinned between Marcus and the doorknob sticking into her lower back. As she gazed up at Marcus, his smile seemed to falter and his eyes appeared to grow suddenly darker.

A second later, his smile twisted into a full, gleaming white grin and his eyes glinted. "Right," he said. "I *am* stuck with you. I guess I might as well enjoy it."

Before Callie could utter one word, let alone draw one breath, Marcus bent his head toward her, placed his lips over her parted ones, then slowly and thoroughly kissed her.

Her senses reeled. Her thoughts faltered. She had wanted to experience a feeling similar to the warmth of his earlier kiss, and, without even wishing on a star or a four-leaf clover, she had been granted a wish far beyond her wildest imaginings.

For this kiss was different from any she'd ever before experienced. Marcus held her close, moved his lips firmly over hers, once, twice, three times, each time kissing her more deeply than the last. It occurred to her that she needed to breathe, but she didn't want the kiss to end, so she slid her arms around his shoulders and held on, certain that at any moment she would lose consciousness.

It would almost be worth slipping into an oxygen-deprived coma, her befuddled mind mused, if it meant prolonging the feel of warm lips on hers, the glory of being gathered into strong arms and drawn into the protection of a powerful chest. *This* man's arms, this man's chest. This man's mouth on hers.

A mouth that was slowly urging hers open, working first on her upper then her lower lip, grazing them lightly before intensifying the kiss, entering her mouth with his tongue, pleasuring her with slow strokes until she was so warm and weak that her legs refused to bear the weight of her fevered body. Even the arms she'd wrapped around his neck felt heavy and feeble. The only thing that kept her upright was the pressure of his body crushing her against the door.

And then that support deserted her.

With a loud click, the door flew open. Before Callie realized the significance of this, she felt herself fall backwards, dragging Marcus down with her. As she tore her mouth away from Marcus's with a gasp, Callie braced herself against the inevitable crash onto the floor.

The fall turned out not to be all that dramatic, however. Somehow Marcus had managed to grab onto the doorjamb as they slid past, and his other arm remained wrapped around Callie's waist, so their descent was slow and controlled. At least until the last foot or so, when the drag of his weight, combined with Callie's, ripped his fingers from their grasp.

The two of them tumbled to the ground in a heap of arms and legs, accompanied by two soft "oofs."

Just before they hit the ground, Marcus had pulled his arm from around Callie's waist and braced it against the floor to keep from crushing her. Still, once his mind recovered from the switch from lust to the sudden terror of free fall, he found that his body was completely covering hers. Her face was mere inches from his, her soft green eyes wide, staring into his with a stunned, glazed-over expression.

"Are you all right?" he asked.

Callie blinked, moved her eyebrows together in a little frown and said, "I think so."

She lay perfectly still after she spoke. Her parted lips were a dark pink, her eyes continued to hold a dazed expression. Marcus felt a little on the dazed side himself. That kiss, which had been meant as something of a joke, a fulfilling of the jesting threat he'd made earlier in the evening, had turned into something totally unexpected.

No. That was a lie.

That kiss, and his response to it, had been building in him almost from the moment he met Miss Callie Chance. He'd been doing his best to ignore his attraction to this woman, to assure himself that she was just an element of a case he was working on, that she was no different from any other woman he'd ever met.

Another lie. She was *nothing* like any woman he'd ever met. In the last ten years he'd developed a knack for hooking up with women who were as emotionally unavailable as he was. He'd meet someone, they'd share dinner and drinks, go to movies, plays, baseball games, whatever, enjoy frequent nights of passion, then repeat this sort of thing over a period of a few months. One day, he would find he was bored, or learn that she was, and the thing would be over. No messy emotions to deal with, no hard feelings on either side.

With Callie, the messy emotions he preferred to avoid had been a part of the package from the very moment they'd met. He'd seen past the forced glitter of her smile to the embarrassment she'd been trying to hide that first night. At the hospital, he'd been aware of her physical pain, despite her show of bravado. He'd stood over her, watching her cry in the night, as if that was the only time it was safe for her to do so, and held her sobbing form in the middle of lunch-hour rush in downtown San Francisco.

Each time, he'd tried to pull back. Tried to keep himself from feeling, fought against the desire to pull her into his arms. But not to offer sympathy. It was clear she had no use for that, nor its buddy, pity. He'd wanted to offer her love.

Good grief.

Marcus pushed himself up, away from Callie and onto his bottom in one swift motion. He sat on the soft carpet, crossed arms around his knees and stared at her.

Love?

Where had *that* word come from? He thought he'd deleted it from his vocabulary years ago, about the time he deleted emotions from his soul. Messy, unreliable things that confused the thought process. He knew better than to let that happen, knew his job would be next to impossible to do if he allowed his mind—and his heart—to grow soft.

He remembered all too well how easy it was for a love-muddled mind to be fooled. And yet, dammit, he sure as hell felt *something* for Callie Chance. Something that went far beyond lust. Beyond the challenge of proving to her that there was no such thing as a jinx.

Callie had pulled herself into a cross-legged position across from him. She shook her head and gave him one of those bright smiles that indicated her armor was back in place. Marcus felt a moment of relief, until he noticed that the shake of her head had sent her hair tumbling down, tempting him to reach across the two feet that separated them and touch it, crush thick ropes of it into his fist, then gently tug her face toward his for another of those heart-stopping, blood-boiling kisses.

The moment he reached for her, Callie leapt to her feet. "Well," she said. "I must say, that was definitely better than a throttling."

Marcus gazed up at her a moment before he rose to stand in front of her. The magic pull was gone. Callie's brittle smile said far more than words that things had gone too far too fast.

And, of course, she was right.

Still, gazing at her curving lips, Marcus felt an almost irresistible desire to reach across, slip his hand behind her neck, pull her to him and capture that smile with his mouth.

But he couldn't. She obviously didn't want that, and it was for the best.

Letting his hand fall gently to her shoulder, he looked deeply into her eyes. "I enjoyed every minute of that," he said. "I'd repeat it again, except for one thing. You're vulnerable right now and I'm..." *Too chicken to risk having you walk away once you regain your strength.* "I'm not what you need."

Callie lifted her chin. Her smile had disappeared. Her eyes glinted as she asked, "How do you know what I need?"

"You want a relationship that will eventually lead to marriage. I'm not marriage material."

He could have said more. Could have explained that the young man who had once looked forward to a house-with-a-white-picket-fence future had died, along with his father and the family business. But it seemed best to say a soft, "Good night, Callie," then step past her and out the door.

He heard Callie's door click shut just as he was slipping the key into his lock. It had a quiet, final sound that should have relieved him, reassured him that he'd done the right thing in walking away. She obviously wasn't ready to start another relationship, and when he thought about it, he didn't need the complication. Instead his hand tightened over the knob as he gave a quick turn and shoved the door inward. Anger rose up from a tight, creaking knot in his stomach as he passed through the living room to his bedroom and began to strip for bed.

He didn't need an alarm to wake him the next morning, for he woke early, as tense with unacknowledged emotions and unsatiated desire as when he'd fallen asleep. After a glance out the window at the early morning fog, he dressed in sweats, then headed out for a long overdue run around Marina Green.

The chill, moist air surrounded him as he jogged past boats groaning at their moorings, past seagulls perched on the rock wall along the water, past other early morning exercisers. Normally, his runs were mindless forays into physical oblivion, working his body to remove the tensions that built up in the course of his job.

The last time he'd run had been the morning of the day he'd first met Callie. And he thought he'd been tense *then*. The frustrations eating at him that morning—the new partner who seemed too cocky, the stupid catnapping assignment taking precedence over murder cases—now seemed like nothing.

True, it still bugged him that Bradford had turned the more

important cases over to Malone, leaving Marcus to focus on one that seemed to go nowhere. Yet today all he could think of was Callie. The musky-flowery fragrance of her hair, the way she fit so perfectly into his embrace, the way her wide mouth shifted beneath his, sending desire spiralling upwards to the tight, hard realms of lust. The shy smiles and wide grins that tugged at his heart. The heart he'd so very long ago hardened so very successfully.

Marcus pounded the pavement, pushing his pace until that heart was nearly bursting from his chest. When he slowed, and his pulse began easing toward normal, he fully expected to have exercised Callie right out of that spot. And by the time he stepped back into Zoe's foyer, he was certain he'd freed himself of those useless, dangerous emotions.

He lived in that fantasy world as he showered and dressed, feeling more in control than he had for days. He had a plan, people to interview, taped telephone conversations to listen to. He had his work. That was all he needed. All he would ever need.

As he started down the stairs, Callie's voice floated up. "I'm waiting for the cab to arrive. Raj isn't on today, and the dispatcher said it might be a while before one could get here, what with people trying to get to work. I hope it isn't too long. Pia Blanchard said she has a day full of appointments."

As he descended the stairs, Callie came into view slowly, slim feet in low, tan heels, then long slender legs leading to a short tan skirt beneath a matching jacket tailored to her willowy form.

And it hit him again—the lust that had transformed last night's kiss into a dance of desire. The sudden need to cross the foyer, pull that slim body to his and explore each of those curves until he knew her body as well as he knew his own, to kiss her until they both fell to the ground again.

"Pia will just have to make time for you." Zoe's sharp retort broke the spell Marcus had fallen into. "This is *her* disaster that you are offering to correct. I'm going to call the

woman and give her a piece of my mind while you wait for
the cab.''

Callie opened her mouth with what looked like the beginnings of a protest, but Zoe had pivoted and disappeared into
her living room.

''Save your breath.'' Marcus forced himself to speak
calmly, past the desire that clogged his throat. ''When Zoe
is on a mission, there's no stopping her.''

As he finished, Callie turned to him. For one moment her
pale eyes reflected a mixture of joy and embarrassment. Both
glints faded, and she gave him a brief nod.

''I'm sure you're right. Well, I guess I'd better go outside
and wait for that cab.''

Marcus reached out to touch her arm as she started to turn.
''If I remember correctly, Pia Blanchard lives up on Washington Street.''

Callie nodded.

''Well, I have to go that way. Why don't I drop you off?''

Five minutes later, after calling to cancel the cab and con-
veying to Pia, through Zoe, that Callie was on her way, Marcus was driving up a steep hill, past the huge mansions that
made up the Pacific Heights district.

''Are you going up here on police business?''

Callie's question caught Marcus off guard. His car's
cramped interior had him trying to ignore her soft fragrance
and tempting proximity. Now he had to glance at her, and
concentrate on what she'd asked, and not his desire to stop
the car and pull her into his arms. He nodded in reply, then
forced himself to speak.

''Yeah, I am. After the news report the other night, we got
calls from two people claiming they'd also had cats stolen
earlier in the month. Both of them live in the same neighborhood as Gerald Harding, and each of them paid the requested ransom without informing the police. I interviewed
one of them yesterday. The other couldn't see me until this
morning.''

''Oh.''

The single-word reply caught his attention. When he

glanced over to see that she was gazing out the window, he wanted to believe she was too awed by the magnificence of the mansions sprouting on the hill in front of them to say much more. But there was a tense, straight-backed look about her that suggested a desire to create distance, rather than pre-occupation.

A few seconds later, Marcus made a right, then pulled to a stop in front of the address Callie had given him. Without one glance at him, she opened the door and got out, giving him a flash of her long, slender legs as she did so.

God. He was in trouble.

Marcus closed his eyes briefly, trying to quell his body's instant reaction to that sight, then just before Callie shut the passenger door, he went ahead and lost control again.

"Hey," he said. "You want me to come back around and pick you up when I'm through?"

Callie seemed to freeze. He couldn't see her face, but her body visibly stiffened. Slowly she bent forward, looked into the car and shook her head. "No. After I'm done talking to Miss Blanchard, I'll be doing some preliminary shopping for ingredients. Since I happen to know what I *need* in the area of food, I prefer to do that alone. But thank you for offering."

As soon as the passenger door clicked shut, Marcus roared away from the curb, quickly shifting into second, then third as he sped up the street. Dammit. He'd insulted her last night, telling her that he wasn't what she "needed."

But maybe, he thought as he slowed to a stop at the corner, it was for the best. He'd meant what he'd said. He *wasn't* right for her. She needed—deserved—someone with an open heart. Someone she could trust with hers. Someone who wasn't completely wrapped up in his work.

His sometimes tedious, frustrating work, Marcus thought a short while later as he interviewed Dr. Robert Ramos.

The man was small, with thick brown hair and thick black glasses. He was in a hurry, had surgery scheduled in less than an hour, and he really couldn't tell Marcus much about the people who'd stolen his cat. The animal made its home in the solarium, and he'd been afraid it had slipped out a partially opened window until he received the ransom demand.

Once he finished his story, the doctor dashed off, leaving Marcus to question the maid about the day Fluffums, a blue-eyed white Persian that looked to be more fur than cat, disappeared. After a lengthy conversation, the clearly distracted woman finally recalled that the "plant man" had come that day to care for the doctor's prized collection of orchids, which shared the solarium with Fluffums.

That hadn't been the man's normal day to come by, however. *Today* was his regular day.

Marcus waited around for Yancy Woods to arrive. The fellow promptly denied being at Dr. Ramos's house on the day in question. When the maid *insisted* that he had shown up that day, the orchid specialist offered to give Marcus the telephone numbers of the people he had serviced that day to verify his whereabouts. After taking down the numbers with the intention of doing just that, Marcus asked the man if his client list happened to include Gerald Harding or Mrs. Marietta Adams.

It did.

Mrs. Adams lived two blocks away, so Marcus left his car parked where it was and walked. He'd spoken to the woman the day before, but there had been no mention of a solarium. Until she heard from the catnapper, she'd been under the impression that the maid had let the animal escape out the back door.

This house wasn't nearly as big as the doctor's, but as Marcus approached he could see the corner of a glass enclosure attached to the back. The small Asian woman who answered the door spoke very little English, but she managed to convey the time that Mrs. Adams was expected to return.

Marcus had already been in Harding's house, and knew that he, too, had a sunroom filled with exotic plants. However, interrogating that man or any of his staff right now was out of the question, given the "unofficial" status of the case.

So, frustrated and with time to kill, he headed for nearby Fillmore Street, and a café that brewed a particularly strong

cup of coffee. As he turned the corner, a woman came out
of the building on his right, darting in his direction so quickly
that he almost ran into her. And, considering how his life had
gone since meeting her, he wasn't at all surprised to find that
the woman was Callie Chance.

As she stood staring up at him, the expression on her face
went from startled to resigned, then to incredibly sad, all in
one swift moment.

"Something wrong?" he asked.

She seemed hesitant to answer.

"Is it that thing you're catering?"

She shook her head. "No," she replied. "I've already
found a deli up the street that can provide me with quite a
bit of what I'll need, and they suggested other places that
might carry the other supplies and ingredients."

"Then what's wrong?"

Callie looked up at him for a long moment before she
released a large sigh and said, "I think I'm in love."

Chapter 10

The expression on Marcus's face was almost comical.

Callie saw a mixture of surprise, fear and something else, an almost blush hinting at pleasure, but she wasn't sure. And she didn't have time to puzzle it out. She needed to correct any misunderstanding her words might have created right away.

"Oh," she said. "Not with *you!*"

That might not be exactly true. She wasn't sure. She wasn't sure of anything after the kiss they'd shared the night before.

"Don't tell me you've decided that you're still in love with Dave?"

Callie blinked away her thoughts to stare in horror at Marcus. "Good grief! Not with Dave—with a cat."

"A cat?"

The incredulous expression on Marcus's face would have made Callie laugh if she didn't find the situation so unbelievable herself. She released a sharp, bewildered breath and nodded.

Marcus lifted one eyebrow. "Rather sudden, wouldn't you say? Mind telling me just how this came about?"

Callie shrugged. "Sure. I was walking up Fillmore Street, checking restaurant prices on their appetizers. I'm going to have to prepare quite a bit of food in a short period of time. Zoe said I could take over her kitchen, but having a place close to Pia's that will fix and deliver some of the hot dishes would be a big help. Anyway, I ended up in that place."

Marcus glanced at the door she'd indicated. "The Cat Connection?"

"Yes. That's the charity that will benefit from this party."

"Oh, I get it. You walked in and fell in love with a kitten."

Callie shook her head. "No. With a full-grown cat that someone abandoned. A *black* cat."

Callie could hardly believe the words, and they had come out of her mouth. So she could hardly blame Marcus for looking momentarily stunned. He stared down at her, his gaze assessing her, before he gave her a wide smile.

"Perfect. Just what Dr. Zoe would order. Adopt it."

"I can't."

Marcus lowered one eyebrow. "Why not?"

Callie stared up at him, a million reasons chasing each other through her mind. Far too many for her to go into here, on the street, feeling as she did about what had just happened to her inside that building, feeling as she did about what had happened between her and the man standing before her the night before.

The connection that had built between them was like nothing she'd ever experienced. From the moment they'd met, there had been something safe about him. Safe and dangerous at the same time. She'd trusted him with so many of her feelings, with her crazy beliefs, and he hadn't laughed.

Callie turned her head to gaze across the street. Marcus hadn't reacted to her warning that she was a jinx like any other man she'd ever known. Because Joshua Michaels had won a part on a soap opera the first day he met her, she became his "good luck charm," until his character was killed off and he couldn't get another part. Dave, on the other hand, had encouraged her belief that Cape Cod was a safe haven against misfortune as a way of keeping her safely away from his other life.

But Marcus had argued with her, denounced any belief in luck, challenged her to "tempt fate," going so far as to kiss her to show how little concern he had for her *curse*. She knew that he was challenging her now, but she didn't think she was ready for that particular step yet.

"Did you have breakfast this morning?"

Marcus's abrupt question cut through her confused emotions. She turned to him with a frown. "Breakfast?"

"You know," he said. "Eggs, toast, orange juice. Something with substance to fuel your brain?"

Callie shrugged. "I grabbed a bite of toast and jelly before I left for Pia's. I didn't really have time for more."

"Well, I didn't eat at all, and I'm finding that my mind isn't working as sharply as I'd like. I was on my way to the coffee shop across the street when I ran into you. Come with me. My treat."

Callie was most definitely tempted. Not only by the promise of food to fill her suddenly growling stomach, but by the tiny telltale twitching at the corner of Marcus's mouth, and the warmth in his dark eyes. Tempted, but wary. She wasn't about to end up unburdening herself to this man again.

"Okay, I'll join you. But I want to pay for mine."

The coffee shop was small, but since they'd arrived between the breakfast and lunch rushes, there were only two other people in the place. They took a table next to the window, and in no time, Callie was enjoying a bagel filled with scrambled eggs and melted cheese. Gradually she became aware that her rushing, panicky thoughts were slowing down, and her seesaw emotions were smoothing out. She took a sip of the strong coffee, just to keep from getting too comfortable.

"This was a good idea," she said. "I have a lot to do in the next few days, mostly connected to food. Ironically, I tend to forget to eat when I get really busy, even when I'm surrounded by the stuff."

"I suppose that explains your great figure."

Callie stared into her half-empty coffee cup. A compliment, she thought. Great. What was she supposed to do with *that?* Get all soft and woozy-minded like she had last night? Get angry for him daring to comment on her body? Ignore it?

The last option seemed the best.

"More coffee?"

Callie looked up to refuse the waitress's offer, but Marcus was nodding and the small, dark-haired girl filled Callie's cup, then his.

"Now..." Marcus placed his elbows on the table and leaned toward her. "I want to hear about this cat."

Callie hesitated. It wasn't really something she wanted to talk about. Her feelings were too raw, too new. She didn't understand them herself. Explaining them to someone else would be impossible.

"I'd rather not talk about it. Besides, aren't you on a case? Don't you have somewhere you should be?"

Marcus gave her a slow smile. "Yes, I'm on a case. As it happens, I need to reinterview the woman I spoke with yesterday, and she won't be back till twelve-thirty. So, I have some time to kill. You know," he said slowly. "Sometimes I find it helps to talk something through with someone else."

"You want to discuss the case with me?"

"No, I want to hear about this cat you've developed a mad crush on. But now that I think about it, if you tell me about this situation and distract me from said case, it just might help me go back to it with a fresh perspective. How about it?"

His expression couldn't exactly be called *pleading,* but it was sufficiently appealing to nudge Callie into complying. She started out with a big sigh. "Well, it probably wouldn't have happened, if it weren't for Zoe telling me to face all the stuff from the past that has contributed to my present fears."

"Your fears. I thought this was about good and bad luck. Are you saying that you're afraid of cats?"

"Just cats in cages," Callie qualified. "And I'm not afraid

of *them,* I'm afraid of what my presence might cause them to do.''

She paused, and shook her head. This was beginning to sound nuts. She was going to have to be more specific.

''You see, I wasn't allowed to be around the animals in the circus. My mother was convinced that I'd somehow rile them up and cause who knows what sort of disaster.''

''Because of Ebony,'' Marcus said with a nod. ''The panther who escaped.''

''Right.'' Callie felt a moment of surprise that he had remembered that detail, then reminded herself that he was, after all, a detective. ''Anyway, I avoided the area where the animals were housed. Sometimes, like when I was helping set up in a new city, that wasn't possible. So, if I had to walk by their cages, I would tense up and hold my breath, and imagine that I could keep everything under control that way.''

Marcus nodded as he finished swallowing a sip of coffee. ''Well, I can understand the rule about staying away from those cats. They could be dangerous even without your supposed curse. But what about a pet?''

Callie shook her head as she lifted her own cup. ''Our motor home was too small. And I could hardly take an animal with me when I stayed with the Manzettis.''

''The Manzettis?''

''The Flying Manzetti Family—a mom, a dad and six kids. I went to stay with them whenever my mother was 'involved' with the latest man she was convinced would become her husband and my father.''

Callie saw the question in his eyes and went on, ''I think I mentioned that our motor home was very small? Believe me, as crowded as it might have been in the Manzettis' trailer, it was far more comfortable than living with my mother when she was with someone. I was always trying to stay out from underfoot, or smooshing a pillow over my head at night to keep from hearing something I just didn't want to hear. Not to mention the fact that my mother watched my every move to make sure that I didn't do anything to jinx this new relationship of hers.''

Marcus was frowning again. "You know, your mother sounds totally self-centered."

Callie took a deep breath, stared silently across the table for several moments, then sighed. "I prefer to think of her as scared and confused. And very needy."

"Generous of you to see her that way."

"I have Mama Manzetti to thank for that. Considering that the woman made a career of swinging on a trapeze forty feet in the air, she was quite grounded. She helped me work through some very angry, wounded feelings regarding my mother, and her words of advice came in quite handy when I turned eighteen and my mother asked me to leave."

"To leave?"

"Yeah." Callie's lips twisted into a wry half smile. "She said my vibrations were wreaking havoc on her love life, and I had to go off on my own."

Callie noted the sudden tightening of Marcus's jaw, and hurried to explain. "Look, she did me a favor. I finally got off the road, found a great little apartment in New York and began to feel centered." She paused. "Well, as centered as I could feel, considering how often my job situation changed."

Marcus stared at her a moment, still frowning. "And your mother. Did she find true love after your 'vibrations' were cleared from her dwelling?"

Callie shrugged. "I'm not sure. We corresponded for a while after she embarked on her search for her soul mate. I lost count after number seven. Then the letters stopped coming. The last I heard, my mother was traveling with a small circus in Europe. Maybe she's having better luck there." Callie paused. Aware that a hint of bitterness had crept into her tone, she forced a bright smile to her lips. "After all, now there's an entire ocean between her and my bad vibes."

Callie's smile and the pain it attempted to hide weren't lost on Marcus. He wanted to get up, pull her to her feet, wrap his arms around her, and absorb that pain. But he was afraid she would either see such an action as a romantic overture, or an expression of sympathy, then interpret that as pity.

He knew she wouldn't accept pity. Besides, that was the last thing she needed. She did, however, need love. That unconditional sort that everyone was talking about these days. The sort that animals were supposed to offer.

"You know," he said slowly. "You still haven't told me about the cat."

Callie's face reflected momentary puzzlement, until comprehension smoothed her forehead. A small shrug told him she'd grown weary of dodging the subject.

"Well, there really isn't much to say. When I went in and explained that I wanted to check out the place because I'm catering the upcoming fund-raiser, the person behind the counter sent me upstairs. I found a huge room filled with rows of cages. Not little, kitty-size cages, but tall chain-link enclosures with wire tops, filled with scratching posts, perches and baskets. No cats, though. The animals were roaming the wooden floor between the door and a large desk set against the opposite wall."

She paused. "Some of the cats were wandering about, while others were playing with balls and various other toys. I stood watching them for several moments, until a young woman looked up from some paperwork and motioned me to the desk. It was so strange. I started forward slowly, half certain that the cats would suddenly rush the door in a mad attempt at mass escape. But they barely even looked at me. Except the black one."

"What did he do?"

"She," Callie corrected. "She walked right up to me, and when I stopped, she brushed herself slowly along my ankle, then turned, sat down, raised bright green eyes to look at me and let out the softest, saddest sound I ever heard. My heart melted instantly. I wanted to pick her up and take her right home."

Marcus gazed across the table. He suddenly recalled seeing Callie in that hospital bed, and found himself identifying with her temptation.

"So why didn't you?"

Callie shook her head. "The young girl, Molly, showed

me that each cage has a sign with pictures of the cats housed in it, along with the animals' names and a couple of lines about their disposition and state of health, if this information is available. I was told that most of the cats are strays, but some have been brought in by people who can't keep them any longer. Anyway, the black cat didn't have a name, and the note said she wasn't available for adoption. Molly didn't know if someone had already asked to adopt it, or if the cat has a medical problem. She said she'd be able to tell me more after eleven o'clock when her boss gets in.''

Marcus glanced at his watch. ''It's almost that now. Why don't we go on over?''

Marcus watched an expression that looked suspiciously like panic fill Callie's eyes. ''Marcus, I don't know a thing about taking care of a cat. And it *is* a black one.''

''Perfect. As I said before, I'm sure that's exactly what Zoe would recommend.''

''And that's another problem. Zoe. Molly gave me this adoption form to fill out and one of the questions is about getting a landlord's permission to have a pet. I know Zoe has cats, but that doesn't mean she would want one up in the studio.''

Marcus reached into his jacket and flipped his cell phone open as he handed it to her. ''Call and ask.''

Ten minutes later, after Zoe had all but ordered Callie to bring the cat home, Marcus escorted her across the street. At the top of the stairs, he opened the door to the adoption area to find a different picture than the one Callie had painted. The tall, roomy cages were there, but now they were all occupied and both the wide alleyway running between the wire enclosures and the desk at the opposite end were empty.

Marcus followed Callie to the nearest enclosure, noting that she held her body taller, straighter, a little more rigid than usual, and that her obvious tension took a little of the swing out of her hips.

Accompanying her from cage to cage, he watched as she gazed through the chain-link wire at orange marmalade cats, multi-hued calicoes and gray tabbies. At first her overtures to the animals could be considered tentative at best, but by the time they reached the end of the first row of cages, she was coaxing them to come to her in a deep, throaty voice.

The cats responded favorably to the sound. And they weren't the only ones. Frowning at his body's response to the allure of her voice, Marcus found himself regretting that he'd suggested this visit. Or at least that he offered to accompany her. After all, it was only fourteen hours earlier that he'd had a long, serious talk with himself regarding Miss Callie Jane Chance and the inexplicable desire he felt each time he was in her presence.

Well, perhaps not so inexplicable. She might not be a beauty according to current standards, but she exuded feminine appeal. At least to him. And this, despite the fact that the last thing he needed in his life right now was someone like Callie, someone who made his mind go suddenly soft, made him entertain fantasies he had denied himself for years. And not just the in-bed-with-her-long-legs-wrapped-around-him sort. The holding hands, getting-to-know-her-fondest-dreams type.

"This isn't a good idea."

Callie's words made Marcus draw in a sharp breath. He noticed that during the time that his mind had been running away with him, they had crossed the room, and were now standing side by side in front of a cage holding the black cat. The animal prowled the enclosure nervously as he asked, "What isn't a good idea?"

"My adopting a cat."

Callie turned to him as she spoke, her eyes wide. Again recognizing panic, he took her hand and smiled.

"Hey, I've known Zoe long enough to realize that when she says someone needs to do something for their best and highest good, she's right."

"Has she ever told you to do something for your best and highest good?"

Something? Sure, the same thing over and over. *Marcus, you must release the past and learn to trust your heart again.*

Well, he had dealt with the past. He'd seen that both Miranda and Ron went to prison for what they'd done to his father, and to him.

"Yes," he replied slowly. "Zoe has sent her share of suggestions my way."

"And did you listen to them?"

Marcus clenched his jaw. How had he missed seeing *that* trap? Too busy, he supposed, resisting the sudden desire to kiss the woman next to him, in spite of their surroundings, in spite of the knowledge that it wasn't the wise thing to do.

As he'd told Callie the night before, he wasn't right for her. He was a police officer, for God's sake. With her belief system, any time his job put him in danger, she would blame her curse. If they were to enter into a relationship, he'd spend half his time reassuring her that she hadn't jinxed him.

And the rest of the time in a state of physical bliss, if the kiss they shared last night was any indication where things might lead.

"Marcus?"

At Callie's questioning tone, he turned to her with a smile. "Listen to Zoe? Well, I'm afraid I usually choose to ignore her orders, even when I know I'd probably be better off to follow them. No need for you to make the same mistake, though. Besides, in this case, you have someone else to think about. I think someone likes you."

He indicated the cat, whose right front leg was stretched halfway out of the cage, gently swatting at Callie's beige flats. When one sharp nail caught the leather at the tip of the toe, the cat stopped moving, determined it seemed to maintain this fragile hold on her.

"Oh, you did come back."

Marcus and Callie turned at the sound of the voice. A young woman, perhaps all of twenty, stood to their right, fingering her long brown braid.

"Yes, Molly, I did." Callie took a deep breath, and blew it out slowly before she went on. "Did you find out whether the cat is available?"

"Well, sort of." Molly glanced at the cat in the cage, then back at Callie as she said, "Mr. Laramie hasn't come in yet, but I spoke to one of the other caretakers here. Janice said that there was a hold tag in this cat's file two days ago, indicating that someone wanted to adopt her. They might have had to check with a landlord or something. I can't find the file now, but we only keep a hold for twenty-four hours, so that means she's available again.''

Marcus watched Callie closely, saw her bend down and gently touch the outstretched paw. The cat's curved nail slid away from the tip of her shoe, then the paw twisted to curl around Callie's finger.

At that exact moment, Molly chose to say, ''Little Miss Blackie here won't stay available for long, you know.''

Callie stood quickly. ''You don't mean that you'd... you'd—''

The young girl vehemently shook her head. ''No. We don't put animals down. We keep each of our cats until someone adopts them, unless they're sick. We give most of those a home here.''

''Most?''

Molly nodded. ''We get some cats who have feline leukemia. The disease is too infectious for us to keep them here, but we have a list of people who'll take these animals in and keep them comfortable for whatever time they have left. And then there are the cats with FIV.''

''FIV?''

''Uh huh. Feline immunosuppressant virus. It's like HIV in humans. With proper medication, these animals can live a very long life, but their disease is highly infectious, which makes it difficult to find foster homes for them. Greg, my boss, is trying to raise the funding to set up a permanent facility to house them. It's hard, though. It would take a bundle, and he has enough on his hands trying to find homes for healthy animals.'' She paused. ''Like Miss Blackie here.''

Marcus had to admire Molly's not-so-soft sell. He watched Callie glance down at the black, outstretched paw then look up at Molly again.

''How soon after I fill out the adoption form would I get her?''

Molly grinned. "If you have your landlady's permission and can pay your fees, she can go home with you today."

As Callie and Molly stepped over to the desk, Marcus glanced down at the cat. The animal was still lying on its side, and as he watched, she twisted her head so that her brilliant eyes met his. He could almost swear that the pleading expression he'd seen as the cat gazed up at Callie had been replaced by a somewhat smug, self-satisfied look.

Behind him, a door swished open, and Marcus's cop instincts pivoted him around to study the man stepping into the room.

He was of medium height, had a trim athletic body, and was dressed in a yellow T-shirt and blue jeans. His hair was dark blond and pulled back into a six-inch ponytail.

"Hey, paperwork," he said as he approached the desk. "I hope that means you found a home for another of our orphans, Molly."

"Sure did," came the reply. "Miss Chance here is taking home that little black cat."

A moment of silence followed. Marcus watched the man stop at the edge of the desk and look at Callie for a long moment.

"Hi, there," he said. "I'm Greg Laramie, the director of this branch. I'm sorry to tell you, but that particular cat isn't available."

Marcus started walking toward the desk even as Molly protested. "Greg, Callie here really wants this cat. The cat wants her, too."

"I'm sorry about that." The man's voice reflected sincere regret. "But you know, all these other kids need homes, too. That little calico over there has a real sweet personality, and she's been lonely since someone adopted her sister."

As Marcus approached, he could see the disappointment on Callie's face. His jaw clenched. As she turned toward the cage Greg was indicating, he took her hand as he spoke to the man.

"Before she does that, would you mind checking the files?"

Laramie turned to him with a frown. Marcus gave his widest smile as he reached into his pocket and flipped out his badge.

"I don't mean to question your honesty or anything. I just know that sometimes paperwork can get mixed up. You know, bureaucratic snafus and all that. I'd hate for Callie not to get the cat she wants, especially if it turns out that this one is available after all."

The man stared at the badge for a moment before nodding. He stepped around the counter to a file cabinet and opened a drawer, flipped through the folders several times, before pulling one out and opening it. Marcus could feel Callie tensing next to him as Laramie studied it for several moment before looking up.

"Well, it seems that today is your lucky day, Miss Chance. The prospective adoptees apparently decided to get a kitten instead of an older cat. I guess the file was misplaced when it was put back in. We have so many people working various hours that this sort of thing happens from time to time."

Callie was quiet for several moments, aware of Marcus's fingers gently squeezing her right hand, conscious of Laramie's dark brown eyes holding hers. She released the breath she'd been holding and slowly uncrossed the index and middle finger of her free hand.

"Thank you," she said. Then, uncomfortable with the man's gaze, she turned to Molly. "How much did you say that would be?"

It wasn't until she and Marcus were halfway to Marcus's car that Callie realized she wasn't at all prepared for the animal nestled in the plastic-and-wire carrier Laramie had placed the cat in.

"What am I *thinking?*" she said as she turned to Marcus.

He gave her one of his half smiles. "Well, maybe that you need cat food, and a bed and a litter box?"

Slowly Callie smiled. "Did you learn mind reading from Zoe?"

"No mind reading is involved." He grinned widely. "I'm a good guesser. Comes with the job."

Callie glanced down as she shifted the carrier in her arms, careful not to jostle the animal inside. A good guesser, huh? Just how much of her feelings had this man discerned? Especially last night, when his kisses had left her too weak and mindless to hide the wave of desire and emotion that had swept through her.

Recalling those moments, a rather lustful chill shot through her. She fought the telltale shiver, and stared at the pavement rising before her as she labored up the hill. A tiny "mew" from inside the carrying case caught her attention as they reached the car. After Marcus had opened the door and she'd slid into the passenger seat, she looked up at him.

"Thank you."

Marcus shrugged. "No problem. According to Mrs. Adams's housekeeper, the woman won't be available to answer my questions for another half hour. There's a pet shop on Chestnut. Probably no parking space nearby, but I'll circle the block while you run in and get what you need, then I'll drop you at Zoe's and head back here."

Callie shook her head and smiled. "I wasn't thanking you for the ride. I was referring to the way you came to my rescue back there, flashing your badge and everything."

Marcus's dark eyes met hers. For a moment she thought he was going to smile again. Instead, his eyebrows lowered in a frown as he shrugged. "Laramie might love animals, but he struck me as a petty little bureaucrat who likes to demonstrate his pathetic measure of power. I don't like bureaucrats very much." He gave her the tiniest of smiles. "Just ask my captain."

Little else was said on the way home. Marcus parked in Zoe's driveway. His arms were laden with Callie's new cat paraphernalia while she cradled the carrier containing the animal as they stepped into the foyer. After calling out for Zoe and getting no response, they carted their burdens up to Callie's apartment.

After Marcus placed the scratching post and bag filled with cat toys in the corner, Callie watched him depart with more than just a little trepidation. After filling the plastic box with guaranteed-to-be-odorless kitty litter, she found an out-of-the-way spot for it, then placed the bright pink cat bed at the foot of hers. Finally she filled one blue plastic bowl with the dry food Laramie had recommended and the other with fresh water.

The moment of fate was at hand.

A very loud *meow* escaped the carrier box. Callie glanced at her new copy of *Caring for Your Cat*, and decided it would hardly be fair to her new pet to keep the cat locked up while she read all 142 pages, just so she could feel a little more confident before giving the animal its freedom.

So, Callie walked over, opened the wire door and stepped back.

The cat jumped out like Jack popping from the lid of his musical box, landing a good four feet away. When the bright green eyes met Callie's, she smiled and leaned toward the animal.

This was apparently not the right move, because the black back arched sharply, and the green eyes narrowed. Taking another deep breath, Callie slowly straightened, then remained motionless as the cat's bright gaze darted around the room. A few moments later, the curved back relaxed. The cat turned and began a slow, ambling inspection of every square inch of the room, except for the three square feet surrounding Callie.

The creature also ignored the bright pink padded basket she was supposed to sleep in. Instead, she jumped onto Callie's bed, circled a spot right in the center, then curled into a black ball and closed her bright green eyes, without so much as *once* looking at Callie again.

Slowly Callie shook her head, and for some bizarre reason she found that she was smiling widely. She had a cat. A pet of her very own. Not exactly the most grateful animals but then, she didn't want gratitude any more than she wanted pity. She wanted love and companionship. Long ago, she'd learned that these qualities were sometimes very slow to grow, so if the cat needed time to get accustomed to her, time was what the little ball of fur would get.

Along with a little bit of space, Callie decided, and went downstairs to fix herself some lunch.

On the way, Callie congratulated herself. She had been in the house with that most unlucky of items—a black cat—for an entire half hour and there wasn't one sign of disaster.

She'd just reached the third-floor landing when she heard a loud pounding on the front door. Picking up her pace, she hurried down, pulled it open and blinked when she found Zoe standing on the other side.

"Oh, I am so glad you are home," the woman sighed.

Callie frowned as Zoe stepped into the foyer. "Did you forget your keys?"

"No," Zoe replied. "They were stolen, along with my purse."

Chapter 11

"Callie, you are *not* to think, for even one moment, that what happened to me had anything to do with your new cat."

Callie blinked at Zoe. The woman was mind reading again. Maybe Zoe and Marcus could open their own carny tent—Scanlon and Zeffarelli, two mind readers for the price of one. Special discounts for schizophrenics.

"That *is* what you were thinking, was it not?"

As Zoe reached back for her grocery-laden cart, Callie helped the woman drag it over the threshold and into the foyer, then shrugged. "Of course I was."

"Well, you must disabuse yourself of that idea. People have purses stolen every day of the week around here. Well…" Zoe frowned as the two of them pulled the cart toward the kitchen. "Perhaps not so often in this neighborhood. But why not? Look at the elaborate homes that surround us. I suppose if I were the sort to steal things, I would choose an area where my prospective victims might be carrying a great deal of money. An area without much foot traffic to witness my nefarious activities."

By the time Zoe finished speaking, she was standing by

the phone on the wall. Lifting the receiver, she punched in three numbers. A moment later, she was explaining that she'd just been robbed, gave her name and address and asked that someone be sent over immediately to search the area in case the thief was hanging around, looking for another old woman to victimize.

Callie found herself smiling in spite of the situation. Zoe didn't sound at all like a victim, or an old woman. She sounded more like a commandant ordering troops on review.

"Good." Zoe turned to Callie as she placed the receiver on the hook. "An officer will be arriving soon. In the meantime, I suppose I should put all this away."

Zoe's voice grew the slightest bit weaker as she finished speaking, just noticeably enough for Callie to glance over sharply and see that the woman's complexion had paled considerably.

Callie didn't need a medical degree to recognize the beginnings of shock. Now that Zoe was in her own house and knew the police were on the way, the trauma of having been accosted in broad daylight, in an area she considered safe, was undoubtedly having its effect. Crossing the room, Callie took the woman's hand. It was dry to the touch, her fingers cold, and when Zoe looked up at Callie, her pupils were slightly dilated. Callie gave her a warm smile.

"Why don't you let me take care of the groceries, Zoe, while you sit for a moment and gather your thoughts. The police will have a million questions to ask you."

Zoe's dark eyebrows flicked together for a moment, before the woman nodded and allowed Callie to lead her over to the table. After she had Zoe safely in the chair, Callie asked, "How about a cup of tea?"

The frown Zoe shot her was much more definite this time, her eyes sharper as she asked, "What do you take me for? Some British her-ladyship with a case of the vapors? I *detest* tea." She paused, then smiled widely. "However, I would appreciate it if you would brew me a cup of coffee. Very strong."

Callie began putting the groceries away while the coffeemaker sputtered and Zoe scribbled notes on a pad of paper. The doorbell rang just as Callie was handing the woman a cup of steaming black brew. Hurrying down the hall, she opened the door to a uniformed police officer, whom she led back to the kitchen. After seating him at the table and getting a cup of coffee for him, Callie finished putting the food away and listened as Zoe described her ordeal.

"It happened less than a block away. A man stepped out of an entryway, jerked on the handle of my shoulder bag and took off running."

"I see." The officer was making notations in a small booklet, reminding Callie very much of Marcus the night they'd met. "Do you remember exactly where this happened?"

"Of course. It was in front of the white Spanish hacienda, two houses from the corner. You will notice that the entryway has two side panels that extend toward the doorway, each with a little arched window set with decorative wrought iron work. It forms the perfect little alcove to wait and watch for some unsuspecting victim."

Callie noticed the officer's lips twitch, and found herself wondering if that engaging little movement was standard issue to the cops of the city, along with badges and revolvers.

"You're very observant, Mrs. Zeffarelli. What can you tell me about the man who took your purse?"

"Ridiculously little."

Again Callie caught a hint of a smile from the officer before he said, "I understand. It all happened in less than a minute. Can you remember hair color, or height?"

"Height? Yes. He was not much taller than me. Five-eleven, perhaps. Hair? I don't know. A baseball cap covered his head. It was black. And he was wearing a jacket—brown, I think." She paused, frowning, then slowly shook her head. "That's all I can remember, for now."

The officer placed his notebook back in his breast pocket. "I hate to say this, but this sort of thief is rarely caught on a description anyway. The guy probably whipped off the cap the moment he turned the corner, then continued down the street with your purse hidden inside his jacket. We might find it stashed in some yard, emptied of all valuables, but I doubt we'll find him, unless someone else witnessed this. Did you scream, or do anything that might call attention to the thief?''

''Scream?'' Zoe pulled herself up very straight in her chair as she spoke. ''Do I look like someone who would scream, like some foolish girl frightened by a mouse? No. I did, however, raise my voice as he was running away, insisting that he come back, immediately. A waste of time and energy, of course.''

At this display of independence and toughness, Callie found herself fighting a grin. Afraid Zoe would see this and misinterpret it as amusement at her expense, Callie turned, opened the refrigerator and began straightening the shelves.

''Not necessarily,'' the officer responded. ''I'm guessing there aren't too many voices raised in this neighborhood. There's a possibility that this brought one of your neighbors to their window, where they may have caught a detail you missed in the heat of the moment. I'll check around, and see what I can find.''

Callie saw the officer to the front door. When she returned, Zoe was ladling some of the previous night's noodles and sauce into a bowl. A second container rested on the counter-top.

''I'm going to heat this up in the microwave,'' she said. ''I had a nice salad at my friend Ruby's house before I did my shopping, but I find I'm suddenly in the need for something with more substance. Would you like some as well?''

At Callie's nod, Zoe filled the second bowl as well, then placed them both in the microwave. In a few moments, the two women were seated at the table, sharing the impromptu meal.

''Well, tell me, how is this little cat of yours?''

Ohmygod, the cat. Callie gasped, almost choking on her spaghetti. After a coughing fit, she managed, ''I can't believe it. I forgot all about her.''

When she started to stand, Zoe grabbed her hand. ''No, no. There is no need to worry. The animal needs time to adjust to its new surroundings. You, she will come to know in time, once she has accepted her new home. You must not rush things.''

Callie nodded. ''Actually, that's why I came down here in the first place. I used to watch Janik of the Jungle, the animal tamer, work with new cats—from a safe distance, of course. I saw how he gave them space, allowed them to become accustomed to their cages, then to the large enclosure in the center ring, before he started actually training them. I figured if this worked with lions, tigers and panthers, it would certainly work with smaller cats. But I would love for you to see her.''

''Perhaps later. I have a client coming soon. But tell me about her. When Marcus called, he said it was love at first sight.''

A blush bloomed hot on Callie's cheeks. Maybe it was hearing the words ''love'' and ''Marcus'' in the same sentence. Maybe it was just because she was suddenly feeling so very silly about her instant reaction to the cat.

''I guess that's a fair description of what happened to me. But now that she's mine, I'm a bit nervous. I...I've never been a pet owner before. I'm not sure I can handle that role, that I'll be worthy of having her.''

''Dear girl, love is not about being worthy. It is an emotion that is expressed in positive, caring actions. It is giving pleasure to another, because making that person feel good also makes you feel good. At least, when it is a healthy sort of love. So, you must remember that when you are with your little cat.''

The woman paused, then smiled widely before going on, ''Or with anyone you care deeply about. Love and fear do not belong together. In a relationship between two responsible adults, love should be offered without tainting it with the fear that the emotion will not be returned. *Que sera, sera,* as the saying goes. Love has its own sort of logic, and we must let it have its wings or it will die.''

Callie gazed into the woman's kind eyes. Zoe wasn't talking about loving the cat, she knew. She was talking about

Marcus. Mind reading again, was she? Or would this be heart reading?

Callie always suspected that if anyone really tried to see past the bright smile she offered, they would easily see the pain she tried to hide, but the number of people who had bothered to do so amounted to a mere handful—Mama Manzetti, Marie and Stan Wilson, and now Zoe.

And Marcus, of course.

That very first evening she'd been aware on some level that he could see past her defenses, and had known she was lying about something. Now that she knew about the lies his fiancée had used to betray him, she marveled at the fact that he hadn't hated her on sight for not instantly telling him the complete and total truth. Instead, he'd given her time—time to get to know him, time to trust him.

Time to fall in love with him.

And oddly, she realized, that had hardly taken any time at all. Despite her conflicted feelings over Dave, despite her fears of bringing some sort of disaster into this house, her heart had instantly been drawn to Marcus.

And what had she done? She'd pushed him away. Oh, she'd told herself that it was for his own good, that it was necessary to protect him from her curse. But she knew better, knew even before Zoe had said it, that love and fear didn't belong in the same place. One or the other would have to win.

She wanted it to be love that triumphed, and yet fear still had such a grip on her.

Fighting off a shiver, Callie blinked away the thought just as the doorbell sounded. Zoe's eyes held hers for one moment further before the woman patted Callie's shoulder.

"Come. I will admit my client, and you will go up and see if the cat is ready to make friends. If she seems comfortable, bring her downstairs in a little over an hour, so that I can meet her. Does she have a name yet?"

Callie shook her head as she stood. "They were calling her Miss Blackie at the shelter, but that doesn't seem right."

"Of course not. You do not know each other yet. Give it time. She will let you know what she is to be called."

Callie considered Zoe's words as she followed the woman to the foyer. While Zoe admitted her client, Callie started up the stairs, frowning slightly. So, the cat would let her know what she was to be called, would she?

Not sure whether to be unsettled or reassured by this idea, Callie stopped in front of her door. She had to forget all those ideas now anyway, and focus on calming herself before she entered the room. After a couple of deep, cleansing breaths, Callie opened the door to her apartment slowly, ready to block the cat's exit should it try to escape.

Her preparations turned out to be totally unnecessary. Slipping into the room, and closing the door quickly behind her, Callie glanced around. All she saw was blue and white, not one hint of black. Callie moved forward, her heart pounding wildly as she remembered that she normally left the windows over her bed cracked open slightly. But, she reminded herself, they had well-fitting screens. Surely the cat couldn't have escaped that way.

Still, she had to check. Stomach tightening into a sick knot, she walked toward the bed alcove, her eyes on the three-inch gap between window and sill. She could see the gray shadow of a screen, apparently intact, but she realized she'd never checked to see if it was securely latched. After all, when she left that morning, she hadn't known she'd be bringing a cat home with her.

Callie had one knee on the mattress and was peering at the window as she leaned toward it, when a pitch-black shadow rose from the nest of pillows, frightening Callie almost out of her wits.

Before she was even aware of moving, Callie found herself two feet back from the edge of the bed, heart thumping against her ribs, staring at the ebony form with the blinking emerald eyes. A second later the cat yawned widely before getting onto all fours and arching her back into the air. Then, with a casual air, the animal walked its front legs forward, until her long sinuous body was stretched nearly flat.

Callie watched all this without moving a muscle. So far, the earlier agitation demonstrated by "Miss Blackie" wasn't in evidence. Still, reluctant to frighten the cat in any way, she simply stood where she was.

After finishing its stretch, the cat once more sat on her haunches and gazed at Callie. Fighting the temptation to approach the bed, Callie decided to let the animal make the first move. Turning, she nonchalantly walked over to the blue chair in front of the balcony windows, sat and stared out over the rooftops toward the bay.

A few moments later, Callie heard a soft thud. Not moving a muscle except her eyes, she slid her gaze toward the bed. The cat was on the floor in front of it, slowly walking toward the chair, pausing every few steps. Callie smiled, took a deep breath and concentrated on relaxing.

The first touch was so gentle that Callie would have thought she'd imagined the soft brush against her calf if she hadn't been able to see the cat at her feet. Still, she didn't move until the cat placed both paws on her knee, and then she only lowered her head so she could look into the slanted green eyes.

The cat held her gaze for several moments, before issuing a soft *mew*.

Callie smiled and said, "Well, what's it going to be? Friends?"

The almond eyes widened slightly, and then the cat leapt lightly into Callie's lap. Still she didn't move, not until the cat had stomped around for several moments, plopped onto her stomach and lowered her head to rest on her paws. It was at that point that Callie lifted her left hand and placed it gently on the cat's head. The animal looked up at her as Callie began scratching behind the soft ears, then slowly closed her eyes and began to purr.

Without warning, tears sprang to Callie's eyes.

It was almost four-thirty when Marcus roared up to the house, tired and in a perfectly foul mood. On top of learning that the plant man, Yancy Woods, had been where he said he was on the day Harding's cat disappeared, eliminating that promising suspect, he'd had yet another run-in with Bradford. The worst yet. He was damned happy to see the driveway empty, because he didn't feel the least bit like searching for the elusive parking space. Pulling into the driveway, he got out to open the garage door, then pulled his car into the dark enclosure. As he came back into the light, he noticed a figure mounting the stairs to the front door—a decidedly male figure, wearing the familiar garb of a police officer.

Now what?

Frustration instantly became concern. Pulling the garage door shut, Marcus hurried up the steps. As he neared the top, he saw Zoe standing in the open doorway, talking to the officer, so he stopped climbing to listen.

"Mrs. Zeffarelli, I had to answer another call before I could get back to you. I tried phoning, but I think you gave me the wrong number."

When the man rattled off the digits, Zoe frowned. "That's correct."

"Well, then something must be wrong with your line. I dialed several times, and kept receiving a recorded message saying that this particular number is no longer in service."

"How very odd," Zoe said.

"No more odd than coming home and finding a police officer on my doorstep," Marcus said as he mounted the last few steps.

The officer pivoted to meet him. Noting the man's defensive stance, Marcus realized he was still scowling about his perfectly disastrous day at the office. He took a deep breath, then managed a smile as he started to reach for his badge. He stopped, and offered an outstretched hand instead.

"Detective Scanlon," he said. "I live here. And you are?"

"Yes, sir. I recognize you from a couple of crime scenes. I'm Officer Erik Randolph."

Marcus nodded, then turned to Zoe. "What? You decided that one cop around here wasn't enough?"

Zoe shook her head. "No. That is, yes. Today, at any rate."

When Marcus raised his eyebrows, Zoe went on. "Come in, please, both of you. Have a seat in my office."

As Marcus approached the French doors leading to the room, he immediately noticed Callie. She was sitting cross-legged on the floor in front of the sofa, grinning widely as she dangled a feather in the air above the black cat, keeping it just out of reach of the feline's wildly batting paws. The moment he stepped over the threshold, Callie and the cat both stopped their game and looked up at him.

The scene brought a slow smile to his lips, and Callie smiled in return. For one moment he felt as if it were just the two of them in the room, wrapped in some little domestic scene. He half expected to hear himself say, "Honey, I'm home," and Callie to tell him that dinner was almost ready.

Then he remembered all the questions he wanted answered, such as what was a uniformed policeman doing here, and what was this business about the telephone. As Zoe stepped into the room, she answered his first question.

"Someone grabbed my purse this afternoon as I was returning from the store. Officer Randolph came here earlier to take my report." She turned to the man. "And I'm assuming he has returned to tell me something about that particular matter."

Randolph was young, about twenty-three, a Scandinavian-type blond with the sort of complexion that colored easily. His face turned a warm shade of pink as he shrugged.

"Well, Mrs. Zeffarelli, I actually came to tell you that I wasn't able to learn a thing. I spoke to several neighbors when I canvassed the area, but none of them saw anything, or heard you yelling at the thief."

"Raising my voice," Zoe corrected. "And my purse? Did you find it?"

"No. I checked several yards, front and back, for several blocks in the direction you last saw the man running. That's unusual. Purse snatchers will normally throw handbags away after removing the wallet, which is easier to conceal. However, the man might have had a car parked nearby, and didn't have far to run."

"Oh, yeah, *that's* likely." Marcus couldn't control his wry tone. When he saw the man turn a bright fuchsia, he took pity on him and smiled. "I'm sure you did all you could for Mrs. Zeffarelli. It was…very considerate of you to come by and give her this information."

"Well, it was the least I could do."

"Oh, I disagree." Zoe smiled up at the man. "I would call this action above and beyond the call of duty."

Officer Randolph's face was now nearly the color of boiled beets. "Really," he protested. "It was no problem. I just wish I could have done more."

"Well, you *have* done more," Zoe replied. "You have informed me that there is some problem with my telephone. If you hadn't come by, who knows when I might have discovered it wasn't working properly? Probably just when I needed it most."

"That's what I thought. Well…"

Randolph glanced from Zoe to Marcus, obviously not sure how to make a graceful exit. Marcus took pity on the man, saying, "I appreciate you coming by."

The officer nodded. "My pleasure."

While Zoe accompanied the man to the door, thanking him, Marcus walked over to the phone on Zoe's desk. When he held the receiver to his ear, he heard nothing.

"He's right," Marcus said as Zoe walked back in the room. "The line is dead."

"How very odd. It was working four hours ago."

Marcus shrugged. "Well, I'll just run up to my room and report this to the telephone company from my phone."

It didn't turn out to be that easy. Marcus discovered that his line was dead as well, and when Callie went to her room, she returned with the same diagnosis: dead telephone.

"Can you call the phone company on your cell phone?" she asked.

"No," Marcus replied.

"No?" Zoe gave him a sharp look. "Marcus, I understand that the cellular is supposed to be reserved for police business only, but—"

Marcus cut her off with a shake of his head. "I don't have the cell phone with me. It's back at the station, along with my badge and my gun. I've been suspended."

Silence met his announcement, interrupted only by a sharp gasp, followed by a soft *mew*.

Glancing in the direction of the sounds, Marcus saw Callie staring at the cat in her arms. Slowly the woman lifted her head to stare at him.

"That's the three," she said softly.

"The three?" Marcus frowned. "The three *what?*"

"The three bad things. You know, as in *Bad things always come in threes.*"

Chapter 12

Bad luck always comes in threes.

These words echoed in Marcus's mind as he watched Callie stare at the cat in her arms. He wanted to shake his head and tell her that she was being ridiculous and fanciful. But the undeniable fact was that three less than fortunate things *had* all occurred after she brought the animal into the house.

Not that he was going to accept that there was any truth to this jinx nonsense.

"You're not going to tell me that you're going to blame that poor animal for these things?"

"Of course not." Callie lifted an insulted face to his. "None of this is *her* fault. It's me. I should never have taken the chance—"

"Yes!" Zoe broke in. "That's *exactly* what you needed to do. Take a chance. Defy what you see as your fate."

Callie turned to the woman. "Why? So that you could have your purse snatched? So that all our phones could inexplicably go dead? So that Marcus could be suspended from his job?"

"My suspension has nothing whatsoever to do with your cat."

As if the animal in question knew she was being discussed, she leapt out of Callie's arms, ran across the room, and bounded into the floral chair. There she sat, still as a statue, staring at the three of them. Callie watched the cat's green eyes widen, then narrow. Aware that their arguing had probably frightened the animal, she turned to Marcus and spoke with a more controlled sort of fury.

"I notice that you didn't say that your suspension had nothing to do with *me*. It does, doesn't it? It's because of that scene at the art gallery, where I couldn't let well enough alone and had to cause even more problems between you and Gerald Harding, over *his* cat."

Marcus's gaze wavered, then narrowed as he shook his head. "The circumstances behind my suspension are far more complicated than I feel like going into at this point. And as for your 'theory of threes,' as far as I'm concerned, each of the things you mentioned has some logical explanation. The telephones, for example. For all we know, the entire neighborhood might be without service. So, before we go on with this conversation, I'm going to run next door and see if Mrs. Hogenbloom's phone is working. If so, I'm going to call the phone company and find out what's what."

With those words, he turned. Callie watched him exit through the front door.

"He is right, you know, about the explanations."

Zoe's soothing words only served to make the muscles in Callie's shoulders tighten further. She wanted so very much to believe it, but at the moment she was feeling so completely the Calamity Jane that she knew she couldn't discuss the issue without bursting into tears.

And *that* she was not prepared to do.

Besides, there was the matter of a frightened cat to see to. Callie walked over to the chair. The animal looked up, eyes wary. Releasing a deep breath, Callie cleared her mind of angers and fears and concentrated on sending soothing thoughts to the animal, until the wild look faded from those emerald eyes. Slowly Callie reached down to scoop the furry form into her arms, then turned to Zoe.

"I think I should take her back to my room. I'll be right back down, though. I decided to cook dinner for the three of us, so I put a chicken and some potatoes in the oven about an hour ago. I still need to prepare some beans, but I don't think the kitchen would be the best place for this one, right now. Tripping over her or stepping on her tail would probably not be the best way to cement our relationship."

Callie didn't believe for one moment that her breezy words could make Zoe think that she'd forgotten all about the dreaded "threes." The woman's hazel eyes met and continued to hold hers for several moments before Zoe said, "No, it would not. Well, while you are cooking, I shall finish transcribing my notes on my last patient. When I'm finished, I shall join you in the kitchen and prepare the salad."

Up in her room, Callie noticed that the last of the evening light was shining through the balcony window, pooling onto the chair's faded blue cushion. The perfect spot to soothe any residual fear from the cat in her arms. The animal did, indeed, settle right in when Callie placed her in the middle of the chair, hunkering into a tight ball, her paws tucked beneath her chest, her tail curved around until the slender tip was just beneath her chin.

Callie smiled, then started for the door. Before stepping into the hallway, however, she paused and looked back. The cat was watching her. For one moment Callie thought she saw an expression very close to fear narrow the green eyes, as if the animal were frightened of being left alone. But the next second those same eyes opened wide, and the cat began to gaze around with an unconcerned, almost regal air.

Feeling a bit like a handmaiden dismissed from the queen's chambers, Callie closed the door and started down the stairs. A tiny smile curved her lips. She'd heard that pets often came to resemble their owners, if not in appearance then in disposition. And, sure enough, already the cat displayed an ability to mask its emotions, much like her own tendency. Not unusual, she supposed, if the animal had been living the life of a stray for very long, searching for nourishment and companionship, not sure if anyone wanted her around.

And so, Callie decided as she reached the foyer, she would take a page from the cat's book. Pretend that none of today's disasters had any effect on her at all.

This plan worked as long as Callie was alone in the kitchen, focusing on the job of rinsing the eight-inch spears of fresh green beans in Zoe's copper colander. While waiting for the pot of hot water to come to a boil, she started butter to melting in a smaller pan. She'd just placed the beans in the water when she heard a deep voice in the hall.

"It was some kind of mistake," Marcus finished as he stepped into the kitchen. He'd removed his jacket and tie and was unfastening the top button of his shirt as Zoe followed him in.

"Of course it was a mistake," she said. "But what *kind* of mistake would shut off three different telephone lines coming into this house, and yet leave my neighbor's working?"

Marcus turned. "I asked that very same question. But it wasn't easy getting an answer, I can tell you. First off, the person I spoke to insisted that his records showed that I had called some time this morning, told a representative that I was moving, ordered the phone disconnected and even gave them a forwarding address for the final bill. It took me ten minutes to convince some man named Bruce that I had never participated in that conversation, then to reassure him that I actually am Marcus Scanlon, before he conceded that *perhaps* the operator who took the disconnect order pulled up the wrong records."

"For three different accounts?"

Marcus ran a distracted hand through his hair, leaving it looking rumpled, much as it had following the kiss he and Callie had shared the night before. Feeling suddenly warm, Callie bent to remove the chicken from the oven. As she placed the hot roasting pan on the counter, she heard Marcus sigh.

"After I asked about that little coincidence, he muttered something about cross-referencing numbers that serve the same house. He said it was possible that when the caller was asked if all services in the house were to be terminated, he might have assumed the representative was asking about extension phones and said yes. That way, your name might never have come into the conversation. If it had, Bruce assured me, the mistake would have been caught right then, and we wouldn't have been *inconvenienced.*''

''Well, how long are we to be, as the man put it, 'inconvenienced'?''

''Just another hour or so.''

As Callie stirred her hollandaise sauce, she heard the refrigerator door open followed by Zoe's reply, ''Perfect. I have several calls I need to make, but I can do so after I have enjoyed the wonderful meal Callie has prepared for us. Callie, are you ready to serve yet?''

Turning from the stove, Callie shook her head. ''Not for another five or ten minutes.''

''Good.'' Zoe nodded as she filled her arms with a head of lettuce, cucumbers, red onions and tomatoes. ''Just enough time for me to make a salad, and for Marcus to set the table.''

Five minutes later, the three of them sat filling their plates in silence. As Callie ladled pale golden hollandaise sauce onto her bright green beans, she decided that with everyone's attention on the food, it was a comfortable silence. Not unlike those moments at the Manzetti table, with everyone passing platters and bowls, anticipating the glorious meal to come.

Almost as if the three of them were a family.

The thought should have cheered her, but she knew that Zoe and Marcus were no more her family than the Manzettis had been. And she didn't truly belong in this house, any more than she had belonged in that overcrowded trailer, or even her mother's less populated but equally cramped quarters.

''Callie.''

Zoe's soft voice drew her attention. ''Can Marcus and I have some of that sauce, too?'' the woman asked.

''Oh.'' An embarrassed smile twisted Callie's lips as she passed the bowl to the woman. ''I'm sorry. I was thinking about something.''

"Well, I hope you weren't thinking about that jinx stuff." Marcus placed the almost empty bowl of beans in the center of the table as he spoke, then glanced at Callie.

"Look," Callie started.

Marcus shook his head. "No. *You* look. We have an explanation about the interrupted telephone service. A college roommate of mine worked part time for the phone company and he was constantly coming home with stories about mix-ups which were very similar to the one I was told about today. Repairmen being sent to the wrong address. Crossed wires resulting in long-distance calls being billed to the wrong people. And, yes, the wrong person's service being disconnected. Now, as to Zoe's—"

At the mention of her name, the woman held up a hand. "Enough. Marcus, I keep telling you, good food is to be honored. We will finish this discussion after we have partaken of our meal. Until that time, only pleasant conversation is to be allowed. Callie, this chicken is wonderful. And the roast potatoes, as well. Is that rosemary I detect?"

Callie forced a smile to her lips, and nodded in response. Then, she answered Zoe's next query: about her meeting with Pia.

"Well, the woman isn't a total flake. She has most of the party worked out, and gave me a list of the wines that have been donated, so I can match the finger food I prepare with the different flavors. I'm a little frustrated, however. The things I'd really like to make call for some rather unusual ingredients." She paused to sigh. "Maybe it's just as well. Considering that I only have four days to prepare, I should probably play it safe and keep the food on the simple side."

"No. I do not agree." Zoe sliced off another bite of chicken breast. "I think that you should make as big a splash as you can. Many of the people who support this cause are the sort who frequently host parties. I can think of no better way for you to quickly attract clients." She paused. "You *are* thinking about starting your own catering business, are you not?"

Having her own catering company was Callie's most fervent dream. It was the one thing she was really good at, the one area in which disasters never seemed to show up. But that had been back on the Cape. What if things had changed? What if she made all this food and it tasted horrid, or the entire party came down with food poisoning? Or—

"Callie?"

Zoe's voice softly brought Callie's spiral of panic under control. "Yes," she replied. "I do want my own business. And you're right, this is a great opportunity to attract future clients, but I need more time to hunt down the ingredients I need. I also need refrigerator space so I can make things ahead of time."

"And, of course, a kitchen to work in," Zoe went on, finishing the sentence as if Callie had been making a to-do list instead of cataloguing problems. Lifting her glass of wine, Zoe said, "Well, you can certainly use *this* kitchen as much as you wish. And as to the refrigerator, well, none of the shelves in this one are anywhere near full. Consolidate what is there, and you should have plenty of room. And I have a great many of those little plastic storage containers, from the days when I had my own parties. As to getting about the city to find those items you need—"

The woman stopped speaking. She turned to smile at Marcus before going on, "I am sure that Marcus will be more than happy to drive you around while he waits out this suspension of his."

Seeing the slight frown form on Marcus's face, Callie shook her head. "No. I couldn't ask him to do that. Not when he's been reprimanded for something that I—"

"Hold it," Marcus said with a scowl. "Let's get this straight right now. The reason that I'm on suspension is because I shot off my big mouth. You remember that I mentioned seeing a reporter near the canapé table at the gallery? Well, today Shirley McIntyre's column carried an account of my confrontation with Harding. The man called the mayor to complain that I was continuing to interfere in his business after he'd ordered the department off the case. The mayor then called the police commissioner, who in turn called Bradford, who, of course, got into *my* face about it.''

Marcus laughed harshly as he shook his head. ''I told Bradford I couldn't see what all the fuss was about. If Harding really wanted to convince the catnappers that I'm no longer involved, what better way than for the suspects to read it in black and white? When Bradford refused to see it that way, I lost my temper and told him if he was so damned unhappy with the job I was doing on this, he could just give it to someone else. And the man took me up on it.''

''I always said your boss was a fool.'' Zoe smiled at Marcus, then turned to Callie. ''And the man is. He and Marcus have been butting heads ever since Bradford was promoted six months ago. Which means that today's ruckus was in the making long before you or your little black cat ever came on the scene.''

Callie had no trouble seeing where this conversation was leading. She did appreciate Zoe's attempt to convince her that there was no jinx involved here. But it just wasn't taking.

''Zoe,'' she said softly. ''I can't do what you want. I can't pretend to disbelieve all the things I was taught as a child. It might be true that everything that happened today has a logical explanation. I'm sure if Officer Randolph were to apprehend the rat who stole your purse, we might learn that the man has been planning for months to rob someone in this neighborhood. But I can't get past the fact that all three disasters happened right after I tempted fate by bringing a black cat to live with us.''

The older woman stared across the table for several minutes, then leaned forward. ''Callie, tell me something. When you were walking down Fillmore Street today, what shops did you notice?''

''What does—''

''Please. Indulge me.''

Callie took a deep breath and forced her mind to take a mental stroll past the varied establishments lining the street. ''A bakery,'' she replied. ''Two delis, several restaurants, a store that sells kitchen items…a couple of flower shops.''

Zoe turned to Marcus. "You've frequented those blocks many times. What other stores would one see there?"

"Well, besides the numerous places selling latte and cappuccino there are a couple of jewelry stores, several places that carry decorator items for the home, and some clothing stores, including quite a few thrift shops. There's a candy store devoted exclusively to overpriced chocolate, and—"

Callie shuddered before breaking in. "I remember seeing that place."

Marcus frowned. "And the memory makes you react like *that?* Most people..." He paused as his eyes widened. "Ohhh. Don't tell me. You have a *chocolate* phobia?"

"I prefer to call it an aversion."

"This is something we can deal with later." Zoe said. "Callie, do you recall seeing any of the other places that Marcus mentioned?"

"I vaguely remember seeing a yellow dress in a window, but—"

"But you were thinking about the affair you are going to cater and your eye skipped past everything that was not connected in some way to food or table ornamentation. Is that not right?"

Callie nodded.

"Well, that is what you do every day as you go through your life. You have been conditioned to be aware of bad luck, to see every little unfortunate thing that happens to anyone around you. What you must learn, and accept, is that just because you *notice* these things, doesn't mean that you have caused them. That would be like Marcus believing that he was to blame for the crimes he sees each day."

The logic in these words was irrefutable. Callie found herself sitting perfectly still, trying to control the sudden sensation that the world as she'd always known it was tilting on its axis, spinning in a new direction entirely.

"So," she said finally. "If I want to stop believing that I'm a jinx, then all I have to do is focus on..."

Her voice trailed off as she wondered just what sort of activity would hold her interest so completely that she would fail to notice cars running red lights, people stumbling and all the mishaps and near accidents that daily filled her with a sense of guilt.

"On anything you choose," Zoe finished for her. "Take this catering job, for instance. Make the most elaborate plans you can. Keep your mind trained upon every little detail. Keep yourself busy. When you are not planning the party, shopping or cooking for it, get out and walk around the city. Look at the buildings, not the people, stare out over the empty sea, focus on the scents of the flowers that line the streets."

"That's quite a tall order," Callie responded. "Wouldn't it just be easier to have you hypnotize me into disbelieving this jinx stuff?"

Zoe shrugged. "Easier, perhaps. But not nearly as effective. Hypnosis can break through emotional and psychological blocks, but it will not eradicate deeply held beliefs. That you must do consciously. Now." The woman got to her feet. "I wish to be alone with my dishes and soapy water. Why don't you two go upstairs and see if that cat is ready to tell you her name."

When Callie reached the door to her room, she placed her hand on the knob, then glanced at Marcus. "You don't have to come in if you don't want. This probably seems silly to you."

"What?" Marcus lifted one eyebrow. "Waiting for a cat to reveal its name? Hey, doesn't sound any sillier than someone being terrified of chocolate. Tell me, what frightens you most, milk or semi-sweet?"

He widened his eyes as he said these last words, revealing an unmistakable glint of amusement. Callie supposed she would find it funny, too, if she'd heard someone list "fear of chocolate" in the same company with a fear of heights or claustrophobia. But at this moment, her sense of humor failed to come to her aid. Unable to dredge up her normal breezy smile or a joking reply, she straightened defensively.

"I told you. It's just an aversion."

"An aversion? What's that mean? That you find the taste revolting, repugnant?"

Callie knew she could end this silly conversation with a simple lie, but she'd lied too many times to this man when they first met. So, with a deep sigh, she shook her head.

"No. As a matter of fact, I was once a card-carrying chocoholic. When I got that job at the candy factory, I thought I'd died and gone to heaven. Then, there was an accident."

"An accident?"

Callie shuddered. "Yes. I was just returning from my break, when something happened to the metal apparatus holding a vat of chocolate above the conveyor belt. Gallons and gallons of the stuff flowed down like molten lava onto the floor. Fortunately, everyone managed to leap onto a table or the conveyor belt before the river of boiling, splashing chocolate rushed by."

"What's this? *Indiana Jones and the Confectioner's Doom?*"

Callie looked up to see much more than a *glint* of amusement in Marcus's eyes. Deep creases fanned out from the outer corners, and two vertical creases at the corners of his mouth accentuated his wide smile.

"Hey," she protested. "Someone could have been badly burned."

By the time she finished speaking, Marcus was laughing. As Callie watched him shake his head in silent mirth, she grew more insulted by the moment.

"It wasn't funny. It was the worst mess I ever saw. There was brown congealing gook ankle-deep on the floor and splattered onto every surface. We had to sit on the tables for an hour, with the doors open to let the January air harden the stuff. Even then, it was so slippery that most of us fell at least once. By the time I got out, I felt like a chocolate-coated icicle."

The more Callie talked, the more Marcus laughed. As he held his stomach tightly and collapsed against the wall, she shook her head.

Best audience she'd ever had, and she hadn't even been trying to be funny.

Marcus managed to stop laughing a few moments later.

Slowly he straightened. God, it felt good to do that. He'd been wanting to let himself laugh like that ever since meeting Calamity Jane Chance.

He'd been wanting to do a couple of other things involving that young woman as well. But the look on her face told him that his timing was, once again, way off.

"I'm sorry for laughing." Marcus pressed his lips together to keep from cracking up again. When he thought he was once more in control, he said. "It's been a long day. I guess I needed a little comic relief."

Callie's gaze flickered from his face to the door leading to her room, then back to him again.

"I understand. But I'm not sure the cat would. She seems to be rather sensitive."

Seeing Callie's very serious expression, Marcus fought off another chortle, forced his lips into serious-business mode and nodded. "I won't laugh at her. I promise."

Callie gave him a dubious look before she turned the knob and slowly pressed the door in, speaking softly. "I'm never sure if she'll be waiting to rush out when I come in, or if I'll find her curled up on… Yep. There she is. On the bed again."

Callie flicked on the overhead light as she stepped into the room. Over her shoulder, Marcus saw the black form raise its head. Deep green eyes watched with studied nonchalance as he followed Callie into the room, shutting the door behind him.

"You see how she is?" Callie turned to him. "She hasn't been here an entire day yet, and already she's lounging around on my bed like the Queen of Sheba."

"Hey. There you go—her name. Sheba."

Callie's eyes opened wide. "Not bad. I knew a tiger named Sheba once. I got to watch her give birth."

She turned and slowly walked over to the bed. Marcus watched her sit down and offer the back of her hand to the cat to sniff, which it did with regal disdain.

"Sheba," Callie cooed. "Is that your name?"

The cat chose that moment to stretch full out, then flop back on its side and stare placidly across the room.

Callie turned to Marcus. "Guess that's not it. Any more suggestions?"

Actually, seeing Callie half sitting, half lounging on the end of that bed, a few suggestions did present themselves to Marcus. Suggestions that would probably get him tossed out of the room even quicker than laughter would. So restraining both his suggestions and his amusement, he shrugged and threw out, "Queeny?"

Callie cocked one eyebrow and sent a speculative glance toward the cat. A few seconds later, she shook her head. Marcus crossed the room to sit opposite Callie. The cat, lounging between them, turned narrowed eyes to him before beginning to lick her left paw.

"I'm not sure she likes me," he said.

"She *should,*" Callie replied. "After all, you and your battle with the bureaucrats of the world were instrumental in freeing her from that cage. She just doesn't know that yet. Give her time."

Marcus gazed at Callie. Give her time, his mind echoed, but his thoughts weren't on the cat. He was thinking about Callie, how close she was, how much he wanted to pull her into his arms. Staring into her opal eyes, he thought he detected a similar spark of desire. Recalling her responses to his kisses the night before, he was fairly certain that he was right. But he also remembered the haunted look on her face when she'd pulled away from that embrace.

The woman was just getting over a man who'd lied to her, he reminded himself. Of course she needed time.

Forcing himself to glance down at the cat, he said. "You don't like the name Molly gave her? Miss Blackie?"

"No. Too obvious."

He looked up at Callie and suggested, "Shadow?"

"Sounds like a dog's name."

"Well, how about naming her for that panther? Ebony, wasn't it?"

When he saw her shudder, Marcus shook his head. "No. That probably wouldn't be a good idea," he said. "And I suppose Semi-Sweet would be out of the question."

Callie stared at him, unblinking, for a long moment. Marcus was just beginning to curse himself for insulting her again, when he caught sight of the tiny twitching motion at the corners of her lips. Focusing his attention on her wide mouth, Marcus grinned.

"Okay," he said. "How about Licorice. It's perfect. She's black like the candy. And she *licks* a lot—providing at least part of the name."

Callie's eyes rolled as she grinned and shook her head. "I don't think that's the sort of thing Zoe was referring to. I think she meant that by watching the cat, I'd just get a sense of what she should be called."

"Okay. You got this creature, in part, to help you counteract your fears and phobias. How about something that accentuates that aspect…something like Charm, or Lucky. Maybe Lucky Charm."

"That's a cereal." Callie gave him a mock scowl, then turned to study the cat again, who was now washing her other paw. "But I think you've moved in the right direction. Lucky sounds like the name of a ranch cat, though. I think she's more refined, a little exotic, even."

"Talisman."

Callie glanced at him sharply. The light in her eyes made him think he'd hit on the right name, but already his mind was rushing ahead.

"No, not Talisman—too masculine sounding," he said. "How about Kismet?"

As the word hung in the air, Callie gazed into Marcus's eyes for several minutes, before turning to the cat and calling softly, "Kismet. Hey, Kismet."

The animal stopped midlick, lifted wide green eyes and stared back at Callie for several moments, then gave the tip of her tail two quick flicks.

Callie smiled, and turned to Marcus. "That's it. Kismet. Someone or something coming into one's life at the right time. I decided I needed a cat, and there she was. The name fits her perfectly. Thank you."

The expression of unmitigated joy lighting Callie's face

went straight to Marcus's heart, making it swell so quickly that he had to take a sudden breath. But not to control the feeling. He was tired of fighting his responses to this woman. She was right. Kismet was the right word, not just as a name for the cat, but to describe Callie's arrival into his life.

Life is what you make it.

He remembered saying that to Callie as a way of denying the existence of luck. But what, exactly, had he made of his life? Holding on to his bitter anger, his life had become a sterile wasteland of duty and the occasional romantic fling. If the word romantic could be applied to relationships that had lacked any sort of emotional depth.

Slowly Marcus reached across to place his hand over the one Callie had rested on her cat's back.

"You know," he said when her eyes met his. "Five days ago, if anyone had used the word *kismet* to describe your arrival in my life, I would have laughed in that person's face. And I would have been dead wrong."

Callie stared at him for several moments after he finished speaking. When her hand slid slowly from beneath his, Marcus thought for sure he'd said the wrong thing at the wrong time. But then, her hand came up to gently cup his cheek. Her thumb moved slowly over his lips as she leaned forward to place her lips where her thumb had just traveled.

Marcus savored her gentle touch for several seconds, relished the warmth of the tenuous contact, until his appetite began to grow, to ask for more. Placing his arms around Callie, he pulled her to him, closing his mouth over hers in a kiss meant to devour. He heard a soft moan and felt her lips vibrate against his, as her arms slid around his neck.

The contact between their bodies was far from satisfactory. Leaning forward, he urged her gently back, planning to press her onto the mattress. However, they were so close to the edge of the bed that they slid right off, once again ending up on the floor. It was a slow gradual descent, however, one that didn't require they break off the delicious, soul-satisfying kiss that joined them. And once on the floor, they pursued further delights.

Sliding his hand down past Callie's waist, Marcus cupped her jean-covered bottom and urged her toward him. As they moaned in unison, Callie began pulling Marcus's shirt out of his waistband. Then her fingers slowly worked their way up the front of his body, unfastening buttons as they went. Not to be outdone in the area of being undone, Marcus slid his hand up her back and smiled against her lips as he snapped open her bra on the first attempt.

Aware of Callie's attempt to remove his shirt, Marcus reluctantly removed first one hand and then the other from her soft flesh, to slip his arms free of his sleeves. As she tugged his shirt upwards, he reached down to grasp the hem of her sweater and pull it over her head.

This maneuver required that their lips part. With both items of clothing tossed onto the bed behind them, Marcus gazed down at Callie's darkened eyes, her well-kissed lips, then the curves peeking out from the lower edge of her loosened bra. As he moved forward to kiss her once more, his right hand brushed over her bare stomach as it traveled up to palm her soft breast. Callie's moan was followed by a harsh hiss, of indrawn breath, he imagined, just before their lips met again.

Then Marcus heard a second hiss, this one louder, coming from somewhere above his head. A moment later, something landed on his shoulders, driving what felt like a thousand needles into his bare skin.

Chapter 13

With a gasp of pain, Marcus reared back violently, dislodging whatever had landed on his shoulder and back.

The next thing he knew, he was sitting in front of Callie's bed, glaring at the animal crouched on the floor in front of him. His upper back stung like the dickens. Reaching across his chest, he gingerly explored his left shoulder. When his hand came away lightly stained with red, he heard Callie gasp.

"Oh, geez. She really dug into you, didn't she?"

By the time Callie was finished speaking, she'd moved to kneel behind him and placed her hands on his shoulders, gently bracketing the stinging area.

"We've got to get you to a hospital."

"A hospital?" Marcus jerked around. "She couldn't have scratched deep enough for me to need stitches."

Callie looked up from her hurried struggle to refasten her bra. "No," she said. "But her claws did break your skin. I've heard that cat scratches can cause all sorts of—"

"Problems." Marcus cut her off as he pushed himself to his feet. "Yeah, I know. But not if the scratches are taken care of properly. I'll just go scrub my back in the shower, then apply some antiseptic cream.''

He turned to find that Callie had also risen and was pulling her sweater over her head. When her face popped into view, it was filled with concern. ''But what if—''

''If I experience any unusual symptoms, *then* I'll go to the emergency room.''

''But why take a chance? It will only—''

''No!''

Callie blinked and backed up as if he'd slapped her. Marcus reached over to gently cup her cheek in his hand. ''Hey,'' he said softly. ''I hate hospitals. Call it an *aversion*. Okay?''

Callie's lips curved ever so slightly, but the concerned look remained in her eyes.

''Look,'' he said. ''I'm sure I'll be fine. But in the event that a problem appears, I promise I'll go to the hospital, if you'll promise not to blame yourself for this. Deal?''

After a moment's hesitation, Callie nodded. Marcus gave her cheek a quick pat, then bent over to retrieve his shirt from the floor. He'd just straightened and turned for the door when Callie's soft, ''Marcus?'' made him turn back to her.

''I really am sorry.''

One side of Marcus's lips curved. ''So am I.'' His entire body shared that regret. Despite the pain in his shoulder, he was still tight with desire for her. A desire that still needed to be held in control.

It was too soon for what might have happened tonight. Oh, not for him, Marcus knew. For a man who had spent ten long years avoiding serious relationships, he was surprisingly ready to take this connection with Callie Chance to the next level, both physically and emotionally.

But Callie's life had been a wild roller-coaster ride the last couple of days, and before they took things further, he wanted her to feel as sure of her emotions and desires as he did. That would take time, and oddly, thanks to Captain Bradford, he now had plenty of that commodity to offer her.

''Anyway,'' he said. ''The next time you take my shirt off,

I'll remember to make sure that your 'watchcat' isn't anywhere near, waiting to defend you.''

When he saw the beginnings of a smile at the corners of Callie's mouth, he bent forward and captured it beneath his lips. For one long, glorious moment he held the kiss, highly aware of her hands when they touched his waist, of the cool feel of her fingers tracing a path up, over his chest, to his shoulders.

Each second of that moment was sheer pleasure. Also sheer torture, because he knew it had to come to an end. Reaching up, he caught her hands in his, then held them gently as he lifted his mouth from hers. Drawing back a scant inch, he closed his eyes against the allure of her scent, her tempting body, reminding himself of his vow to give Callie the time she needed to be sure that she wanted him. Not just in her bed, but in her heart as well.

''You'd better get that shower,'' Callie said in a hushed voice, then backed away.

As Marcus opened his eyes and followed her progress with avid attention, Callie felt once again the tiny twist of pleasure low in her stomach. Forcing a smile to her slightly bruised lips, she said, ''Um. You know, I have a soap made of lavender, thyme and tea tree oil, which all have natural antiseptic properties. Let me get it for you.''

It only took her a couple moments to retrieve the soap from the box near the chair, just long enough to catch her breath. Not long enough, however, to quiet the pounding of her heart as she crossed the room toward Marcus again, nor to halt the trembling in her still-weak knees. When he wordlessly held his hand out to receive the soap, she quickly dropped the bar into his palm, afraid he would see how badly her hand was shaking.

''Thanks,'' he said.

Callie forced herself to meet his gaze again. ''Don't mention it. It was, after all, my cat who scratched you. I only wish I could do more.''

Like join you in the shower and make sure that every inch of your back is well scrubbed.

Callie froze as Marcus grinned at her. When she realized she hadn't actually said these words out loud, that he was already turning to leave, she drew in a quick, relieved breath. When he stepped into the hall and closed the door behind him, she continued to stand before it, breathing slowly, until the trembling and heat eased from her body.

This took several minutes, and by the time her heart rate had lowered to a pace somewhere near normal, she barely had enough strength left in her legs to stumble to the chair and collapse into it. Elbows resting on the overstuffed arms, she let her head loll against the back of the seat.

Never in her entire life had she ever been kissed the way Marcus Scanlon had kissed her. The first brief touch of his lips two nights ago had completely taken her breath away. The next meeting of lips, before they'd fallen into her room, had been completely intoxicating. But this last kiss had taken her far beyond the state of inebriation, to a place where she felt hot and cold at the same time, invigorated and weak, nervous and yet safe. His strong embrace and the feel of his hands on her body had completely muddled her mind, then threatened to turn her flesh and bones into a helpless puddle of jelly.

And she'd loved every minute of it.

"Meeooow."

The plaintive cry brought Callie's eyes open, just as Kismet leapt lightly into her lap. As the cat cocked her head to one side, her eyes seemed to ask what was going on.

"I wish I knew," Callie responded as she ran her hand over the animal's thick, luxurious coat. When Kismet closed her eyes and started purring loudly, Callie sighed.

She knew all too well what was happening. She was falling—no, she had *fallen* in love with Marcus Scanlon. Tonight she had been more than ready to give that love to him, heart, soul and body. Without any reservations, without any fears.

Callie shivered. Okay, she had some fears. But she didn't think they were unreasonable ones. After all, five days ago she was preparing to marry Dave Johnson. And now, she was hopelessly besotted with Marcus Scanlon.

Seeing that the cat had opened her eyes again to stare into hers, Callie rubbed the animal's ears and leaned forward to say, "All right, Kismet. You tell me. Am I some kind of fickle strumpet? Or the luckiest woman on earth?"

When the cat blinked and yawned, Callie answered the question herself. "I'm going to go with lucky. I'm going to believe that fate decided to step in and show me that the man I was about to marry was a two-timing jerk, then make up for all the bad stuff in my past by bringing Marcus into my life."

The following morning, Callie was still so filled with the conviction that luck had, indeed, finally decided to shine on her and those around her, that she barely touched the steps as she hurried down to breakfast. Tucked in the back pocket of her faded jeans was a piece of paper filled with a list of ingredients, and the phone numbers of establishments she planned on calling in search of them. Once she knew where to go, she would use some of her store of cash to pay Raj to drive her around town.

After she had breakfast.

Callie came to a sudden halt in the kitchen doorway. The dark-haired man leaning against the counter, wearing a dark blue T-shirt tucked into snug Levi's and sipping a cup of coffee while reading a folded newspaper, bore very little resemblance to suit-and-tie-clad Detective Scanlon. Just as she was deciding that this version of the man was even more attractive, if possible, he looked up from his paper, and gave her one of those rare, all-out dazzling smiles of his.

Drawing in a steadying breath, Callie said, "Hi. How's your back?"

His smile dimmed slightly as he shrugged. "So far, so good. But, you know, I understand that it takes several days for gangrene to set in."

Callie frowned.

"That's the truth." Marcus placed his mug in the sink and straightened from the counter without taking his eyes off her.

"So, I was thinking that you really should keep a close eye on me for a while."

Callie forced a reluctant expression to her face. "Well, I suppose." She sighed. "Seeing as it was my cat who scratched you, and all."

Marcus stepped forward. Placing an arm across her shoulders, he guided her toward the hallway as he said, "Well, since we are in agreement on that point, let's get going."

"Going? I kind of like to eat breakfast before—"

Marcus cut her off with a quick shake of his head. "We're going to be eating breakfast out today. It's part of the tour."

"The tour?"

"Yes." He led her toward the foyer as he spoke. "Marcus Scanlon's patented full-day get-acquainted-with-San-Francisco tour."

"All day? Sounds nice but—"

"But what?"

"Well, for one thing, I have a huge list of ingredients and stuff I need to locate, and—"

"Got that covered. While we eat, you're going to tell me what you need, and I'll arrange the tour to fit your list. Any other problems we need to solve before we start?"

"Kismet."

Marcus shrugged. "That's not a problem. I have no doubt that as the day goes on, the right items will appear at the right time."

"The cat, Marcus. *My* cat."

"Oh, *that* Kismet." Callie noted that Marcus was doing a poor job of hiding his amusement as he went on. "Well, as it so happens, when I told Zoe my plans for the day, your cat was one of her concerns, too. She's with a client right now, but she has the rest of the day free, and she's volunteered to cat-sit. She said something about taking Kismet to her apartment, and letting your pet get acquainted with her cats, Victor and Hugo. So, any more dragons to slay before we get astride my black charger and thunder off to the sea?"

Marcus's low-to-the-ground Karmann-Ghia was a far cry from "charger" status, but it did emit a satisfactory roar as they raced up and down the hills of the city, heading west. The top was down, and it was a decidedly relaxed Marcus Scanlon who sat beside Callie in the slightly worn bucket seats. Each time Callie glanced over to see the wind ruffling his dark hair and caught his wide grin, she recalled that first smile he'd given her at the hotel.

At the time she'd suspected his disarming grin was nothing but a ploy, meant to break down her defenses so he could reach into her heart and tear out her secrets. But that smile had also revealed a glimpse of the man behind the badge, and to that man she was more than happy to open her heart.

"Oh."

A gasp of pleasure escaped Callie's lips as the car crested a hill, then started down a long curve toward the Pacific Ocean. The sea shimmered a deep blue-green beneath the pale blue sky. Several huge rocks rose from the surf just offshore, and as the car approached, a series of waves rushed forward to foam white and pale green as they broke against them.

Before Callie had more than a moment to notice the collections of buildings at the bottom of the hill, Marcus turned sharply to the right, parking in front of a single-story brown building. Callie was staring at the oval sign over the door that proclaimed the place belonged to Luis, when Marcus came around to open her door.

"Best breakfast and most spectacular view in town," he said.

And he was right. The simple meal of eggs, fried potatoes and an English muffin was delicious. While Callie ate, she gazed out the bank of windows to watch the ocean rush forward, then retreat, while Marcus explained that the large rectangular area filled with water just down the hill and to the right of the restaurant had once been a series of swimming pools, built at the end of last century, and enclosed beneath a huge glass and iron structure.

After breakfast, they took their shoes off to stroll hand in hand along the water's edge. The scent of salt, the roar of the breaking waves and the warmth of the sun wove a particularly sensual form of magic, relaxing Callie deeply, making her tingle with awareness of the man at her side.

She turned to look at him, and noticed a combination of joy and longing in the dark blue eyes that watched the progress of a curling wave. As she gazed up at him, he turned to her and asked, "Have you ever surfed?"

Callie shook her head. "You?"

"Yeah. But it's been a long time. Too long."

"Your job takes up most of your life, doesn't it?"

"It has. I think that's something that needs adjusting, however." He paused to give her a quick smile. "And speaking of jobs, I'm falling down on mine. I think it's time we get on with the tour."

Once they were back in the car, Marcus drove south along the shoreline for several blocks before turning into Golden Gate Park. Towering pines and eucalyptus trees shaded them as they skimmed past several small lakes and various gardens.

"This is just a peek, to whet your appetite," he said as they pulled back into city traffic. "Some other day, soon, I'd like to bring you back and show you this place in depth."

Some other day.

Callie nodded as her chest suddenly filled, not just with the fresh bracing air, but with a quiet, certain kind of joy she'd never felt before. Marcus Scanlon meant every word he said. She had no doubt that "some other day" would come, and it would come soon, as he promised.

While they ate, Callie had given Marcus a list of items she needed, so the first shopping stop came at the Japan Center, where Callie found a small store within the two-story mall that carried packaged kelp and Asian rice.

A stop in Chinatown garnered the wonton wrappers she needed, along with two kinds of soy sauce. Following a quick tour of that area, they moved onto North Beach, otherwise known as Little Italy. After lunch overlooking Washington Square, they explored various shops, where Callie purchased freshly roasted coffee beans. In a deli filled with the scents and ambience of the Italian Riviera she found a huge bottle of pale green olive oil, the Mediterranean olives she was looking for and some soft goat cheese.

As they got back into the car, Marcus said, "You did say you needed seafood, didn't you?"

Callie nodded.

"Okay. Next stop, Fisherman's Wharf. And more walking."

Callie stifled a groan. She wasn't sure her legs were up to more of *that* particular activity. However, the little car crept so slowly through the early rush-hour traffic that by the time Marcus pulled into a parking space, Callie felt almost rested.

Good thing, because after strolling along the wharf, inspecting the salmon-colored crab and shrimp displayed atop snow-white beds of shaved ice, she found a place that would deliver a quantity of both, freshly caught, directly to Pia's house on the morning of the benefit.

After taking care of that piece of business, Callie was beginning to droop as they stepped into a tall brick structure filled with shops and restaurants, until Marcus led her to a store called the Cannery Wine Cellar and Gourmet Market. Here, she revived, snapping up various crackers, some hors d'oeuvre-size loaves of bread and a selection of small, pre-baked pastry shells for quick-to-make, yet impressive-looking canapés.

It was after seven when they got back to the car. With the tiny front storage compartment already filled with previous purchases, Marcus put the top up so Callie could store her most recent packages in the small rear jump seat. As he shut and locked the door, he smiled at her.

"I hope you're ready for dinner."

"That depends," she replied. "Does it mean more walking?"

Marcus chuckled. "Just two blocks, back to the wharf. And up one flight of stairs. But I promise, the view will be worth it."

Marcus was right. The view from the second floor of Alioto's was so magnificent that when Marcus asked Callie if a cracked crab salad sounded good, she simply nodded, reluctant to pull her eyes from the sight.

The entire San Francisco Bay stretched out in front of her, from the glow of the well-lit Golden Gate Bridge on the left to the string of lights that marked the Bay Bridge way down to the far right. The huge body of water lay black beneath the dark blue sky, and the lights of the surrounding communities encircled the bay like a diamond tiara set on black velvet.

"It looks so peaceful."

"At night, yeah," Marcus replied softly. "But during the day, between the huge ships that come in and out on a regular basis, the fishing and sailing boats, kayaks, windsurfers and wave runners, the traffic on the bay can be almost as bad as the congestion in the middle of downtown."

After that conversation, they sat staring over the water in companionable silence until the waiter delivered a basket of warm, crusty bread and two glasses of white wine. Callie broke off a piece of the bread, popped it in her mouth, then took a sip of wine.

Marcus, she noticed, was still gazing out to sea. Noting his expression of intense concentration, she took a guess at his thoughts.

"Wondering if Mr. Harding has managed to get his cat back?"

One corner of Marcus's mouth quirked up as he turned to meet her gaze. "And you accused *me* of being a mind reader. Are you sure you didn't learn some mind-reading skills from your mother?"

At the mention of her mother, Callie felt some of the day's glow fade. "My mother only read palms."

"Yeah? Was she any good at it?"

Callie shrugged. "She thought she was. We were never in one place long enough to learn if any of her predictions came true, so who knows?"

"Do you miss having your mother around?"

Marcus watched Callie take another bite of bread, then chew slowly as she gazed in the direction of the Golden Gate

Bridge. Her face was in profile, but he didn't need to see into her eyes to guess that some of the light had gone out of them.

"Hey," he said softly. "I'm sorry. I guess I've forgotten first-date etiquette. I think I remember some rule about avoiding subjects that are too personal."

Callie's head swiveled toward him. "First date? Is that what this is?"

"That was the general idea."

"Really." Callie's eyes narrowed as if she were considering a totally foreign concept. Slowly her lips eased into a warm smile. "Well, considering the unconventional way we met, and how much you already know about me, I don't think we need to worry about that particular rule. And to answer your question..." She paused for a quick sigh. "Well, I can't miss something I never had. You see, my mom never did 'motherly' things. The person who dressed and fed me when I was really little was Madame Zorokova, the fortune teller who first hired and trained my mom. And by the time I was five, when we moved up from the carny to a real circus, I was in charge of doing these things for myself. And even though my mother was convinced that I was the source of anything that went wrong in our lives, as soon as I learned math, it became my job to pay the bills, along with cooking the meals."

She paused again. This time the sigh she released was almost too soft to hear.

"But I do miss her. She was really fun to be with when things were going well. She was lighthearted and silly, and she told great stories, too. And I believe, in her own odd way, that she truly loves me. She just feels that she's better off without me in her life."

Marcus reached over to take her hand. "I think it's the other way around." When Callie started to shake her head, he squeezed her fingers. "Callie, no one needs someone belittling them, telling them ridiculous, self-serving lies. If the things that Zoe has been telling you haven't sunk in yet, then listen to me. I have complete and total proof that you are no jinx."

The look Callie shot him was half hopeful, half dubious. Marcus grinned.

"You want to know what it is?"

Slowly Callie nodded.

"Okay. I think I've told you that parking spaces in San Francisco are nearly as hard to find as four-leaf clovers. Well, today, with you in the car next to me, I found not one, but *three* legal spaces, without circling for hours."

Callie stared at him silently. When he saw a suspicious hint of moisture glimmering in her eyes, Marcus tensed. But Callie's voice didn't waver at all as she asked, "Are you telling me having me in your car today was *lucky?*"

"Of course not. You know that I don't believe in luck." He leaned toward her. "But I do believe in miracles."

Bending forward just a little more, he touched his lips to hers, felt them tremble ever so slightly before deepening his kiss. She was just beginning to respond when a bored voice said, "Excuse me."

When they slowly parted, a waiter placed a plate laden with chunks of pink crab and bright red tomatoes and green lettuce in front of each of them. With a quick, steadying sigh, they turned their attention to the food.

During the meal, conversation drifted back to the catnapping case. Marcus admitted that he'd been ruminating on the few clues he had, searching for some detail he might have overlooked. In spite of his suspension he wanted to check a few things out the following morning, unless Callie needed him to help hunt down more ingredients. She replied that the rest of the things on her list could be obtained at the nearby market, or further up on Fillmore Street, a short bus ride away.

When they were finished dining, Marcus walked Callie back to the car, then drove the short distance to the house. As he pulled into the driveway, he noticed that the windows were dark. Checking his watch, he saw that it was only nine-thirty. He knew that Zoe retired each night at the stroke of ten. However, the last couple of days *had* been rather eventful, so after garaging the car, he suggested to Callie that they be as quiet as possible as they went about storing her purchases in the kitchen.

Following Callie up the stairs, he noticed her nervous backward glance when he walked past his own apartment and continued up the stairs to the landing outside her room. The windowed alcove to the side of the stairway let in enough moonlight for him to see her face as she reached her door and turned to him.

After a moment of tense, expectant silence, she whispered, "Would you like to come in?"

Marcus shook his head.

"You afraid of the cat?"

Marcus bent toward her and asked, "Did you just call me a 'fraidy-cat?"

Callie's barely muffled giggle brought a quick smile to his lips. Placing his hands on the door, bracketing Callie's head, he bent closer and whispered, "I just want a first-date, good-night kiss."

Callie answered with a smile and a nod, her eyes shimmering.

The kiss wasn't like any first-date kiss Marcus had ever delivered before. He started out with the best of intentions, brushing his lips softly over Callie's before slowly increasing pressure and intensity.

His reaction to her answering kiss lit a veritable bonfire of a response that leapt to life in one whoosh of spontaneous combustion. The kiss went from gentle, to sweet, to one of instant, intense hunger. Of their own volition his hands slid down the flat, hard surface of the door to search out the warmth, the softness of Callie's waist. Pulling her to him, he pressed his hands lower, molding his palms to her bottom, urging her hips toward his.

Callie responded with a soft moan of pleasure. Her hands moved upward, testing the firm surface of Marcus's stomach, the hard curve of his chest before closing over his shoulders, giving her fingers something to cling to while she arched against him. The sound of his deep-throated groan accelerated the pounding of her heart, increased the temperature of her skin, intensified the throbbing of her desire. She answered with another soft moan.

Soft enough for her to hear a loud thump. Not from her heart, though she was certain that organ was knocking hard enough against her breastbone to be audible.

The sound in question had come from her room. But just as her passion-drugged mind figured that out, the thump was followed by a loud screech, definitely feline in nature.

Chapter 14

From inside the room came another loud yowl, followed by a stifled but decidedly human curse. Callie's body tensed immediately. Marcus broke off both kiss and embrace as he pulled away.

The next few moments were a confusing tangle of hands and fingers as both Callie and Marcus grabbed the doorknob and struggled to turn it. When it finally twisted and the door clicked open, they stumbled together into the room, then stopped just inside the threshold.

The balcony windows were wide open, the filmy curtains floating on the breeze. Callie's packing box lay on its side, spilling an odd assortment of items onto the floor. The cat stood next to the box, facing the balcony with her back arched as if prepared to attack. A dark, limp object hung from Kismet's mouth.

Marcus moved first, stretching his arm toward Callie in a warning to stay where she was as he crossed the room, through the open French doors and onto the balcony. He was only out there a few moments before he stepped back into the room.

"Seems you've had company," he said.

"Company?"

"Yep. A grappling hook is wedged between the wrought iron bars out there, attached to a very long rope. And, it appears that your uninvited guest left a calling card."

Marcus's attention had shifted to the cat, which was now crouching down, still clutching her prize in her jaws. Moving slowly toward the animal, he crooned, "Hey, Kismet. Whaddaya have there?" As Marcus reached the animal's side, he hunkered down and continued in a smooth-as-honey tone, "Now, don't you glare at me, you little beast from hell. You can be a good girl, can't you? Oh, give it a try, you little fiend. Calm down now. That's right, relax that back of yours, retract those flesh-ripping claws. Okay now, Miss Devil's Spawn, let me see what you've clamped your sharp little teeth on."

Caught between feeling insulted on behalf of her pet and the almost irresistible desire to laugh, Callie watched as the cat responded by slowly rising to sit on her haunches. However, Kismet was obviously still wary, leaning away as Marcus slowly reached toward her.

"Come on, Kismet." Marcus had managed to grasp the corner of the object, but Kismet kept her mouth clamped shut. Marcus tugged at it. "Be a good little brute." The cat spat the item out with disdain, rose to all fours again, turned and walked away, tail held high.

The prize they'd struggled over now dangled from Marcus's thumb and forefinger. "A glove," he said as he stood up. "A brown leather glove, with the tip of the index finger almost completely bitten through. Interesting."

As he walked toward Callie, his tone and bearing told her he'd slid right into detective mode.

"You and I are going to go downstairs and call the police," he said. "We'll have to shut Kismet in here until they arrive. I want you to close the door behind us, but don't touch the inside knob. The feline screech and the curse we heard suggest that this glove was on the burglar's hand until just before he made his escape. But you never know how long the guy was in here before we—''

Marcus had stepped into the hallway and Callie was just closing the door, when he stopped speaking abruptly. Rounding the banister quickly, he rushed down the stairs. It only took Callie a moment to realize what he was thinking and to follow him.

She found Marcus on the next landing, knocking on Zoe's door. By the time Callie joined him, he was shouting, ''Zoe! Are you in there?''

Both of them leaned forward, listening for a reply. Nothing. After repeating the procedure and getting the same result, Marcus crossed the landing to enter his apartment. Callie was barely aware of the light flowing from his doorway. All her attention was on the raised panelled door in front of her, visualizing Zoe on the other side, gagged and bound.

''Callie, I need you.''

She responded immediately. Stepping into his room, she glanced past a brown overstuffed couch and empty white walls until she spied Marcus in front of an intricately carved desk, rummaging through the center drawer with his left hand. The glove still dangled from his right.

''I'm looking for the key to Zoe's rooms,'' he said. ''While I search, can you run down to the kitchen and get a baggie for this glove?''

Callie muttered, ''Yes,'' as she turned, clattered down the stairs to the kitchen, then thumped her way back up. By the time she reached the landing again, Marcus was once more in front of Zoe's door, bending down to fit a key into the lock.

''Here,'' Callie said. ''Put the glove in.''

With only the slightest break in his concentration, Marcus dropped the glove into the open plastic bag, then reached down and twisted the doorknob. When the door swung open, he called out, ''Zoe?''

Again no answer. Callie's heart, still racing from her sprint down and up the stairs, came to a thudding stop. When Marcus flicked on the light, Callie followed him into the room.

Her eyes quickly scanned the rustic yet elegant country French decor. But nowhere, not on the green couch or the pink-and-green plaid chair or the floral area rug, did she see any sign of the woman they were looking for, just two long-haired cats, one smoke-brown and one calico, who looked up from their spots on the couch to blink placidly at the intruders.

"You stay here," Marcus said softly as he stepped away. "I'll check the bedroom and the bathroom."

Callie watched him approach an open door, cross the threshold and flick on another light. He took two steps into the room before turning to the right, disappearing from sight. As she waited, Callie's heart pounded. She'd just realized that she was holding her breath and biting her lower lip, when Marcus reappeared.

Callie knew from the relieved expression on his face that he hadn't found Zoe, gagged and tied, or in any other form.

"She must have gone out tonight," he said as he reached Callie's side. "Unusual for her not to let me know, but she *is* an adult, and I'm just her tenant. Let's just check downstairs to be sure."

Callie followed, still clutching the bag containing the glove in her hand. A quick search revealed that they were the only two people in the house.

"And it doesn't look like anyone has been ransacking down here either."

Marcus frowned as he approached the kitchen wall phone. He punched in several digits, identified himself to the woman who answered and explained the situation. When he turned back to Callie, he could see she was disturbed.

"Hey, you get Kismet as soon as the detectives and forensics arrive."

"Oh." Callie blinked. Her mouth twisted into an embarrassed grimace. "Some cat owner I am. I wasn't even thinking about her. I was wondering why anyone would choose to break into my room."

Marcus had been wondering the same thing. He had a couple of theories. ''Do you remember that article in the paper the day after we attended that art show?''

''The one about your argument with Harding?'' Callie rolled her eyes and nodded.

''Well, further on it mentioned several society types who were also there that night, including Zoe. Now, she doesn't really do the society thing much these days, unless it's for charity. Apparently she's donating a collection of valuable Venetian art glass to be auctioned off sometime soon.''

''Okay, that would provide motive. But why break into a fourth-story room? Wouldn't it have been easier to pick the lock on the front door?''

Marcus crossed the room and placed his hands on Callie's shoulders. ''Hey, I must be rubbing off on you. You're thinking like a cop.'' She gave him a weak smile as he gently kneaded her tense muscles. ''The front door to this place is very well lit, in clear view of several of the houses across the street. Both my balcony and Zoe's can be seen from the street as well. However, your balcony is at the back of the house, and the rear neighbor's roof is close enough to make access rather easy.''

''What makes you think the thief might have been after Zoe's art glass?''

Marcus shrugged. ''Well, after the article ran in the paper her purse was stolen.''

''True.''

Marcus frowned. It made sense, but something about the scenario just didn't feel right.

Maybe because, now that he was standing so close to Callie, breathing in that musky-floral scent of hers, his mind was once again becoming clouded. Memories of the good-night kiss they'd shared, and the desire that had erupted within him, weren't helping the situation. Neither was the fact that the light green eyes gazing up at him hinted that Callie was recalling those very same sensations.

The arrival of Rick Malone and two members of the forensics team shattered the moment.

Back in cop mode, Marcus led the troops up to Callie's

room. He had her check everything out, and after she decided that nothing was missing, he instructed her to take Kismet downstairs, then let the guys loose with their little brushes, plastic baggies and cameras.

"Be sure you dust the balcony and the doors leading to it," he told them. "Callie's cat ripped the guy's glove off before he left, so that area's the best bet for finding any usable prints."

Leaving them to their work, he went downstairs, where Malone led Callie to take her statement. Hearing voices in the kitchen, Marcus headed that way. When he entered the blue and yellow room, he was surprised to see Zoe sitting at the table along with Callie and his partner.

"Dr. Zeffarelli returned just as I got to the bottom of the stairs with Miss Chance." There was no hint of a smirk as Malone spoke Callie's name, then went on, "From what she's told me, it sounds like someone wanted your landlady out of the house tonight."

Zoe nodded. "I received a desperate fax from a friend of mine. The message was very urgent: she said her daughter was in trouble again. This particular friend is also a client with an anxiety disorder. She needed to talk to someone, she said, but didn't want to leave the house or tie up the phone in case her daughter should call. However, when I arrived, the woman greeted me with a smile and looked at me like I'd lost my mind, and said she'd never sent me a fax. Of course, then I had to wait for another cab to bring me back here."

Marcus remained silent for several seconds after Zoe finished speaking. Little puzzle pieces were falling into place, but the pattern still seemed askew.

"This might explain those hang-up calls we've all been getting the last couple of days," he said slowly. "I'd dismissed them as some glitch caused when the phone company restored our service, but someone might have been trying to see which of us was home. Tonight, when neither Callie or I answered, you were the only one left. In that purse that was stolen, didn't you carry a small address book?"

Zoe nodded.

"Ah." Malone jumped into the conversation. "Then the burglar simply found the name of one of your friends and sent you a fake message from her."

Marcus nodded slowly, a reluctant frown brewing. "Maybe. Except the would-be thief seemed to know that the person he was pretending to be not only had a daughter, but one who'd been in trouble in the past. That indicates someone who knows Zoe and her circle of friends."

"So the guy is clever." Malone shrugged. "Maybe he called several numbers in the address book, and used a census-taking scam until he learned what he needed to come up with a story that would get Dr. Zeffarelli's attention. Not unheard of."

"True."

The forensics team walked in at that point to inform Marcus that they'd found two bloody fingerprints on the balcony railing, as well as a full palm print and another bloody impression of a finger on the frame of the French doors. After printing Callie to eliminate hers from the mix, they collected the torn glove and left.

Malone decided to depart shortly after. Marcus walked the man to the door, and asked him to see that the prints were run through the system as soon as possible.

"Frustrating, isn't it?"

Aware that Malone was referring to his suspension, he nodded. "Yeah. How are you coming with our caseload?"

The redhead's mouth twisted into a half grin as his narrow shoulders lifted in a shrug. "Not too bad. The Grisholm case is now closed."

Marcus lifted eyebrows in surprise and admiration. "Really. That one's six months old. Jerry and I worked like mad on that, but couldn't get the proof we needed."

"Well, you were on the right track."

"The man's brother?"

Malone nodded. "But I can't really take much credit, unless it would be for being at the right place at the right time."

"How's that?"

"I went to talk to Ted Grisholm, you know, friendly-like, asking how he was managing after his loss. All of a sudden the guy broke down and admitted to committing the murder. Fortunately for me, I got him to stop talking, took him to the station where I got my Miranda warning and his confession on tape."

"Bradford must be pleased."

"Oh, yeah." Malone paused. "And you? Enjoying your little vacation?"

Recalling his day, and the way it might have ended, Marcus felt his lips curve in what he was sure would appear a rather silly smile. He turned it into a so-so grimace and shrugged. "Today was okay."

"Well, don't get too used to it. The police commissioner came barreling into the station this afternoon, and spent some not-so-quiet time with Bradford. Seems there was some discussion, of the rather loud sort, as to why you were put on the street with the catnapper still on the loose."

"Is that so?"

"Well, that's what I hear." Malone stepped on to the cement landing, then paused. "So, I wouldn't get too accustomed to sleeping in, or anything."

Malone was right. Marcus's phone rang at seven on the dot the following morning. He responded with a groan.

He hadn't slept well at all. After Malone left, Marcus had gone back to the kitchen to explain to Zoe why he'd let himself into her apartment. She had reassured him that she understood his motives, then suggested the three of them have some hot chocolate to soothe their nerves before turning in for the night.

Which was exactly what they did. After accompanying Zoe to her door, Marcus had followed Callie up to her room, where they'd shared another good-night kiss. This one had been much more subdued than the earlier one, primarily due to the fact that Callie was holding Kismet in her arms.

Still, Marcus hadn't come away from the kiss unaffected. In fact, it only seemed to whet his appetite further, an appetite that led to dreams of a rather erotic nature, featuring the long slender legs of Callie Chance tangling with his as they made love in his bed.

The shrill ring of the phone brought him out of that dream. Marcus fought the sheets wrapped tightly around the lower half of his body as he rolled toward his nightstand and lifted the receiver.

"Scanlon," a male voice barked. "I have a badge, a gun and a cell phone sitting on my desk. You be here in one hour, and they're yours."

Before Marcus had a chance to reply, he was listening to a dial tone.

"Good morning to you, too, Captain," Marcus muttered. As he replaced the receiver, he kicked the twisted sheets from his legs, rose and dressed in record time. He considered running up to Callie's to explain that he wouldn't be able to help her shop today. But when he recalled how weary she'd looked as she turned to enter her room the night before, he took a detour to the kitchen, penned her a quick note, then hurried down to the garage.

Not much later, Callie was fighting off another yawning fit as she entered the kitchen. Her feet were still a little sore from all the walking she'd done the day before, her legs slightly stiff, but she'd allowed herself to sleep in, so she felt rested, if a little lazy. As she shuffled toward the coffee maker, she spied a folded sheet of paper on the table with her name printed on it.

"Well, I am glad to see you have found something to smile about."

Zoe's bright words made Callie look up from Marcus's note, and blush. Folding the slip of paper in half again, she shoved it into her back pocket.

"Marcus has been called back to work," she said.

"Of course." Zoe grabbed the bag of fresh coffee beans Callie had purchased the day before and began measuring them into the grinder. "His boss may be a fool, but he is not an idiot."

As if to punctuate her words, Zoe pressed the on button. When the machine was once again silent, she asked if Callie would need any assistance preparing the food.

"No. I'm going to pick up the rest of my supplies today, then get started. Most of the things I'm preparing can be made ahead of time and refrigerated. I *am* going to pretty much take over the kitchen for the next two days, however."

"Well, that's no problem at all. Tomorrow night I dine with my friend Ruby. And tonight I am to attend the auction of Giuseppe's art glass over in Oakland. So, the kitchen is all yours. In fact, because the auction may not be over until late, I've arranged to stay in a hotel. Tonight, then, the entire place will be at your disposal. And Marcus's, of course."

Of course.

Callie managed to keep her thoughts off the possibilities that could arise from this situation as she went about her shopping. Once she returned, with Zoe's little wheeled cart filled to nearly overflowing, she took on the challenge of organizing the refrigerator. Once she'd freed up all but the top shelf, she arranged the ingredients she'd bought yesterday with today's finds.

When she got to the last bag and saw the cans of cat food and the cat toy at the bottom, she shook her head. In her rush to get the food refrigerated, it had once again slipped her mind that she had taken on a new and important responsibility.

Upon entering her apartment, Kismet greeted Callie with much more enthusiasm than Callie felt she deserved.

"Miss me?" Callie knelt in front of the animal. Kismet responded with something that sounded like a chirp, then came forward to butt Callie's hand with her head.

Callie gave the cat a thorough and gentle ear rub, then picked Kismet up and grabbed the cat bed. "I have a ton of work to do," Callie confided as she carried the cat down the stairs. "But I don't want you to feel neglected. So, I'm going to let you stay with me, if you promise to stay on the floor, and away from the food."

She had already fed Kismet first thing that morning, but

after shutting the door to the kitchen, she placed the cat in front of a bowl filled with canned food, hoping that once she had satisfied any lingering hunger pangs, Kismet wouldn't be quite so interested in the food for the party.

And it seemed to work. Kismet chased the tiny plastic mouse Callie had purchased that morning, then curled herself into the pink bed and snoozed while Callie washed her hands and got down to business.

After much chopping of various fresh herbs, she pitted the olives she'd purchased the day before, then blended them in the food processor with the olive oil and anchovies. The resulting tapenade would keep for several days in the fridge and transport easily to Pia's house on the day of the wine fest. There it would be a simple matter of spreading it onto rounds of sourdough bread, then artfully arranging them on one of Pia's lovely serving platters. The same could be said for the goat cheese and herbs, which she mashed together.

The rest of the afternoon, Callie kept the food processor busy, blending several different cream cheese mixtures which would eventually be stuffed into or sit atop a wide array of vegetables, crackers and toast squares. The grinding noise seemed to have very little effect on Kismet, for the cat was still snoozing by the time all the chopping, snipping and mixing was done.

It was past six o'clock by the time Callie was finished with everything she'd scheduled for her first day's work. With airtight plastic storage containers filling one entire shelf of the refrigerator, the kitchen was once again a place of order.

And Callie was hungry.

Far too tired to fix any sort of a meal, she walked over to the wall phone and reached for the list of take-out places Zoe had pointed out on her get-acquainted tour of the room. She'd just decided that Chinese sounded good, when she heard the front door open.

A little nervous after last night's uninvited visitor to her room, she froze where she stood, barely breathing as the door clicked shut again. Marcus, she thought as she heard the sound of heavy footsteps on the foyer floor. She was sure it was Marcus, she told herself as the footsteps started down the hallway toward the kitchen. It *had* to be Marcus.

It was.

When Marcus rounded the doorway into the room, Callie released a huge sigh. And when she saw the brown bag cradled in his left arm, she squealed with delight.

"Happy to see me?" he asked. "Or are you just hungry?"

"Both," Callie replied as she walked over to peek into the large brown bag he carried. Eyeing the top layer of white cartons, she breathed in the scent of soy and rice.

"Do you like Chinese?"

"You won't believe this, but I was just about to order some."

"Hey. Maybe I do have some mind-reading talent, after all. Let me guess. Now you're thinking, *We can have a picnic under the stars.* Am I right?"

Actually, no. But Marcus made it clear that this was his plan.

"I thought we could eat on my balcony. But first," he glanced toward the cat, who had left her bed to stand by Callie "I have a peace offering for someone."

As he spoke, he reached into his jacket pocket and drew out something red that looked like a stuffed fish.

"It's a catnip toy. Think she'll like it?"

Callie shrugged. "Let's take her to my room, and we'll find out."

Up in Callie's studio, she placed the cat on the floor and Marcus bent forward to offer the toy. Kismet lifted her nose slowly to sniff daintily, then pounced, tearing it from Marcus's fingers. Falling to the ground on her side, the cat writhed in mindless ecstasy as she pawed the toy.

"Yeah. I'd say she likes it." Callie turned to Marcus. "My turn now? I won't promise to react quite as strongly, but I *do* like Chinese."

Callie fought a moment of nervousness as she stepped into Marcus's apartment, a feeling that trembled in her stomach as he led her through the living room, then past the massive four-poster bed to his balcony.

The balcony projected only three feet from the wall, just enough to allow the French doors to open. Marcus lit a large candle atop a wrought iron stand in the left corner, then spread a thick sleeping bag and several blankets to pad the slats of iron that formed the floor. Telling Callie to make herself comfortable, he disappeared. When he returned, he carried a tray that held a steaming pot and two tea cups, which he placed on the blankets, along with the cartons of food and two sets of chopsticks.

Sitting on either side of the tray, they ate in silence until Callie asked, "Make any progress on the catnapping today?"

Marcus shrugged. "Not exactly progress, but I have some new stuff to work with. The final results of the forensics workup from the motel room finally came back. It seems that the "big hair" you recalled seeing on the woman was a wig. I have a list of manufacturers that use that particular blend of synthetics in their wigs, and tomorrow we should know which places in town carry these. While I'm working on that, Malone will continue to investigate last night's break-in. The grappling hook and rope were brand-new. He's going to see if he can track down whoever purchased them."

"Sounds like frustrating work."

Marcus's noodle-filled chopsticks hovered above the carton as he gave her a half grin. "It can be. A lot of what we do ends up being a waste of time and the taxpayers' money. But, believe me, it's all worth it when the effort pans out. And with a little bit of luck, I think it will on this one."

Callie swallowed her sip of tea. "Luck? Did I just hear Marcus Scanlon, skeptic extraordinaire, use the word *luck?*"

Marcus pinched a shrimp with his chopsticks, took a bite and gave her a cockeyed grin as he chewed.

The day's heat radiated off the stucco walls and blended with a soft breeze from the bay as they finished their meal. The silence that fell after the white boxes were empty was soothing. So soothing, that when Marcus removed the tray, Callie turned to lie on her back, her feet stretching into the room.

She felt the day catching up with her, tugging her toward

sleep. When the scent of freshly brewed coffee opened her eyes, she continued to lie there, gazing at the night sky until she heard Marcus approach.

"You take cream, don't you?"

Callie sat up as Marcus placed the tray between them again. The flickering candle in the corner glinted off matching black mugs. Callie nodded in reply to his question and reached for the small white pitcher in the center of the tray, sitting next to a small rectangular box. The box was brown, and as she glanced at it, the candlelight picked out the embossed word, Ghiardelli.

As in, chocolate.

"Marcus," Callie said, as she slowly pulled her hand back from the tray. "You know that I—"

"That you're afraid of chocolate."

"No." Her gaze met his. "I am not *afraid,* I—"

"Oh, right. You have an *aversion* to chocolate."

He grinned. She frowned.

"Knowing this, you bring it out as our dessert course, because?"

"It's my attempt at aversion therapy. You see—" one side of his mouth rose in a wry grimace "—I really like the stuff. And I hate to think of you missing out on something so great. I figured if you were brave enough to get a cat, it was time to prove you can eat chocolate without upsetting the balance of good and bad luck. *Not—*" he held up his hand to stop her from speaking "—that I believe in all that, of course."

Callie stared at him for several moments. "Why don't you?"

One dark eye squinted at her. "Why don't I what?"

"Believe in luck."

Watching closely, Callie saw Marcus glance away, his features suddenly tight. She was just about to tell him to forget she'd asked, when his gaze met hers again.

"I'll tell you," he said. "*After* you eat one piece of chocolate."

He reached for the box as he finished speaking, opened it,

then offered it to her slowly, as if it contained the world's most valuable treasure.

The scent reached Callie before she saw the contents. She braced herself for the feeling of dread that normally accompanied that smell. Instead she found herself drawing in the rich, sweet fragrance, and feeling suddenly languorous and just slightly giddy.

It had been so long.

The box, with its neat rows of brown squares, half creamy and warm, the other half dark and shiny, wafted toward her as if borne on the air. But she knew that was not the case, knew that she was being tempted by the devil himself.

"Damn you, Marcus Scanlon."

With these words, Callie grabbed the package from his hand. Taking a deep breath, she fingered out one square of dark chocolate then popped it into her mouth.

It melted slowly into her taste buds with such sweetness, that Callie had to fight the moan clawing up her throat. She held the sinful warmth in her mouth until it liquefied, then swallowed slowly.

When she let her eyelids drift open, she found Marcus's dark eyes staring at her. She dropped her gaze, then primly set the box on the tray.

Strong, lean fingers trapped hers as Marcus groaned, "Do that again."

Callie looked up to meet his slightly dazed expression. "After you tell me why you don't believe in luck."

Marcus stared at Callie, sensing a now-or-never moment. Lifting the tray, he set it to one side as he organized his thoughts, then turned to her with a sigh.

"Actually, at one time I believed that I was the luckiest man on the face of the earth. I had my future with Miranda and the family business and a house with a picket fence all lined up. Then everything fell apart. When I tried to figure out where I had gone wrong, I realized my belief in luck had blinded me to what had really been going on. I decided that I couldn't let that ever happen again, especially once I became a cop. After all, a guy could get killed relying on luck. Rather logical, don't you think?''

Marcus watched Callie carefully. When the light faded from her eyes and she nodded, he spoke again.

"There was just one thing wrong with all of this. I not only stopped believing in luck, but in anything else. I didn't realize, until just a few days ago, how empty my life had become. Until you stepped into it, looking like a half-drowned kitten.''

Callie's eyes widened as he paused. As her lips began to curve ever so slightly, Marcus reached across to cup her cheek in his hand.

"I'm ready to believe in luck now," he said as he leaned toward her. "And in love.''

Marcus kissed Callie before she could say a word.

He didn't want to tell her he loved her, he wanted to show her. Show her that the two of them could overcome her so-called jinx. So he deepened his kiss, sliding his tongue into her mouth to mate with hers and savor the lingering flavor of chocolate.

Callie was leaning into the kiss, gripping his shoulders to pull herself closer. Wrapping his arms around her, Marcus pulled her with him as he leaned back, holding her tightly until her body was stretched out atop his.

Her legs tangled with his. As they strained against each other, they rolled to the left, until they lay on their sides, still kissing, hands tugging at clothing between caresses. Marcus's body grew tight with desire, ached with need. Callie's soft moan, and the feel of her body arching against his, spoke to him, told him she wanted this as badly as he did. But he needed to be sure that she was sure.

Gently drawing his lips from Callie's, he looked down into her eyes. "Callie. Tell me now if you want me to stop.''

A blend of pale green and blue lights glittered in her eyes as she gazed up at him. After several heart-pounding seconds, she shook her head. "No. I don't want to stop. But...''

She hesitated. Marcus's pounding heart thudded to a stop

as he watched her blush in the candlelight, waiting for her to continue.

"I'm taking the pill," she said finally. "But—"

"We should have more protection," Marcus finished.

When she nodded, he released a sigh of relief and pushed himself up, saying, "I'll get that right now."

When Callie started to follow him, he nudged her back onto the blankets. "Stay where you are. Considering our track record, I don't see any point in moving to the bed. We'll only end up on the floor, anyway."

She smiled at this. She was still smiling, Marcus saw, when he returned with his foil packets, to lie next to her beneath the stars. It was an irresistible smile, one that demanded to be captured. And as he kissed her, held her, pulled her body to his, Marcus felt the joy from that smile enter him, and fill all the empty spaces.

A desire to do the same for Callie fueled his physical passion, tempered each long, deep kiss, every hungry, gentle caress. As clothes brushed away, Marcus held himself in check, slowly, slowly moving against her, until she told him with her body that she was ready to receive him.

Chapter 15

Callie sighed as Marcus entered her, sighed with pleasure, with pure joy. The joy and the pleasure filled each and every corner of her body, her mind and her spirit as she answered the thrust of his love, rising to meet him, glorying in each second of joining, breath coming in short, hot gasps, blending with his ragged gasps, her pleasure climbing and climbing to peak in a burst of physical and soul-shattering wonder.

As the sweet waves rippled through her, Callie felt Marcus join her, smiled as he groaned his bliss against her mouth, then held him tightly as his lips trailed along her cheek. His hot, shuddering breaths tickled her ear. A giggle bubbled in her throat.

Marcus rose on his elbows to look down at her. Callie saw that one eyebrow was cocked, his eyes glinting and narrowed.

"Laughing, are you?"

Callie started to shake her head, but she was already grinning widely, and another giggle escaped before she could reply. "I do that when I'm happy. And satisfied."

Marcus stared at her for several moments before raising the other eyebrow and smiling. "Satisfied, are you? Then I suppose you wouldn't—'' he lowered his head toward hers as he spoke ''—be interested in a little more of this.''

The kiss that followed started as a gentle, tender nibble, which built to a soul-deep meeting of lips and tongues, hearts and souls. They finally did end up in his bed, where they made love once more, then fell asleep in each other's arms.

The following morning, Marcus's alarm woke them early enough to repeat the night's pleasures once again before they both had to move into their day.

Callie's was spent in the kitchen again. Zoe arrived home about noon, and made Callie stop to eat some lunch. Callie played with Kismet for a while, and when the cat curled up for a nap, she resumed work until six, when Marcus arrived back at the house, frowning and all business.

''Where's Zoe?''

Callie looked up from the sink, where she was washing out the food processor.

''At her friend Ruby's. Having dinner. Is something wrong?''

The tiny, ever-so-slight note of fear in Callie's voice brought Marcus up short. Looking into her eyes, he saw a combination of emotions, joy at seeing him, shadowed by a hint of morning-after nerves. He crossed the room in four steps to take her into his arms, ignoring the wet hands that dripped soap onto the floor as he pulled her into a long, warm kiss.

''No,'' he said softly as he released her. ''Nothing's wrong. Except that I finally figured out what puzzle piece I've been missing. I think you might have it, but I need Zoe to help me get it from you.''

Callie's completely confused expression made Marcus shake his head and laugh. ''I'm sorry. I'm not making much sense. You're something of a distraction, you know.''

''Oh, really?'' Callie said. Smiling as she slid from his arms, she turned back to the sink and returned to her washing up. ''Does this make it easier for you to think?''

Marcus gave her a half smile. ''It'll do. Anyway, that missing puzzle piece I was babbling about? It's the license plate of the car that almost ran you over. I was so intent on getting Zoe to extract a description of the man and the woman from the motel when she hypnotized you the first time, I completely forgot that I'd suspected the driver of that car might have been one of our catnappers.

"So—" he reached over, placed his fingers beneath Callie's chin and tilted her face up so he could look into her eyes "—would you mind being mesmerized again?"

"Like last night?"

Callie's slow smile awoke a warm curling sensation low in Marcus's belly. Before he could lean in for a kiss, Callie spoke.

"I'm totally comfortable with Zoe hypnotizing me when she gets home. In the meantime, have you eaten dinner?"

As Marcus shook his head, his stomach rumbled softly. Callie grinned.

"Perfect. I'd like you to sample some of the stuff I made today and see what you think."

Marcus devoured Callie's offerings. He particularly enjoyed the California roll, consisting of strips of crab and avocado encased in Japanese rice, wrapped in seaweed then sliced into rounds. But the thin cuts of ham spread with herbed cream cheese and rolled tightly around a slender bundle of chives were quite tasty, as were the tiny tomatoes stuffed with cream cheese and the cucumber cups filled with a crab mixture.

Zoe came in the front door just as he finished helping Callie wash up from their little morsel meal. Marcus frowned as he broached the subject of hypnotizing Callie. "You look tired," he told Zoe. "It can wait until tomorrow morning, if that would be better for you."

After a moment's hesitation, Zoe nodded. "The last couple of nights have been rather late for me. Callie should get to bed early, also. She needs to be rested and relaxed for tomorrow."

With that, the woman bade Callie and Marcus good-night

and started up the stairs. When he heard her door click shut, Marcus turned to Callie.

"Need some relaxing, do you?"

A warm pink blush accompanied her tiny smile. Grabbing her hand, he tugged her toward the door.

"Wait," she said as she tugged back. "I need to get Kismet."

Marcus followed her gaze and saw the cat, snoozing in her bed in the corner. "Some detective *I* am. I didn't even see her there. Has she moved at all since I came in?"

Callie shook her head. "Zoe had her up to her place, playing with Victor and Hugo much of the day. I think she's all worn-out. I'll take her up to my room."

"And I'll meet you there. I have to pick up some things that, I hope, will make for a most *relaxing* evening."

His plan started off with a warm bubble bath, which Marcus insisted on running for Callie. She made her own contribution, adding a few drops of sandalwood and lilac oil. As she rested in the huge tubful of scented water, Marcus knelt behind her, slowly kneading the muscles in her shoulders, grinning at the soft moans of pleasure his ministrations elicited from Callie's smiling lips.

As the scent of oils rose to perfume the air and the bubbles dwindled to reveal more and more of Callie's wet curves, Marcus decided that he needed some relaxing of his own. It took him only moments to remove his clothes and join Callie. Soon both of them were thoroughly relaxed, falling into a tangle of naked arms and legs to sleep in Callie's bed.

Kismet woke them in the morning, jumping from the foot of the bed into the tiny space between their bodies. When Marcus opened his eyes, he found the cat staring at him placidly. Telling himself that neither he nor Callie had time that morning to make love again, he forgave the cat for her protective stance, rolled out of bed, and pulled on his rumpled clothes. After waking Callie and reminding her of her hypnosis date, he descended quietly to his room to shower and dress for the day.

Callie hurried through her own shower, and threw on jeans

and a pink T-shirt. She packed the white shirt and black trousers that would be her catering uniform for the day, along with her black bow tie, in her large purse. Praying that Pia had arranged for help in keeping the platters filled, as promised, she hurried down the stairs to Zoe's office.

In spite of her keyed-up nerves, she felt the now-familiar melting flow into her muscles and mind as she listened to Zoe's soothing voice. It seemed like only seconds before Zoe was telling her to awake, refreshed and energized.

As soon as she opened her eyes, she saw Marcus grinning at her. "Got what I needed," he said. "Six out of the seven license plate numbers, anyway. By noon today I might have a catnapper or two. Good luck at Pia's."

Leaving Callie blinking at his use of the word "luck," he was out the door, and she was rising from her chair to call Raj.

The cab driver had agreed to transport her food to Pia's. The chilled trays of prepared appetizers fit nicely in the large trunk, atop the box that held the plastic containers filled with mixtures that Callie would spread onto vegetables, breads and crackers. She'd arranged for fresh baguettes to be delivered directly to Pia's, as she had with the crab and shrimp, and was pleased to find that everything was there when she arrived.

After paying Raj for delivering her and her food, she went to work, slicing bread and toasting buttered rounds in Pia's large oven for the tapenade and goat cheese spreads. As she assembled the trays of food, Pia ran about in a bright pink caftan, supervising the placement of tables on the flagstone patio just outside the large room off the kitchen and beneath the large white-and-green striped awning that had been brought in for the late afternoon affair.

Callie and the man in charge of the wine servers were in the middle of determining which combinations of food and wine would go on which table, when Pia entered the tented area. Behind her a line of people trooped down the three stairs leading to the patio, carrying large plastic boxes.

"I have a separate little tent set up just past this one. These cages go on the table on the right,'' Pia was saying, waving red-tipped fingers toward a table draped to the floor in white linen.

She turned to Callie. "That will keep the animals away from the food, and yet shelter them from the sun. Or the rain. The weather doesn't seem to want to make up its mind today, does it?''

No, it didn't. It had been sunny when Callie left that morning, but Raj's radio had been tuned to the news, which had mentioned possible afternoon thunderstorms. At Pia's words, she looked up to see that the blue sky was now dotted with several large gray clouds.

But Callie was more concerned with her mention of animals. Standing to one side, Callie stared at the containers that were being carried past. When she saw the furry animals behind the wire mesh on the front, she realized that the plastic "boxes" were cat carriers like the one she'd brought Kismet home in.

"Pia," she said slowly. "What are these? And don't tell me they're cats. I can see that. What are they doing here?''

The woman blinked at Callie. "Why, they're from the shelter, of course. Greg Laramie thought it would be a good idea to have some of the animals on display. With all the cat lovers who will be here today, at least *some* of these little guys might get a home. No, no, my dears!'' This was directed to two of the cat-cage bearers who'd headed for a second table under the separate awning. "All the visitors go on the right only.''

Turning to Callie, Pia continued. "Mr. Laramie has asked several of our more distinguished guests to bring their cats. He'll be giving these people special awards for the generous way they've contributed to his organization, and he wants to give them a chance to show off their blue-blooded animals. Oh dear. That reminds me. He told me to be sure to have you bring your cat.''

"Mine?''

"Yes. Apparently you recently obtained an animal from his shelter? Well, he wants to use you and your pet as an example of a successful adoption, hoping to get others in the mood to take home one of the orphans.''

"That's a lovely idea, but..." Callie shook her head. "I can't go home and get Kismet now. I barely have enough time to get all—''

"Don't worry, my dear," Pia interrupted. "I'll call Zoe, and have her bring your little kitty with her. And as for the time, I'm sure everything will be ready before the guests arrive."

Amazingly, two hours later, everything was ready. Nestled among the soft yellow flower arrangements Pia had ordered and surrounding bottles of wine, Callie's food was being oohed and aahed over by the arriving guests.

Standing to one side, Callie watched the formally garbed crowd mill about, filling their plates as a tuxedoed server at each table poured their wine. Pia had just stepped up, exclaiming over the good turnout, when Greg Laramie shouldered his way over. The cat cage he cradled in his arms looked somewhat out of place with his tuxedo and white gloves.

"Thought if I'm going to play master of ceremonies, I should look the part," he said. "And I brought along one more orphan. Where can I put her?"

When Pia started to motion for one of the wine servers, Laramie shook his head. "Don't bother him—just point me in the right direction."

Callie watched the man go. As his ponytail disappeared into the crowd, she decided to follow and check on Kismet. When Callie reached the "guests of honor" cages, she didn't see any sign of Laramie or the new addition for the adoptee table. Figuring he'd been stopped by a member of the crowd, she walked past the enclosures that held Dr. Ramos's white Fluffums, Mrs. Adams's rather vocal Burmese, an adorable Scottish fold named MacDougal, a tawny Abyssinian called Cleo, and a beautiful gray cat belonging to Gerald Harding.

This was another Russian Blue, one of the missing Electra's offspring, named Jinx. Zoe had arrived with Kismet shortly before Harding stepped up to place his animal's cage on the table next to hers. Callie had fought off a shudder at the name. As the man turned to walk away, completely ignoring the animal's plaintive, lonely cry, Callie's misgivings became anger. Before she could stop herself she'd asked, "Is that how you treat *all* your cats?"

When Harding turned to her, his gray eyes narrowed, she'd finished, "Or do you pay some attention to the ones who win blue ribbons?"

After staring at her a moment, he'd had the decency to turn to the cage and speak in a soft tone to his animal for a moment before walking away without a second glance at Callie.

He was nowhere in sight now as Callie peeked in to see Jinx curled up in the front of his cage, sleeping. When she moved to Kismet's carrier, however, emerald eyes glowed wide from the rear of the enclosure, where the cat crouched, ears flat.

"Too many people for you?" she crooned. "Well, don't worry. No one will hurt you. Here. Will this make you feel better?"

Callie drew several chunks of cracked crab from her pocket, then stuffed them between the openings in the wire. After Kismet unwound from her tight ball, stepped forward and began to eat, Callie bade her pet a reluctant goodbye.

Crossing the tented enclosure, she checked the status of the food trays as she wove between the chatting guests. Several items were already in need of refilling. Hurrying to the kitchen, she pulled prepared morsels from the fridge, placed them on a serving dish, and returned to the tables.

"This is truly lovely," a voice said from Callie's right. "You've done a great job. This spread is every bit as good as Monique's."

Looking up to respond to the compliment, Callie found herself looking into Sunny Johnson's large brown eyes. Callie's lips froze into the smile she'd already started to form. She replied, "Thank you," before turning away with the empty platter.

Holding her breath, Callie walked quickly toward the kitchen, hoping Dave hadn't seen his wife talking to her and leapt to any conclusion. She'd caught him frowning at her earlier as she searched for trays that needed replenishing. The expression in his light eyes had chilled her to the bone.

As she returned with the last plate of crab legs, Callie found Greg Laramie at the center of the tent, halfway through a speech thanking everyone for their donations. As Callie placed the food on the table, the man began handing out awards to people he called "special contributors."

Callie was called up last. After Laramie explained about her recent adoption, he handed her a small gold charm in the shape of a cat. When she glanced at the crowd to acknowledge the polite applause, her eyes met Dave's. A dark scowl marked the features she'd once found so handsome.

Pia stepped forward as the surrounding crowd turned back to their conversations. "Callie, dear, I just heard some thunder. I think it would be a good idea to put the dessert things out now."

In the kitchen Callie asked the young men who'd been pouring the wine to carry the two large coffee servers, one filled with regular brew and the other decaf, out to the dessert table, located near the "cats of honor."

Callie followed to the soft rumble of thunder, carrying two trays of petits fours and various fruits dipped in chocolate, resting in individual fluted paper cups. As she approached the table, she noticed Dave, wine glass in hand, standing in front of Kismet's cage, glowering at her. Shaking off a chill, she set the platters in position, then stepped back slowly to check on the placement.

A tap on her shoulder jerked Callie around. It was Sunny Johnson, looking puzzled and angry as she said, "I finally figured out where I've seen you."

Callie opened her mouth to insist that it *must* have been in Soho, but before she could say a word, someone shouted, "Hey. Get away from that!"

The voice was familiar. Callie turned toward the house. Atop the steps leading to the patio, a pair of uniformed officers flanked a redhead in a pink smock. Three men in suits stood in front of them. Two of them were Marcus and Malone.

A low, ominous roll accompanied Marcus as he descended the short flight of stairs, scowling across the tented pavilion. Callie turned to follow his line of sight, and saw that Dave now had his hand on the latch to Kismet's cage.

The next few moments blurred as the cage door flew open and Dave bent forward like the fullback he'd once been, angling his shoulder toward Marcus's stomach. Marcus managed to block the blow. A black streak flew between the two men as Marcus dodged Dave's widely swinging fist, then came back with a left hook that threw the blond man against the table holding the prized cats.

Another clap of thunder matched the crash of the table as it fell backwards. Cats yowled and screeched, and moments later, similar sounds filled the crowd as three of the animals escaped cage doors that had sprung open in their fall, then snaked through the forest of legs. More tables toppled, women screamed and men shouted. The air was filled with noise, flying food and wine as cats raced by and owners tried to catch them.

Callie felt as if she were standing in the eye of a hurricane, turning around and around, watching as a tuxedoed man managed to grab Fluffums, and a blond woman in gold lamé snagged Tiki, then held the spitting animal at arm's length, cooing to the cat as she tried to avoid flailing claws.

When some semblance of order slowly returned, only Kismet was unaccounted for. Callie started toward the direction she'd last seen the animal, only to have Marcus's voice stop her.

"She's over here, Callie."

Callie turned to see that the "distinguished cats" table had been righted. On it sat two cages. One held the Russian blue, Jinx. His beautiful fur still ridged along his back, his emerald eyes stared wild and wide. In the other cage, eyes of exactly the same green stared out of a coal-black face.

Kismet. Callie frowned. She'd definitely seen the animal escape. Rushing forward, she wondered if someone had captured Kismet in all the confusion, and returned her to her carrier.

Gerald Harding stepped in front of her to block her path. "That's not your cat," he said. "It's mine. It's Electra."

"No, it isn't," she protested.

"Yes, it is."

Callie turned to find Greg Laramie looking at her, shoulders slumped forward. Behind him stood Rick Malone. A soft *click* drew her attention to the fact that Laramie's gloved hands had just been cuffed behind his back.

The man's eyes shifted to Harding's. "We had to give Electra a little dye bath. As my message said, though, the cat hasn't been harmed in any way. Her fur will grow out in a month or so, as beautiful as ever."

"A lot of good that will do me," Harding growled. "It won't be in time for the show. You've cost me a grand champion, and you're going to pay for this. But first you're going to explain—"

"Not here," Malone interrupted. "At the station. Detective Scanlon will be glad to escort you."

"Detective Scanlon is going to be in cuffs himself," a muffled voice said.

Dave Johnson stepped forward, his hand covering the lower part of his face. Blood seeped through his fingers as he turned to the third suited man. "Bradford, your man accosted me without any provocation. I demand you arrest him."

Marcus moved behind the man, handcuffs at the ready. "I had plenty of provocation. Johnson, you are under arrest for—"

"Hold it," Bradford barked. "We're not going to settle any of this here."

Turning to the two uniformed officers, the captain ordered both Marcus and Dave to be placed in custody.

Callie watched as Bradford waved Harding to join him, then led the parade of cuffed men up the stairs. At the top, Marcus paused to look back and give her a smile she assumed was meant to be reassuring.

But when she looked at the wreckage around her, the food on the cement, the torn dresses and ripped nylons, the wine-stained shirts, the tent poles leaning toward the center to leak the rain that had just begun to fall, she knew she'd been living in a dream.

She was, and always would be, a jinx.

Chapter 16

Marcus's stomach tightened as he pulled into the garage.

It wasn't bad enough that dealing with Dave Johnson, Greg Laramie, both of their wives and their lawyers, not to mention Gerald Harding, had gone on endlessly. But here he was, ready to tell Callie and Zoe how the case had been solved, who had done what and why, and there didn't appear to be one damn light on in the entire house.

Granted, it was almost eleven-thirty. He knew that Zoe rarely allowed anything to interfere with her ten o'clock bed time. But Callie, Marcus thought as he unlocked the front door, he would have expected her to be sitting on the doorstep, dying to hear all the details, no matter how tired she might be.

The entire time he'd been asking and answering questions, then filling out form after form, a portion of his mind had been worrying about her. He kept picturing the confused and resigned expression on her face as he was led away in handcuffs.

The resigned part had concerned him the most, he decided as he unlocked the front door. It reminded him of the expression he'd seen in her eyes that very first night they'd met, as she surveyed the devastation around her, accepting total blame for everything that had happened.

More than once, he'd reached for the telephone to call her. But each time, a suspect had demanded to be released, a lawyer had insisted on an interview, or the chief of police had called for an explanation. Just as well, Marcus told himself. What he had to say would be best said face-to-face. And it would be said tonight.

After he made one little stop.

Marcus quietly opened his door, then walked to the ornately carved desk in his living area. It was the first piece of furniture produced by Scanlon's Fine Furnishing, made entirely by his father's hands. It was the only thing he had left of his father, and inside the top right hand drawer rested a faded velvet box that held the only possession he had of his mother's.

Putting the box in his jacket pocket, Marcus turned, closed his door softly behind him, then walked up the final flight of stairs to Callie's room. A faint streak of light outlined the space between the door frame and the not-quite-shut door, but the apartment beyond was silent.

The situation felt suddenly all too familiar. The dark house and the silence reminded him of the recent break-in, putting Marcus's instincts on immediate cop alert. Hurrying up the last few steps, he told himself that the man who'd broken into Callie's room was now in jail. Still, he didn't hesitate when he reached the door. Hand inside his jacket, flipping the snap on his holster, he slowly pushed the door inward, eyes scanning the room as the swinging door revealed each corner.

The white curtain had been pushed to one side, so he could see that the bath area was empty. As the door swung past the bed, he found the source of the light. An iron-and-glass wall sconce cast a soft glow onto the large cardboard box on the floor in front of the bed, and another, smaller one next to it. The powder blue spread was littered with various items of clothing, books and several tissue-wrapped bundles.

Marcus scowled at these, and at the possible import of their presence, before continuing his inspection.

By the time the door had finished its half-circle, coming to rest against the wall to his left, Marcus had ascertained that not one soul was in the room. The balcony, however, was another matter. Through the gauzy curtains, he could just make out a tall, slender shadow standing at the railing. Walking quietly, he pushed the filmy fabric aside and softly called her name.

Not softly enough, apparently, for Callie started. Marcus grabbed her arm as she turned toward him.

"What's going on?" he asked.

Callie's eyes glittered as she gave him a bright smile. "Nothing," she replied. "Just looking at the moon."

Marcus let his gaze slide skyward, where sure enough, a huge round ball of silver hovered above the Golden Gate Bridge. The perfect romantic setting for what he had in mind.

Or it would be, if he hadn't seen the box on the floor and things waiting to be packed into it. He turned back to Callie. She was still smiling, that wide, beautiful smile he'd come to recognize as her armor.

"Well," she said. "I see that you're no longer in handcuffs. Does that mean that Dave's charges against you didn't stick, or are you just out on bail?"

She stepped into the room as she spoke. Marcus followed her. When she turned to him, her eyes were bright with interest. Too bright. He had an idea what was going on behind those eyes, of the effort she was making to pretend her inquiries were lighthearted and casual, but he knew her too well by now, knew she was hurting. He thought he knew why, was tempted to call her on the cause right now, but decided that could perhaps be avoided if she knew what had led up to that debacle at Pia's.

"The man didn't have a leg to stand on," he replied. "And because I'm a decent guy, I didn't add resisting arrest to his indictment."

Callie shook her head. "His *indictment.* I'm confused. Are you telling me that Dave was involved with the catnapping?"

"No. He's facing charges of felony hit-and-run. We traced those license plate numbers you gave us to his wife's car. When he realized you'd seen him greet his wife and child that first day, he called Raj's cab company and learned what motel you'd gone to."

"Then he tried to kill me?"

Marcus took in her stunned expression, and gentled his tone. "No. He hadn't planned on hitting you, just coming close enough to make you question your luck, so that you'd go running back to the safety of Cape Cod. When you showed up at his father-in-law's gallery, he decided to take things further, snatching Zoe's purse and arranging for the telephones to be shut off. He said he thought you'd freak out when three bad things happened."

Callie seemed to be staring at the tie he'd loosened sometime during the evening's interrogations. Her eyes narrowed as she sighed.

"And he decided to let Kismet out because he saw Sunny talking to me and wanted to keep me from telling his wife why I'd showed up on their doorstep."

"You got it. Except the cat he released wasn't Kismet."

Marcus waited until Callie's eyes met his, then continued, "Laramie had brought another black cat with him. He'd stashed its carrier under the table, then switched the cages at some point during the party. This would put Kismet—I mean Electra—under the table, where Harding had been told she'd be."

"So Harding knew I had Electra?"

"No, he just knew where he was supposed to find his cat. Laramie had E-mailed a message to Harding, telling the man to wire the ransom money over the Internet to a certain account. As soon as the money cleared, Harding would receive another E-mail with directions for recovering his cat."

"And Harding went along with this?"

Marcus shrugged. "He wanted that grand champion ribbon. Besides, he figured once he got the cat, he'd have us trace the E-mail and the bank deposit. Laramie had all that figured out, however. There's more to his wife than dye jobs and wigs. She's apparently an accomplished hacker.''

''Dye jobs?''

Callie's puzzled look brought a reluctant grin from Marcus. ''Do you remember me telling you I was going to check out places that carried the brand of wig worn by the female kitty-snatcher? Well, at two o'clock this afternoon, Malone and I walked into a beauty salon on Fillmore Street and asked for the owner. A redhead came to the desk. It took us all of two seconds to recognize the woman in Wong's sketch, then arrest Felicia Laramie, wife of Greg. I knew her husband was at Pia's, so we called for uniformed backup. That's where Bradford came in. Knowing that Harding would be at this function, he wanted to be along to get some of the credit.''

Callie nodded slowly, but her frown deepened. ''As you walked away, I thought I heard Malone say something to Laramie about breaking and entering.''

''Yep. On the way to the wine fest, we were called with the make on the license plate of the car that hit you, along with the owner of the prints lifted from your balcony. Seems that Laramie was arrested when he was eighteen on a minor breaking-and-entering charge.''

Callie's arms crossed tightly around her body. ''And he broke into my room to get Kismet, who is really Harding's Electra?''

''Yes,'' Marcus replied gently. ''Laramie's wife is so allergic to cats that they decided to dye the animal black so no one would recognize her as the famous stolen cat, and keep her at the shelter. When I flashed my badge the day you were trying to adopt the cat, Laramie was afraid I'd get suspicious. He let you take her, figuring he could break in and carry her out in a bag strapped to his back. The cat bit him when he tried stuffing her into the backpack.''

Callie's lips twitched slightly at this, but Marcus saw her blink and look down. Watching as she bent toward something on the ground, he went on, ''With the blood and prints, we'll be able to put him in jail for attempted robbery, even if Harding refuses to press charges on the catnapping.''

Callie stood, gripping something in her fist, her eyes wide. "Why would Harding refuse to press charges?"

"Believe it or not, the guy has a soft heart."

"Oh, right. He thinks nothing of keeping his cats in tiny little cages, but he won't send a man to jail? He doesn't deserve to own a cat—especially not one like Kis…"

Her voice trailed off as she turned and dropped the item from her hand into the smaller of the two boxes. Marcus saw the red catnip-filled fish sitting atop the cat's other toys, her bowl and bed, all neatly packed away. Gently he took Callie's hands in his and said, "Hey, I'm sorry."

Callie blinked, sniffed, then shook her head and lifted a bright smile. "I'm all right. I mean she was only my cat for five days. We weren't lifelong pals or anything. I'd just feel better if I thought Harding really cared about his animals."

"You know, as much as I dislike the man, I think he does. When he ordered his chauffeur to take the other cat home, I heard him tell the guy to be sure to release Jinx in the solarium and give him a treat. At the station, Harding took Kis— Electra out of her cage and kept stroking her till she settled down. And the reason he may decide not to press charges is because Laramie wanted the money to set up that shelter for cats with FIV."

Callie continued to frown for several moments. Slowly her features relaxed. Shrugging, she turned and stared out the window.

Marcus glanced from her to the items on her bed.

As he'd gone through the hassles of nailing down each detail to successfully wrap up this catnapping case, *this* was the concern that had nibbled at the back of his mind—that Callie would assign the blame for the mess at Pia's to her "curse," and would once again decide that her presence had the power to endanger the people she cared about.

As he stared at the cookbooks on the bed, he felt his concern harden into anger.

In the last ten days Callie Jane Chance had completely turned his life upside down. When they met, he'd been content to sidestep any sort of emotional involvement. She'd changed all that. Made him laugh, made him feel, made him love.

Yes, love. He could say it now without turning and running in the other direction. Not only say it, he was willing to offer his heart to Callie on a permanent basis, no matter where that might take them.

She, however, didn't seem ready for such a commitment. She seemed all too ready to turn her back on all they'd shared and let the day's disaster frighten her into running, leaving him with all these emotions and nowhere to put them.

His growing fury lent a bitter note to his words. "So, just when were you planning on leaving?"

When Callie turned to him, her eyes puzzled, he pointed to the items on the bed.

Callie glanced in the direction Marcus indicated. She stared uncomprehendingly at the stack of books, at the clothes and shoes she'd taken out of the box earlier in the evening. When she realized what this must look like, she looked up to Marcus's frowning eyes.

They were hard and unreadable, just as they'd been the first night they met. Callie shook her head slowly.

"I'm not packing. As a matter of fact, I was finally getting around to *un*packing all this. I've been hired to cater a small party next week, and I thought it was time I organized my cookbooks."

Marcus's expression softened slightly. "Someone hired you today, after everything that happened at Pia's?"

"No," Callie replied. "Not some*one*. Three people booked my services. And, yes, after everything fell apart."

"I see. I thought—"

"You thought that today had convinced me that I'm a terminal Calamity Jane, that I was getting ready to run away," she broke in. "Well, to be honest, when I saw you dragged off in handcuffs, I couldn't help but wonder if my staying here might someday put you in real danger, and I thought it might be best for you if I left. But after I got these job offers, I decided that if these people could risk their good china and crystal by having me cater parties, who was I to argue? I decided, well…''

She'd done so much thinking after she got back to the house, not to mention packing and unpacking this box at least three times. It was when she decided to put Kismet's things away that she realized she didn't want to face another loss. More than that, she didn't want to be like her mother, drawing love to her, then pushing it away.

"I decided that maybe you should have a say in whether I stayed or left,'' she finished. "I guess the question is, are you willing to keep me around and continue to tempt fate?''

Callie watched Marcus carefully. His eyes held hers as he shook his head. Callie's heart dropped to her stomach, and before she even knew it was happening, traitorous tears filled her eyes. She turned to hide them, only to feel strong fingers cup her chin, urging her head up.

"Callie.'' Marcus's voice was deep and thick, as he demanded, "Look at me.''

She blinked until her vision cleared. His eyes were as dark as ever and the look of concern was still there, but so was a smile. "I don't want to tempt fate,'' he said. "I want to defy it. I want you to marry me.''

Callie blinked again. "Look, you don't have to—''

"I *want* to,'' he said as the hand cradling her chin dropped down to his jacket pocket. Callie watched as he drew out a small blue velvet box. His other hand took hers and turned it over. He placed the box on her palm.

"I stopped in my room to get this on my way up here tonight,'' he said as he flipped the lid open to reveal a thin gold band set with a solitaire diamond that winked white in the dimly lit room. "It was my mother's. I promise you the diamond is real.'' He tipped her chin up again. "As real as everything I feel for you. Marry me, please.''

Callie didn't bother to blink back her tears. She just let them trickle down her cheeks as she forced a "yes'' past the lump in her throat.

Epilogue

In keeping with their vow to defy fate, Callie and Marcus planned a less-than-traditional wedding.

It was held on Friday the thirteenth. Callie did wear white, but she made a point of letting Marcus see her before the ceremony, when they met to exchange gifts. Marcus admired his new, neon-blue surfboard, while Callie tore the paper off her large, flat…rectangle.

She stared in mute wonder at the framed, slightly creased, brightly colored poster dated twenty-eight years ago, featuring a man with wavy reddish hair, hanging by his knees from a trapeze. The curved lettering across the top proclaimed "The Great Gregorio."

Marcus was still dabbing the tears from the corner of Callie's eyes as Zoe came in, carrying a large silver-and-white wrapped gift with orders that it was to be opened immediately.

Together they ripped the paper off, then stared at the cat carrier. At the soft "mew," Callie's trembling fingers unhooked the latch and drew out a thickly coated gray cat with bright emerald eyes, while Marcus read the attached note.

"Tradition has it that Russian Blues make for lucky wedding gifts. I don't know if the luck goes to the giver or the receiver. I only know this cat hasn't been happy since I got her back. Take her, along with my wishes for a wonderful life. Gerald Harding.''

Because Callie had to redo her makeup after this, she and Marcus were late getting to Pia's, where a canvas tent protected the waiting guests, along with Zoe as Callie's matron of honor, and Rick Malone serving as best man. With Marcus watching her every move, Callie walked down the aisle to the strains of "Here Comes the Bride,'' played on a rented calliope.

One of the traditions Marcus and Callie agreed to break was shopping for wedding bands together, preferring to surprise each other on the day of the ceremony. After pledging to stay together for better or worse, richer or poorer, in good luck and in bad, they prepared to exchange the rings.

Marcus went first, sliding his offering over Callie's finger. When his hand moved away, Callie looked down to see that the band held a horseshoe made of small opals that fit around his mother's diamond.

Her eyes filled for the third time that day. Blinking, she fought a smile as Zoe handed Callie the band she'd had specially made for Marcus. Just as he'd done, she was careful not to let him see the design until the ring was firmly on his finger. Slowly she slid her hand back to let him see the wide yellow-gold band set with a single diamond in the curve of a white-gold horseshoe. Fighting both laughter and tears, she looked up to see that Marcus's lips were twitching as well.

But it wasn't the time for laughter. That would come later. It was time for a long, slow, deep kiss to seal the vows they had just made. And the good fortune that was to be theirs always.

*   *   *   *   *

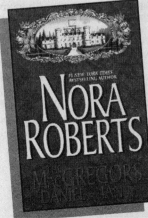

If you enjoyed what you just read,
then we've got an offer you can't resist!

Take 2 bestselling
love stories FREE!
Plus get a FREE surprise gift!

Clip this page and mail it to Silhouette Reader Service™

IN U.S.A.
3010 Walden Ave.
P.O. Box 1867
Buffalo, N.Y. 14240-1867

IN CANADA
P.O. Box 609
Fort Erie, Ontario
L2A 5X3

YES! Please send me 2 free Silhouette Intimate Moments® novels and my free surprise gift. Then send me 6 brand-new novels every month, which I will receive months before they're available in stores. In the U.S.A., bill me at the bargain price of $3.57 plus 25¢ delivery per book and applicable sales tax, if any*. In Canada, bill me at the bargain price of $3.96 plus 25¢ delivery per book and applicable taxes**. That's the complete price and a savings of over 10% off the cover prices—what a great deal! I understand that accepting the 2 free books and gift places me under no obligation ever to buy any books. I can always return a shipment and cancel at any time. Even if I never buy another book from Silhouette, the 2 free books and gift are mine to keep forever. So why not take us up on our invitation. You'll be glad you did!

245 SEN CNFF
345 SEN CNFG

Name	(PLEASE PRINT)	
Address	Apt.#	
City	State/Prov.	Zip/Postal Code

* Terms and prices subject to change without notice. Sales tax applicable in N.Y.
** Canadian residents will be charged applicable provincial taxes and GST.
   All orders subject to approval. Offer limited to one per household.
   ® are registered trademarks of Harlequin Enterprises Limited.

INMOM99   ©1998 Harlequin Enterprises Limited

Silhouette Romance
proudly presents
an all-new, original series...

Six friends
dream of
marrying their
bosses in this delightful
new series

Come see how each month, office romances lead to
happily-ever-after for six friends.

In January 1999—
THE BOSS AND THE BEAUTY by Donna Clayton

In February 1999—
THE NIGHT BEFORE BABY by Karen Rose Smith

In March 1999—
HUSBAND FROM 9 to 5 by Susan Meier

In April 1999—
THE EXECUTIVE'S BABY by Robin Wells

In May 1999—
THE MARRIAGE MERGER by Vivian Leiber

In June 1999—
I MARRIED THE BOSS by Laura Anthony

Only from

V *Silhouette* ROMANCE™

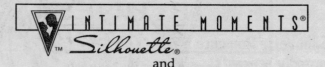

FORTUNE'S Children™

**The Fortune family requests
the honor of your presence at the weddings of**

The Brides

Silhouette Desire's scintillating new miniseries,
featuring the beloved Fortune family
and five of your favorite authors.

The Secretary and the Millionaire
by Leanne Banks (SD #1208, 4/99)

When handsome Jack Fortune asked his dependable assistant to
become his daughter's temporary, live-in nanny, Amanda Corbain
knew almost all her secret wishes had come true. But Amanda
had one final wish before this Cinderella assignment ended....

The Groom's Revenge
by Susan Crosby (SD #1214, 5/99)

Powerful tycoon Gray McGuire was bent on destroying the
Fortune family. Until he met sweet Mollie Shaw. And this sprightly
redhead was about to show him that the best revenge is...
falling in love!

Undercover Groom
by Merline Lovelace (SD #1220, 6/99)

Who was Mason Chandler? Chloe Fortune thought she knew
everything about her groom. But as their wedding day
approached, would his secret past destroy their love?

Available at your favorite retail outlet.

Silhouette®

Coming in May 1999

BABY *Fever*

by
New York Times Bestselling Author

KASEY MICHAELS

When three sisters hear their biological
clocks ticking, they know it's
time for action.

But who will they get to father their babies?

**Find out how the road to motherhood
leads to love in this brand-new collection.**

Available at your favorite retail outlet.

INTIMATE MOMENTS®
TM Silhouette®

COMING NEXT MONTH

#925 CATTLEMAN'S PROMISE—Marilyn Pappano
Heartbreak Canyon

Guthrie Harris was shocked when Olivia Miles and her twin daughters showed up on his Oklahoma ranch—with a deed!—and claimed it was *their* home. But since they had nowhere else to go, the longtime loner let them stay. And the longer Olivia stuck around, the less Guthrie wanted her to leave—his home *or* his heart.

#926 CLAY YEAGER'S REDEMPTION—Justine Davis
Trinity Street West

Clay Yeager hadn't meant to trespass on Casey Scott's property—but he was glad he had. The emotions this ex-cop had kept buried for so long were back in full force. Then Casey became a stranger's target, and Clay knew the time had come to protect his woman. He was done with moving on—he was ready to move in!

#927 A FOREVER KIND OF COWBOY—Doreen Roberts
Rodeo Men

Runaway heiress Lori Ashford had little experience when it came to men. So when she fell for rugged rodeo rider Cord McVane, what she felt was something she'd never known existed. But would the brooding cowboy ever see that the night she'd discovered passion in his arms was just the beginning—of forever?

#928 THE TOUGH GUY AND THE TODDLER—Diane Pershing
Men in Blue

Detective Dominic D'Annunzio thought nothing could penetrate his hardened heart—until beautiful but haunted Jordan Carlisle needed his assistance. But Jordan wasn't just looking for help, she was looking for miracles. And the closer they came to the truth, the more Dom began wondering what was in charge of this case—his head or his heart?

#929 HER SECOND CHANCE FAMILY—Christine Scott
Families Are Forever

Maggie Conrad and her son were finally on their own—*and* on the run. But the small town of Wyndchester offered the perfect hideaway. Then the new sheriff, Jason Gallagher, moved in next door, and Maggie feared her secret wouldn't stay that way for long. Could Maggie keep her past hidden while learning that love *was* better the second time around?

#930 KNIGHT IN A WHITE STETSON—Claire King
Way Out West

Calla Bishop was desperate to save her family's ranch. And as the soon-to-be-wife of a wealthy businessman, she was about to secure her birthright. Then she hired Henry Beckett, and it wasn't long before this wrangler had roped himself one feisty cowgirl. But would Henry's well-kept secret cause Calla to hand over her beloved ranch—and her guarded heart?